GAME

GAME

TREVOR SHEARSTON

ALLEN&UNWIN
SYDNEY·MELBOURNE·AUCKLAND·LONDON

Published by Allen & Unwin in 2013

Allen & Unwin
Sydney, Melbourne, Auckland, London

83 Alexander Street
Crows Nest NSW 2065
Australia
Phone: (61 2) 8425 0100
Fax: (61 2) 9906 2218
Email: info@allenandunwin.com
Web: www.allenandunwin.com

Cataloguing-in-Publication details are available
from the National Library of Australia
www.trove.nla.gov.au

ISBN 978 1 74331 521 7

Text design by Lisa White
Set in 11/20 pt Bohemia by Bookhouse, Sydney
Printed in Australia by McPherson's Printing Group

10 9 8 7 6 5 4 3 2 1

FOR CORIN

1

The light was grey and they were riding down through thick scrub with shed bark slippery under the horses' hooves and loose stone beneath. Jack was being their eyes, but both the younger men knew the country south of Marengo better than Ben did. He was content to ride tail with the pack mare.

Jack had overnighted once at the place with a mob when still a stockman, had even then, he claimed, noted its perfection to a bent purpose. By his account, a mile from Jugiong the Yass road climbed to a saddle cupping a shallow valley part-cleared as a layby, there being a spring. The entrance was blind, through boulders. The coach horses and those of the escort would be badly blown after the climb. The men too would have nothing

on their minds but a drink of cold water. He had anticipated
Ben's rejoinder. 'None of it any damn use, I know, if the bastards
get wind of us—they'll double the bloody escort. So we make
ourselves scarce.'

The three had disappeared for two days into the hayloft on the
Murrumburrah farm of Jack's maternal uncle. The man didn't
want them there but took a wad of quids for gin and bread and
a mutton stew. He asked where they were headed next and Jack
told him back up to Fogg's to fence a few bits of stuff. When
they left he watched them out of sight. On Jack's instruction
they rode north for an hour, then east and by dusk were on the
Galong following the stream south. Ben said nothing, the man
was Jack's affair. They were seated at a low fire eating warmed
sardines from the tins when Jack said out of a brooding silence,
'He'd shop me except he's too worried I'd get away.'

John turned to Ben and waited. When he offered no comment
John looked to Jack. 'What—his own kin?'

'He'd have sold the wife if he run out of Old Tom.'

The youngster strained forward into the firelight. 'And you
haven't shot the mongrel?'

'That what you'd do, John?'

Ben heard the dangerous edge. He caught Jack's eye. The
return glance said keep your hair on.

'My oath! Any dog back home that turned got a bullet!'

Jack grinned without showing any teeth. 'That so. Well that wouldn't look too good on his stone. Shot for turnin, RIP.'

John erupted into a guffaw, then his face froze, until Ben chuckled and Jack himself began to laugh. Jack stopped first. He waited for John to see he'd quit.

'I reckon we'll make that our last word on him but, eh.'

They'd slept till the moon rose, then ridden to Jugiong, skirting the sleeping village and climbing the ridge that would bring them down onto the saddle and the road. Knowing Jack's weakness for putting gain above risk, Ben wanted a look at the place before they began stopping travellers. It was possible too that a mob was being overnighted.

The scrub between the ash and stringybarks thinned and past the two in front of him Ben caught glimpses of a bowl of native millet with silver-grey ringbarks standing and the road a grey stripe that would be white dust later. He caught movement, looked again and was sure, and was about to call to Jack in the lead, but Jack had already seen and was pulling his mare. They sat their mounts in the shadow of the trees and watched the four figures trudging clumped together along the road. The light was still too thick to be able to make them out other than the fuzzy red of a shirt, the dull glint of a pan, but the long handles of the shovels strapped across their backs identified them. Diggers. Going north to Lambing Flat. In the still air the clanking that tolled each step sounded as close as the breath of the horses.

'Buggers are on the move early,' Jack muttered. 'We want em?'

'They're goin in the wrong direction. Anyway, too bloody early to start standin guard, I want some breakfast.'

They watched till the four climbed to the rim, sank into the road. In those ten minutes the valley grew into being, dark blurs becoming shrubs, pale humps boulders, the line of the stream from the spring a green scribble through tussocks. Ben gave the diggers a further minute, then dropped the pack mare's reins and rode from the trees and halted his mare and studied the nest of boulders from which the coach would emerge. The driver would be looking ahead to where placed stones made a roadside trough. A fallen ringbark up the slope to the right was the spot to hold the captures, behind his line of sight. From the log she was a straight run, no boulders, down to the road. They'd be halfway to the coach before the traps had the carbines out of the scabbards. He swivelled in the saddle and nodded.

.

By mid-morning of an already hot November day, thirty-four people sat in discrete groupings about the fallen tree. In deference to the presence of a woman all the men, including the three, had retained their coats. She was the wife of a surveyor. She sat on a horse rug beneath a white parasol, he on the step of their buggy, both angry and neither looking at the other. Two drays piled high with wool bales resembled the walls of a ruin, the resigned teamsters sitting straight-legged in its shade, backs against the wheels. A clerk sat alone at one end of the log holding the reins of a nag the three had not given a second glance. At the customary distance from the Europeans, but close enough to include in the same monitoring sweep, a party of Chinese coming from the diggings squatted on their haunches, faces hidden beneath conical hats, each man's belongings in a tied mat in front of him. A retied mat. Like all there they'd been ordered to empty their pockets and open their loads. Only the purse of the surveyor's wife remained inviolate.

Ben was alone with the captures. Firearms had been demanded at gunpoint and the caps and bullets removed and dropped in a sack. The lifeless weapons lay where tossed on a filthy tarpaulin from one of the drays. Even so his gaze swept the downcast faces constantly as he stood talking to a squatter named Hayes. The two knew one another slightly. When still a cocky with a wife and son Ben had driven a herd of store beef to Lambing Flat and been levied five pounds by Hayes on behalf of the committee towards building new saleyards. The five pounds had, half an hour earlier, gone into the take bag along with seventeen in interest and a fine gold watch. The squatter had responded tersely to Ben's attempt now to converse. But curiosity about a man he'd read much of, but didn't till today realise he'd already met, had got the better of him. Ben asked whether the new yards had in fact been built. Hayes assured him that they had. Then, knowing it was without doubt the only chance he'd ever get, the squatter asked whether Ben had been, as the newspapers asserted, one of the two men never identified by the informer, Charters, in the gang under Gardiner at Eugowra Rocks. Mr Gilbert's presence was known, certainly, Hayes added quickly, he having been named at both trials. But because they were working together now did not of course mean, he granted, that their association went all the way back to the day of the famed robbery. Ben ignored the flattery and stared into the squatter's eyes, trying to read there his motive in asking. It was no secret in the company he kept, but why should this man know and be able to swear on oath if it came to it.

'How does it concern you, Mr Hayes?'

'In no way directly, Mr Hall, I admit. I'm simply moved to enquire. As a reader of the newspapers.'

'And that, you'd have me to believe, grants licence to ask anything.'

'Not at all. My apology.'

Ben shifted his gaze to one of the Chinese, who had stood and was touching his crotch to signal that he needed to piss. Ben nodded and pointed to a tussock, there, no further. He watched the man shuffle away in his slippers and squat as they did to relieve themselves. His mind, though, was still debating whether to answer. How much did it matter? If ever he was taken the traps would charge him with being there and set about trying to prove it.

'Yeah. I was there. I shot above the nags though, not into the coach.'

He didn't know why he'd added that. It was true but the man didn't need to be told. It sounded as if he was begging off.

'It was a savage sentence Gardiner got.'

'More savage than Manns, you reckon.'

Ben was watching the Chinese return to his companions but his eyes grazed the squatter's face. Hayes's cheeks had flamed.

'Ah, quite, yes. I'd forgot.'

'So's Harry. Everythin.' He flicked his hand to dismiss apology before it could be spoken. Jack was escorting a second, smaller, party of Chinese up the slope. 'Beg pardon.' Ben turned from the squatter and strode down to meet them. Two in front were wearing striped miner's shirts and corduroys, the rest were in the uniform of black cotton pyjamas and woven hats. Jack carried across his thighs a double shotgun with tooled barrels and walnut stock.

'Whose is that beauty?'

'Jesus you're a hungry bastard.'

'It ain't for me.'

Jack pointed with his chin. 'In the red shirt.' He lobbed the gun to Ben, who broke and closed it, then led an imaginary bird. The owner of the gun watched like a hawk. He wore a gold ring in his right ear and had his hair pulled tightly over his skull and tied, rather than plaited into the pigtail his brethren wore. Ben lowered the gun and read the maker's mark. 'Tower, eh? No trash for you. Get him where, John?'

'Not John—Lee. I buy him Bathurst. Twenty quid.'

'I give you ten.'

The man shook his head. 'Not sell him.' His companion tugged on his sleeve, the man jerked his arm free.

'Then I bloody take it.'

He spun on his heel. The man looked in disbelief at Jack, then touched himself on the chest and pointed after Ben. Jack nodded. The man broke into a half-run.

'Orright, ten quid.'

Ben spoke over his shoulder. 'Too late, John, I give you the chance.'

The man stopped and turned his distressed face back on Jack. A two-fingered whistle spun all faces towards the nest of boulders. The youngster was out from their cover. He raised and whipped his arm, then kicked the stallion into a canter.

Ben stooped and lay the gun across a tussock, ran to the mare and vaulted into the saddle. The teamsters had stood and others too were climbing to their feet in expectation. Ben drew a Navy and rode in among them.

'Sit down! All of yous! There's your job, Hayes, keep em sittin!'

The squatter began flapping his arms like a bantam her wings and calling 'sit, please'. Ben touched the mare with his knees and she picked her way intelligently through the panic. She was beginning to trust him. She hadn't yet, though, had a revolver go off in her ear. He turned her towards the Chinese climbing the slope and raised the Navy. At the click of the hammer each man broke into a run.

John had slowed the stallion to a trot to come the last twenty yards. Jack called to him, 'They comin behind or in front?'

'Behind, it looks, I just seen the coach.'

'There one on the box?' Ben said.

'No uniform but I'd say so—he's got a carbine.'

The youngster didn't like the police carbines, the roar of them and the size of the slug they threw.

'We're down there quick bloody carbines don't matter.'

When the coach emerged from the boulders it was barely moving, the spokes visible. All on the hillside could hear the blowing of the horses and the driver telling them they were a grand pair of boys and she was only a mile now to the inn and oats and the most of it downhill. On the box beside him was a trooper in plainclothes with a carbine across his lap as John had said. He was looking down into his hand as if at his watch. Neither man had seen the crowd on the hillside. The driver gave the horses' flanks a light flick of the reins, then took all four straps in his left hand and gripped the brake lever with his right as the coach started downhill. Two troopers rode from the boulders into the pillow of white dust in the coach's wake. The bearded one saw them immediately, spoke to the other and pointed. Ben waited for the man then to swivel in the saddle and signal but he remained facing the hillside. Jack had been watching for the same give.

'Just the two of the bastards.'

The troopers kicked their mounts forward and yelled to the driver, who threw a wild look up the hillside and began heaving with both hands on the reins. A man's face, mouth open, appeared in the coach window and quickly withdrew. The trooper on the box had unbuttoned his coat to get at his Navys and was checking the priming of the carbine. The two on horseback swerved off the road and started up the hillside. Jack let out a yip and heeled his mare hard in her ribs. Ben and John took up the yipping. Revolvers in both hands, the three launched into a charge downhill, working the mounts with their knees. The troopers wheeled and separated. The bearded man unslung his carbine, the other chose the lesser range but six shots of a revolver. Ben yelled, 'John—with me!' and rode at the bearded man.

He was no raw recruit. He ignored their opening shots, levelled the carbine and calmly chose Ben. Finding himself staring into the barrel's eye, Ben jinked the mare and in the same instant heard the whine of the heavy slug pass his right ear. He fired both revolvers into the bloom of smoke and followed. The man was waiting. He speared the now-useless carbine and, not waiting to watch, reefed hard on the reins, needing to draw a revolver. The stock struck Ben full in the chest. He felt himself toppling and lunged for the mare's mane, fingers in a tangle of horsehair and trigger guard. John reined in beside him.

'Jesus, Ben! You hurt?'

'No, bloody get after him!'

John heeled the stallion hard in the ribs. Unused to such treatment, the horse half-squatted, then sprang off his haunches. Ben found the left stirrup. When he looked round the bearded trooper had turned his horse and was coming again at him and John, firing left and right. Ben saw a puff of wool as a bullet from John clipped the shoulderpad of the man's coat. The two passed like jousters and then he was on Ben, the snatched shots of both going wide, but giving Ben his first decent look at him as they passed three yards from one another. He was in his forties, ginger beard and red hair, fierce blue eyes with sweat in the sockets, sun-cracked lips flecked with spit. John came hot on the man's tail. Ben pulled hard on the left rein and the mare responded. She wasn't worried by the guns, far from, she had her blood up. A touch and she broke into a full gallop. The man glanced over his shoulder and saw how close he was being pursued and fired a shot blind from below his left armpit, the first sign of panic he'd given. Ben fired and saw the left flap of the man's coat belly like a sail. John had the nose of the stallion nearly up the arse of the trooper's mount. He leaned and spoke in the animal's ear and in three strides the stallion took him abreast of the other horse. The youngster twisted in the saddle and presented the barrels of both revolvers at the man's head. He wasn't asking him to bail, his snarl said he was going to pull the triggers. The man heaved on the reins and stood in the stirrups and his blown mount staggered sideways and collided with a ringbark. The man bellowed in pain, dropping reins and revolver and clutching his thigh in both hands. The horse walked to a halt, lifted her tail and shat.

Ben and John rode each side of the animal into the rich smell rising around her and levelled revolvers at the man's face. All were breathing too hard to speak. The man's teeth were bared and he was closing and opening his eyes and hissing as he pressed thumbs hard into his thigh. John jumped down to retrieve the dropped weapon. Ben pointed a barrel at the man's second Navy. The man opened the flap of the case one-handed and offered the revolver by the butt and gripped his thigh again. Ben pushed the weapon into his belt. The roar in his ears was lessening and through it he heard a shout, 'You're licked, mate, give it up!' Jack and his man were still at it. He'd forgotten them.

'John, stay with this bastard!' He pulled the mare round. The two were fifty yards away, Jack circling the trooper first in one direction, then the other, but the Navy in his right hand steady on the man. They'd flattened the grass in a wide oval so they resembled equestrians on a field. Unlike Jack, the trooper was maintaining a grim silence, but on a slower and heavier horse was finding Jack always just behind his shoulder. To Ben it was clear the contest was over. His arrival would certainly end it. But as he kneed the mare forward the trooper, sick of being outridden, changed tactic and charged. The move caught Jack in mid-taunt. The man rode at him, his revolver arm straight. As he fired Jack dropped in the saddle and thrust his revolver at the man as if to impale him and pulled the trigger. At a range of feet the bullet tore through the man's chest and out between his shoulderblades in a spray of blood and fabric. Uttering a cry like a startled child's, he threw up both arms and slid backwards over the rump of his still-charging horse.

Ben reined in beside Jack and both looked at the body sprawled face down on the ground, the last shudders running through it, fingers opening and clenching, boots drumming on the flattened grass. In the centre of the coat back was a hole the size of a fist, bloody at its flayed edges. The face rested on the right cheek. The left eye was open and coated with grit. Ben repressed the urge to get down and wipe the eyeball. Jack coughed and turned his head to the other side of his mount and spat.

'I thought he'd bail, Ben. The bastard's hung us.'

'What choice he give you?'

'None, the bastard. Jesus Christ!'

They heard bootsteps and swung towards the sound, revolvers up and levelled. But it was the squatter, Hayes. He halted, eyes on the revolvers. Ben lowered his. Still half wild, Jack kept his at the man.

'Where are you bloody goin?'

'I know him, Mr Gilbert. Parry. Will you permit me to see if there's anything I can do for him?'

'I'd reckon he's well and truly copped it. But if you want. Why didn't the bloody fool bail? He a married man?'

'No.'

'That's somethin, anyway. What rank?'

'Sergeant, Mr Gilbert.'

'Chasin inspector, was he? He might've got it too with a decent nag under him, you can tell the bloody reporters that!'

Ben heard in the rush of words how worked up he was still.

'Jack. We got a coach to do.'

'Yeah. While we're here, eh.' He pointed to the revolver lying by the outflung right arm, the fingers extended as if still seeking it. 'Hand me that up, matey—butt first.' The squatter walked to the weapon and stooped, lifted it by the barrel and walked to Jack's stirrup. Jack blew grit from the cylinder and counted the full chambers, clicked through to a fired chamber, and pushed the revolver into his belt with his own. He wheeled his horse and put her into a canter towards the coach.

Ben nodded down at the body. 'Nothin I could do, Mr Hayes. Too keen for his own good, your mate.'

He turned the mare and followed Jack.

The driver was throwing the mail bags onto the roadside. The passenger, a gent in a suit and paisley waistcoat, was out and emptying his pockets onto a linen handkerchief spread on the coach's step. Jack brought his mount to a halt where the bags were falling.

'Where'd the bastard get to was up beside you?'

The driver straightened with a canvas bag in each hand. 'I already told Mr Dunn here, he bolted.' He hooked his head towards the scrub on the far hillside.

'Stay this side of the coach, but,' John said, his gaze moving between the gent's pockets and his hands. 'Bastard's still got a carbine.'

Jack dismounted and drew his pocketknife and picked up one of the bags by its padlocked leather collar. John had finished milking the gent. He pointed towards the arena of trampled grass.

'Looks like you settled him.'

Hayes had removed the coat and turned the body over and was in the act of draping the chest and face.

'Bastard's settled us all. Ain't that sunk in?' He worked the point of the knife into the heavy canvas and ripped down with his fist.

Ben steered the mare to the bearded trooper sitting hatless on the grass still clutching his thigh in both hands, his face beneath the ginger beard white as paper. The man heard him but didn't look up.

'What's your name?'

'O'Neill. Sub-inspector.' The man spoke at the ground.

'Your sergeant's copped it. Like I just told Mr Hayes over there, too keen for his own good.'

The man didn't answer. His cheeks, though, had lost their look of paper and were an angry red.

'In a bit we'll want your watch and chain and that ring. You should dismiss that bastard was up on the box, leavin yous to take on three.'

'The ring was my father's.'

'Give your word and you keep it.'

The man glanced from beneath his brows and back down. His cheeks flamed a brighter red.

'I give my word.'

Ben turned towards the coach. 'John—our friend here's got a watch and chain for us. We'll have his wallet too.'

•

A half-hour later he rode up the hillside to fetch the shotgun. He had worked out a short speech, that in the life they were leading it was them or the traps and the dead trap could as easily have nailed Jack, or any of them. But the averted eyes, and the shock or plain disgust in those that fleetingly met his, told him words were useless. Feeling his unease, the mare had slowed. He kneed her forward. In the new and fatal light in which he'd begun to sense he now rode, it was relief to see that the same light had not touched the shotgun. It lay across the tussock as he'd left it. He jumped down almost gaily, gripped the gun at the breech and remounted and lay it across his thighs. Its weight felt good. He ran his thumb over the engraving on the left barrel of a hare and hound. Then, leaving his thumb there, he turned the mare's head from the sullen crowd, having to resist kicking her into a gallop, and swept his gaze over the scene at the road, taking it in. The coach standing idle, its pair cropping. The pile of slit mailbags white in the sunlight. The bearded sub-inspector, O'Neill, seated now on a bag but still clutching his thigh. And the squatter, Hayes, keeping vigil by the body, its legs sticking out from under the spread coat. Nothing he could do to change any of it. He clicked his tongue and the mare, released, broke into a canter towards the nest of boulders where Jack and John waited with the dead trap's horse, now a second packhorse.

.

They cut the tracks they'd left coming down, climbed to the ridgetop and stayed on the high ground, coming after an hour into a natural clearing that gave a view of the road north past Jugiong. Jack uncorked the Old Tom and they sat their mounts and passed the bottle. They'd lowered the gin to half when they saw the coach emerge from a belt of trees, the sub-inspector's horse tied behind. It was forty miles to Yass.

They sorted on Jack's poncho, the take bag first. John upended it. They separated the notes from the jewellery, the gent's dress ring and ruby tiepin, a silver snuffbox and five gold watches and chains. The oddity was a leather opium pouch in which one of the Chinese had thought his nuggets safe. Ben picked up the watch taken from Hayes, clicked it open, closed it.

'Should've give this back, he was presented it.'

'He should've bloody said, then,' John muttered.

Jack drew the cord tight again round the neck of the pouch. 'We done good here.' He lifted the pouch and shook it. They heard the dull heavy rattle.

They dealt the banknotes by denomination into piles, then started on the mail, Jack and John slitting the registered letters with their red wax seals, removing any notes then shoving the letters back into the envelopes, Ben working his way through a bag of parcels. Jack slit a promisingly fat envelope but found the fatness to be a square of folded silk. He pincered one corner and shook the folds out. The square broke into a scarf of blue and yellow fleurs-de-lis on a purple ground. He draped the scarf over gobleted fingers and held it into the sunlight, the colours against gum trunks and scrub as foreign as the flowers patterned. He scrunched the silk into his hand and placed it balled beside his hip and checked the letter, finding five one-pound notes. John nodded down at the ball.

'Who's that for?'

When the silence grew Ben, too, stayed the pocketknife in his hand. On another day Jack would have had the scarf already wrapped around his throat. He reached for another envelope.

'Dunno.'

'Won't say, more like.'

The youngster sent Ben a wink.

'Either way none of your damn business.'

John made a snorting giggle. 'Not till I seen her anyway.'

Ben rested the knife on his knee. A dead trap was a lark, so too the prospect of hanging.

'I reckon he means it, John.'

'I know he do. Why I'm pushin.' His hand darted out and slapped Jack on the right boot. Ben tensed, ready to grab Jack's arm should his hand move to his belt. John was already speaking. 'Coulda been me that done for us! I was set to blow out his brains, that bastard of ours, before his nag run him into that tree. Bastard knew it too. I didn't need to remind him neither how close he come, he couldn't look at me while we was doin the coach. But it wouldn't be eatin me if I *had* potted him! Ben near got a busted face from his carbine! So why's it eatin you? Your bastard's far from the first bloody trap you've shot at. Eh? Or's had a shot at you! Coulda been any of em before today. So now it's bloody happened.'

Jack looked at Ben, caught between anger and plea. Ben shrugged.

'Forty people seen you fought him fair.'

'Not how the traps or the damn papers'll see it.'

'Course they bloody won't, we was bailin a coach. But John's right—his slug come a couple of inches lower she'd be you under that coat and him crowin about the notes comin to him.'

'Still might've, if he'd had a better nag under him. Nothin wrong with his pluck.'

He reached to his belt, not with intent, slowly, and pulled the dead man's Navy free and held it flat on his palm to read the stamp on the frame. N.S.W. POLICE No. 204. There was dust fine as talc in the mechanism and in the pores of the metal. The sweat of the man's hand had darkened the timber of the butt till the grain was near invisible. He lobbed the revolver onto the poncho. John looked at it, then up at him, not believing the meaning of the gesture.

'You don't want her?'

Jack shook his head. The youngster snatched the revolver up. He sighted it on a trunk, clicked his tongue, lowered it onto his left hand and turned the cylinder through a revolution.

'Two left. Shoot em back at the bastards.'

'I reckon they'll be lookin to give you the chance, too,' Ben said quietly.

.

Camp that night was in a wattle-choked gully where a fire wouldn't show. Rolled in his blanket, coat for a pillow, John was already asleep. The dead trap's Navy, fully loaded and capped, was tucked barrel first into the coat's folds. Before lying down the youngster had extracted from his shammy the wad of notes and using his blanket as table had lain them out by denomination in the firelight. He knew what his share amounted to, he'd just wanted to stare again at the piles of crisp paper. The day's take had been fourteen quid shy of two thousand. His sleeping face still bore a faint look of amazement.

Jack, riding back from Victoria, had found him at Adjungbilly. He was hiding out by day and coming in to the shanty at night, having absconded from bail at Yass on a charge of robbing a drayman. Jack had taken a shine to him. Probably, Ben suspected, because at seventeen John was near as young as Jack had been when he'd fallen under Gardiner's spell and left working stock to join him on the roads. Jack had woven the same spell, telling the youngster drays were nothing, the real money was in coaches, and if he was serious about going on the cross and not just talking, Jack would introduce him to a friend. Three nights later, at Fogg's, Ben had shaken his hand.

The youngster was breathing through his mouth. The full lips were a strange match with the narrow face and beaky chin. Ben wondered if he'd ever kissed a woman other than his mother. He hadn't himself for so long it was hard to remember. The girl Fogg found for him, it would be, not the last time at the shanty but the time before. A touch of the tarbrush and a nice meaty arse. Her face was gone, though. And her name. He came back and found his gaze still on the youngster's mouth. He turned quickly to the fire and took a swallow of gin.

'Too much excitement for the young fella, we've wore him out.'

Jack was nursing his pannikin and staring into the flames. Ben guessed what he was seeing, he could see it himself, the body face down in the dirt and the last shudders running through it.

'Took its time but it was always comin, Jack. And damn sight better one of them. They owed us.'

'I could've shot the bastard sooner. I thought he'd bloody bail.'

'Thinkin's what Old Tom's for.'

Jack half laughed and looked at him. Ben saw himself reflected orange on the dark brown and black of his eyes.

'You'd reckon it was their quids, wouldn't you, the fight the bastards put up.'

'Damned if I'd be doin her for six bob a day. Might start a few of them thinkin the same.'

Jack swigged from his pannikin, then snatched up a stick from the fire and began to jab its glowing tip into the coals, sending a fountain of sparks up into the overhanging wattles. Ben was about to chip him about the glow, then told himself the restlessness was a good sign. The old Jack couldn't sit, he needed always to be stirring things, making something happen from nothing. Ben had known him before the escort robbery, but not well. Jack had been Frank's acolyte. Although five years younger than Ben he'd been on the roads longer, since he was sixteen. He'd learned a ruthlessness Ben knew he could never aspire to. Jack had emptied both barrels into the escort coach. When the hunt got hot and Frank disappeared into Queensland, Jack, abandoned, had come looking for Ben. He'd always admired Ben's calm head, he said. And that he wasn't a drunk. In the two years since that morning, aside from Jack's jaunts into Victoria to see his family, they'd worked together, as a pair or with pick-ups. One of their pick-ups, Micky Burke, had turned his gun on himself after being shot in the guts. At Goimbla each had taken a wrist and dragged Ben's friend from youth Johnny O'Meally, his throat blown away, to the foot of a she-oak, cleaned out his pockets and left him for his killers to glut on. A dead trap went some way to balancing the ledger. Jack was still knifing the coals with the stick. Ben picked up the bottle. Jack paused the stick and held out his pannikin. Ben poured it nearly full, then half-corked the bottle and propped it back against its warming rock.

'So where is he now do you reckon?'

'Our trap? Coffined up. They'd be takin him back to Gundagai.'

'No. I mean . . . you know—his . . . soul. He didn't get no rites.'

'You won't neither. Unless they hang us.'

'I'm askin serious, Ben. Where do you reckon he is?'

'You forgotten it all?'

'Never got much.'

'Well the name don't tell us. But if he was our church they'd have got a father to him, give him absolution. I suppose the Prots have the like. So he's with the Lord.'

'In heaven.'

'Made whole and clean.'

'But we go like him, we'll be damned. Especially me.'

'No! Why? You reckon you're damned for not lettin yourself be killed? Who made a choice today, Jack? Eh? Weren't you. Weren't none of us but him.'

Jack was hunched, staring into the fire. Ben went on speaking to the top of his head.

'The Lord's watchin what we do, that's the truth. But we choose. And your man Parry did. And when our time comes we'll have to.'

He fell silent and waited. Jack picked up the stick again and jabbed it into the coals.

'Comin straight at me like that he didn't give himself much slack.'

'None.'

They were both now watching the smoking point. When it burst into flame Jack stabbed the stick into the heart of the fire.

'The bastard gonna keep comin at you all night is he?'

'No.'

'Damn hope not.'

Jack grinned. 'Give us a kick if he starts.'

The grin was the first Ben had seen since Jack had lobbed him the shotgun.

'Give you more than a kick, might give you a hidin.'

'That's brave talk comin from an old man.'

The Jack he knew was returning.

'Yeah, well yous won't have him to wipe your noses for a few days.'

'Where you goin—Taylor's?'

Ben nodded.

'You ever show yourself to him? The boy I mean.'

'No.'

'How old is he now?'

The sharp questions too were a good sign.

'Seven. I reckon but after today I might need to. Try gettin him over to Will's. Have to square it with him first.'

'They watch his place?'

'He lets em think they do.'

Jack raised his pannikin but didn't drink, instead swirled the gin and watched it settle.

'She had any by him? Taylor?'

'No. His wife neither. Reckon he's a steer, eh.'

'World can do without his get.' He took a gulp from the pannikin, lowered it, swirled the gin again. 'Tell me shut up if you want. Just I never been game to ask about none of this.'

'None of what?'

'Your boy. Biddy. She was gone, eh, before Eugowra.'

'Yeah. I heard Taylor was sniffin around. Didn't get me back there. Little thing named Susan Prior had me by the nuts. I wasn't complainin. At the time.'

'Why would you. So when he last seen you, the boy?'

'Back then.'

'That's a while, Ben. You ever wrote her? Or sent word? About seein him.'

'I see him.'

The centre of the fire fell in with a sigh. Both men felt it a signal. Ben realised only when he looked down that he still held a pannikin. He took a swallow and lowered the pannikin again to his knee.

'Where will I find yous?'

'I reckon the lad here and me'll head up to Strickland's, put some miles between today.' Ben smiled inwardly at 'the lad'. 'Anyway, always nice to see Susan.'

That wasn't so amusing.

'You keep your nose well out of there. And somethin else.'

Jack shrugged. 'You know the sayin about a cut loaf.'

'Not that loaf, matey.'

Jack put down his pannikin, sprang to his feet. 'Reminds me.' He walked from the firelight unbuttoning his fly.

Ben looked over at John. The youngster was lightly snoring. On another night he might have trickled gin into the open mouth. He sat up and drained his pannikin and inverted it on the slab of bark he was using as seat, then reached for the bottle and corked it properly with a thump from the heel of his hand and lobbed it onto Jack's bedroll.

2

The boy stood at the splitting block balancing sawn lengths of stringybark on top of one another until he'd made a column the height of a short man. When sure the column would stand he picked up a knot lying on the chips and old bark and ran back to the line gouged with his bare heel. He made a revolver of his left hand, his thumb the hammer, and took aim, his right arm cocked and holding the knot.

'Pchrr!'

The knot struck the man in the chest, toppling him. The boy fired a second finishing shot from his finger, then ran again to the block and picked up the chunk of stringybark that did for the waist.

His christening name was Henry, after Ben's uncle, but Biddy had insisted on the name Harry. She lived with the ex-policeman Taylor on fourteen hundred acres at Reid's Flat, half a mile from the Fish. The man grew feed corn—when he could be bothered—along the creek, but preferred to live from the cattle running semi-wild on the rough-cleared land rising to the ridge along one boundary. The slab hut the boy had left a half-hour earlier had a roof of stringybark sheets with a wattle and clay chimney at its lee end. The pitched roof joined a flat roof over an antbed and granite verandah running the length of the hut. At each side of the flagstone steps geraniums struggled in tubs of adzed-out logs. It was one of the boy's daily jobs to lug water from the creek to the geraniums. Another was filling the box beside the door with the wood he was supposed to be fetching. If Biddy and Taylor weren't up Ben had witnessed the shooting game go on for an hour. One morning he'd seen the boy arrive at the steps with two filled cans on the carrying pole, lower them to the ground and stand watching the door, listening Ben supposed. After a minute he'd pissed on the geraniums and tipped the water into the horse trough. Ben had been torn between laughing and wanting to stride down and give the boy a clip over the ear.

The timber man stood erect again on the splitting block. Harry ran back to his mark. Just as he fired the door of the hut opened

and Taylor, a black-haired man not much taller than the column
of blocks, came out carrying a bridle, his other hand raised against
the glare. He heard the shot and saw the column fall. Ben rose
instantly to a crouch. He didn't know what he was going to do
but he was not going to have the boy thrashed before his eyes by
this man. Taylor had halted but not dropped the bridle.

'Hey! What do you bloody think you're doin? Your mother
wants wood!'

The words carried clearly to the ridge. Ben had decided on a
shot in the air but the man didn't move. He stood watching while
the boy squatted and began piling wood into the crook of his left
arm. Then he turned abruptly and strode along the verandah,
glancing towards the woodheap as he jumped to the ground.
Anticipating the glance, the boy had loaded his arm full. When
the man disappeared round the corner of the hut the boy dumped
two chunks and started towards the steps.

Taylor had not disappeared from Ben's sight. Many times,
watching the actual man, or doing so in his mind, he'd entertained
visions of waiting for him on the Burrowa road and putting a
slug in his heart. What stopped him each time was Biddy. She'd
know who'd held the revolver. It would be like her to clear right
out, somewhere he couldn't come. Goulburn. Sydney, even.

The urge was still there, though. Better that he didn't see which way the man rode. The horse had spotted her owner and was trotting towards the yard sliprails. He'd soon have her bridled and saddled. Ben took a last hard look at the small figure now juggling the load up the steps. Then, moving in a crouch, he wove up through the boulders towards the treeline and the ridgetop where he'd left his own mare hobbled and grazing.

·

In the hot afternoon of the same day another boy was working to feed fires. The creek flat was a forest of stumps. The severed branches lying on the ground still held the shapes of trees, but the trunks were gone, sawn and split for fence rails. The second boy's name was Charlie Hall. He was cousin to the first, and a year older. In blackened canvas trousers and a singlet and his mother's boots, their toes stuffed with rag, he was dragging a branch towards a fire burning in a stump hole. The fire had been burning since the day before and the stump was well devoured, but he was under orders to keep the wood up to it and he was a boy who took orders seriously. The wall of heat ringing the hole was invisible in the sunlight. He got as close as he could, lobbed the branch and without pausing turned and headed back to the pile he was working his way through, no pause because twenty yards from the hole he'd fed was a new stump, lit that morning.

The same distance the other way his father was digging a trench around yet another, its butt a yard across. He was shirtless, back and arms glistening, sweat dripping from his beard. He was down to dry orange clay and going at it with a mattock. Axe, bar and long-handled spade lay to hand on the trench rim. The spade was good steel and the rock which struck the blade and bounced made a ringing clang. The man had ducked instinctively, but now straightened, fright turning to anger. Believing it Charlie playing the fool, he opened his mouth to roar at the boy. A whistle spun him round. Ben was standing at the edge of the cleared land.

The last time he'd been to the farm he'd had Dunleavy and 'the old man', James Mount, with him. Jack had been five months in Victoria. Will knew both men and didn't like or trust either, and late at night on the verandah had told him so. Ben had defended them, halfheartedly he admitted to himself as he walked between the stumps towards his brother, who'd climbed from the hole and now stood wiping his neck and arms with his bunched shirt. A month after that night Mount had cleared out and been taken next day without a shot fired. Two days later Dunleavy announced he was turning himself in to the priest at Carcoar. If Will mentioned either, though, he'd have a bite of him. His brother had never bailed a man, never mind twenty at a time, day after day and alone, no one at your back and your eyes everywhere. He'd never lain down nights on end in the bush with a revolver beside each ear and nothing but his thoughts for company. Any company, even useless, was preferable. Will knew of the life, Ben himself had told him. But he'd not lived it. Ben saw the stern lecturing look that had appeared about his brother's eyes. But he couldn't yet have heard about Jugiong.

Will confounded him by clapping his son on the back and pointing.

'Every time we see this fella, Charlie, eh, he's wearin a new coat!'

He thrust out his hand. When Ben took it his brother pulled him into an embrace and held him hard. His neck stank of sweat, his hair and beard of smoke. Ben eased himself free and shook the hand the boy offered shyly, then drew him in to his hip and ruffled his hair.

'Christ, you smell like sweeps, both of you.'

'Jack with you?'

Ben searched his brother's eyes for duplicity. There was none. He was simply repeating what he'd read or been told, that Jack was back and they were working together. He had a world of time for Jack.

'No.'

'He was gone a while. How is he?'

'The same, wild and wilder.'

He hadn't got the smile or the voice right. Will stared at him.

'Charlie,' Ben said.

The boy jumped alert. 'Yes, Uncle Ben?'

'My nag's up at the split boulder. There's two bottles in the blanket roll, a half and a full. Fetch us the full, eh.'

The boy sprinted away. Ben followed him with his eyes, admiring the sureness of foot, but felt Will's eyes never leave his face. He spoke watching the shrinking figure.

'He's shot a trap stone bloody dead. Jugiong, two days ago—we done the Gundagai mail. Fair fight—he'd have put a nail in Jack if Jack hadn't got in first.'

'Holy Mother of God.'

'Yeah, well, bit late for her intercession.'

'Curb your tongue. What was the fellow's name?'

'Parry. Edmund.'

Will bowed his head. He spoke under his breath, crossed himself. Ben waited for him to open his eyes.

'He was near worth it—we copped two thousand quid. I got three hundred of that here if you reckon she'll hand him over. That's if yous are still willin to have him.'

'Course we're still willin—have been all this past year! We're gunna discuss, let's get out of this bloody sun.'

He started towards the trees lining the creek, pushing his arms roughly into the sleeves of the shirt but leaving it unbuttoned, its tails flowing. He glanced to see that Ben was in hearing.

'Taylor'd hand him over in a blink—lookin at him's damn near lookin at you.'

'Yeah, well if he weren't a steer he could've had some looked like him. Poor bastards.'

He didn't expect an answer and didn't get one. They ducked through tea-tree and entered the shade of the she-oaks. Will led him to a log. Ben saw it bore two shone patches, large and small, where they'd sat, father and son, on other days. Picturing them brought a tightness to his throat. Will took his habitual spot. Ben couldn't sit with his coat buttoned and four revolvers in his belt. He knew what his brother felt about displaying the weapons in front of the boy.

'I gotta open me coat.'

Will nodded, his eyes remaining on the creek running noisily between granite boulders. Ben unbuttoned, drew the rear Navys from his belt and sat, placing the revolvers on the log at his hip and spreading the flap of the coat. Two inches of the barrels showed.

'So, can you get him here? Even just a few days? Put it to him?'

Will propped his elbows on his knees and flipped his beard forward so as to rest his chin on his clenched hands. Ben knew better than to hurry him. Two and a half years had passed, but neither had forgotten that he'd been arrested with Ben in the round-up after Eugowra for no reason other than that his name too was Hall, spending three weeks in the lock-up. Will spoke at the creek.

'I'll talk to Ann. Where you gunna be?'

'The Billabong—Jos Strickland's.'

Ben brought the chamois bag from his inside jacket pocket, untied the drawstring and extracted a roll of notes. He thumbed off five ten-pound notes and placed them like a small tent on his brother's thigh. Will made no move to touch them.

'They ain't from Jugiong.'

Will let a further minute pass. Then he picked up the notes, folded them small and pushed the paper into the pouch on his leather belt and closed the stud, glancing over his shoulder as he did and making Ben glance also. Charlie was doing a half-skipping jog across the flat, wanting to run but afraid of tripping with the bottle. Will dropped a callused hand onto Ben's knee and gripped, then knotted his fingers again.

'We had the Pinnacle traps here last week lookin for a grey racin mare. Plainclothes the three of em. You think y've got honest stockmen comin across your paddocks and they turn out to be traps. Anyways, I told em there was more than one "Hall–Gilbert gang" liftin nags.'

'I reckon Jack's shot a hole in that game too.'

The thud of feet reached them. Charlie rounded the log and arrived breathless before them with the bottle of port. He shoved it at his uncle, his eyes already on the barrels poking from beneath the jacket flap. Ben feigned dismay.

'By crikey, Charlie Hall, you gunna make us drink it out of our fists, are you? Where's the pannikins?'

The boy clutched his temples. 'Sorry, Uncle Ben!' He scrambled over the log and started back across the flat at a run towards the stump where the satchel with their day's provisions lay in the shade.

'When they expectin you?'

Ben read the question behind the question. Every stump at their backs needed grubbing or burning before the flat could be ploughed.

'When I ride up.'

Half the bottle later the brothers, stripped to the waist, were in the circular trench and Charlie was in the fork of a tree with a view up the valley as far as the farm track. It was years since Ben last grubbed a stump. He was working with the bar, lifting it high, driving the blade into the clay around the roots and levering out clods. At the lip of the hole on his spread shirt lay his revolvers. Both men were going at the work, not speaking.

3

Approaching dusk the following evening their two voices hailed him from boulders below the knob of rock overlooking the southern edge of Rankins plains. Jack had taken seriously the warning about Susan Strickland and waited for him there.

Next morning, the air already dry and hot in their nostrils, the three climbed the knob and sat on its bald crown watching the Billabong creekline for smoke or any other sign that said traps were about. Sighting none they clambered down, saddled the horses, and an hour later rode out of the gully that gave onto the plains. Just past noon they came in sight of the familiar yards and hut, a trickle of smoke rising from the stone chimney. Jack, behind, made a low whistle to get their attention and lifted his chin towards the cow paddock. There was now a third milker. In a new yard attached to the barn three or four poddies were butting one another. 'Nice to see your funds bein put to good use.' Beyond the hut the fruit trees were in full leaf and in the vegetable garden behind the waist-high fence of woven wattles the dark leaves of beet and the lighter green of runner beans on sapling tripods displayed themselves against the yellow grass of the paddock. The three brought the horses to a halt and searched for strange mounts in the yard behind the barn or tied in the shade of the low gums left unfelled about the hut. There were none. Ben wondered where the dogs were. If Jos was working beasts they'd be with him. He kneed the mare forward and as he did the blue dog came from the barn and began to bark.

'Riley!' Jack yelled. 'Shut your face!'

The dog did so and began wagging its whole hindquarters. The hut door was snatched open and Jos Strickland came out, sleeves rolled to the elbow as if he'd stood up from a plate. Seeing three riders he slowed and walked to the edge of the verandah and shaded his eyes, the glare and the wide brims of their hats forcing him to squint to make out their faces.

'Day to you, Jos.'

The man's body fell into a welcoming slouch. 'Ben. Didn't know you with that crop of whiskers. Jack. John.'

'Jos.'

John nodded, having met the man only the once before, at Fogg's.

A woman appeared in the doorway, then vanished, forcing Jack to swallow his greeting. They rode up to the small bimble box pollarded and left standing in the yard as a hitching post and dismounted and tied the reins. The woman came onto the verandah carrying a pitcher and pannikins. She was twenty-three or -four, her beauty careworn but still there, the dark blonde hair which had been free when they'd glimpsed her in the doorway now caught up and held with a bone comb. She stood the pannikins on the verandah rail and smoothed her dress over her hips then threaded the handles again on one finger and started for the steps.

'Good day there, Susan,' Jack called. 'You're lookin trim as ever.'

She didn't look at him, watching instead her feet on the granite slabs. 'This place sees to that.'

'Place is lookin trim too. You'd make a dab midshipman.'

Now safely on the ground she met his frank gaze and laughed, thrusting a pannikin at him to hold while she filled it, then doing the same for Ben. When she moved to John she transferred the pitcher to her left hand with the pannikin and put out her right. 'Susan Strickland.'

Ben had raised his pannikin. He splashed his boots as he quickly lowered it. 'Christ, my apology, Susan—this's John Dunn. Forgot he's only met Jos.'

John had snatched off his hat. He swiped his palm across the belly of his shirt and took her offered hand. 'Pleased to make your acquaintance, Mrs Strickland.'

'I'd rather Susan. You're a Dunn from where, John?' She withdrew her hand and gave him the pannikin.

'Bit north of Yass.'

'From another line of lags.'

She halted the pitcher at half-pour and gave Ben a stare.

'Why you givin me that look? He'd turned before he met us! Eh, John.'

John looked her in the face and nodded. She gave a shake of the head, I don't want to hear, and finished filling his pannikin.

'I'm from down your way. Binda. I was Quade before I married.'

'I know Quades but they ain't Binda.'

'And I only know Dunns in Forbes. My mother moved us when my father passed. Her brother's there.'

Ben and Jack had emptied their pannikins. Ben held his out towards her. 'That's a good drop, Susan. Touch of limes, eh.'

'There is.'

'What I said!' Jack saluted her with his pannikin. 'Should be runnin a clipper!'

Uneasy with the banter, her husband waved towards the steps. 'Come out of this bloody sun.'

Jack walked to the far side of his horse and stood fiddling with the buckle of a saddlebag then the girth strap until the woman had climbed the steps with pitcher and pannikins and disappeared inside. When they were standing at the verandah rail Ben pointed Strickland's gaze in the direction they'd ridden from. They'd passed animals with dull coats, the bones of their flanks showing. He still had enough cocky in him that he took note of stock and feed.

'We come through your south paddock. Your beasts could do with a bit of condition.'

'Ain't got the pick except along the creek. Thank Christ that don't go dry.'

'What's a beast fetchin?'

Strickland glanced towards the open doorway, lowered his voice. 'Sold fourteen head for twelve a head a month back. Good'ns, not them yous seen.'

'And not yours to sell I'd wager.'

Again the man glanced towards the doorway. 'Mine once they're in the pound. I cop half for the movin. She's in the dark, mind.'

'So you'd like to reckon,' Jack said, climbing the steps. He was holding his right hand behind his back. He called the woman's name.

'I'm doing the fire,' she called back. 'Don't you want to eat?'

'She'll wait, come out here.'

An apron now over her dress, she came to the doorway.

'No, right out.'

Eyes alert for some trick she stepped onto the verandah.

'I reckoned this'd suit you better than me.'

He brought from behind his back the silk scarf and draped it over her shoulder. Taken aback, and not at all sure of the meaning of the gift, she stared at the purple lying down her left arm.

'My goodness.'

She wiped her hands quickly on the apron, then lifted the silk from her shoulder by a corner, took the opposite corner in finger and thumb, and opened the scarf in front of her. Her husband forced an awkward grin.

'Cripes—have to buy you a new dress to go with her.'

'Good luck you're in funds,' Jack said. He diverted the enquiring look she began to give her husband. 'Put her on.'

The men watched as she knotted the scarf around her sun-darkened neck and tugged it out to shawl her shoulders. She coloured, acutely conscious of the four pairs of male eyes on her. Strickland broke the spell.

'We might go in, eh. I reckon yous could go somethin stronger than lime water.'

The four men were seated on the benches either side of the plank table, the same pannikins in front of them and an uncorked port bottle in the centre. The hut was stringybark slabs, at one end the bed hidden by a curtain of hessian sewn with stars cut from an old velvet dress and at the other the granite fireplace. Susan was at the fire, the scarf put away. Two skillets were on the rails. A bowl of eggs was beside her, and she was carving thick rashers from a flitch of bacon. Jack drained his pannikin, then winked at Ben and reached for the bottle.

'So, how's the duffin business, Jos?'

The man mouthed 'Jesus!' and flung a look at his wife. She didn't look round but all saw her shoulders stiffen. There was a hiss as the first rasher hit the fat, followed by another. Jack held the man's gaze and tilted his chin towards the fierceness at the fire. What'd I say. There came the successive crack and sizzle of six eggs. She scooped up chopped shallots in both hands and scattered them over the bacon.

'That's smellin good, Susan.'

She gave no sign that she'd heard. Jack swivelled on the bench and turned down his mouth. Ben was watching Strickland. Pulled between anger and fear of Jack's ready temper, the man was trying to grin. It was a dangerous game. To end it Ben drew the shammy from inside his jacket, broke the bow and tugged out the wad of notes. He saw Strickland's eyes widen. He peeled off two ten-pound notes and lay them in front of the man, who picked up and folded them in the one motion and slid them into his shirt pocket. Ben peeled off three more and dropped them in the centre of the table.

·

Their camp on Strickland's was a pool in a bend of the creek a mile from the hut. She-oaks crowded both banks. Further out, near-impenetrable belts of white cypress walled the creek off from the plain. Floods had scoured the creekbed down to granite boulders. A small beach of fine gravel ran to the foot of a more ancient bank. Halfway up the old bank was an undercut deep enough to be a cave, a half-exposed boulder buttressing one side of its mouth, the clay of the roof veined through and held by the roots of a massive grey box. A log laid across the mouth silled a flooring of she-oak and cypress brooms. In summer the place was a bowl of coolness and shade, in winter a haven from the wind.

No one could get within a quarter-mile of either bank without they or a nag hearing the crackle of litter. The seclusion didn't mean they dropped their guard, but they did take their ease.

Ben and Jack were naked in the tea-coloured water. John was seated cross-legged on a flat rock smoking his pipe. Now clean-shaven, Ben was working up a lather in his thick brown hair with a half-bar of Susan's soap. Jack had the other half and was crouched at a stone at the pool's edge scrubbing the corduroys he'd worn since Jugiong. His laundered shirt was coiled on another stone. A third stone, greasy with soap, held scissors, razor, a small hand mirror and curls of beard hair. Ben sniffed his hand. She'd boiled the soap with lemon rind and honey. He was going to smell like a girl dressed for mass. But at least the itch in his scalp was gone. A shift in the air brought a whiff of pipe smoke. He looked across at the youngster. He'd closed his eyes. The pipe stem was below his chin and he was tapping his right knee to a tune in his mind. There was old dirt in the webbing of his fingers, the nails were black. Ben tried to recall the last time he'd seen the youngster wash, properly wash, not just dash water into his face. Standing at the water butt at Jack's uncle's place it had to be, the day before Jugiong. Even then he'd only stripped to the waist. It was lucky Susan hadn't looked at his mitt before she'd shaken it. He dunked his head, flicked the water from his hair, then called, 'John!' He waited for the youngster to open his eyes, then threw the soap hard at his chest, forcing him to catch it and spattering his hand and sleeve.

'Damn you, Ben!'

His eyes went to the pipe.

'Your turn in here.'

Satisfied the bowl and stem were unspattered, he placed the half-bar beside his hip and wiped his hand across the dry rock. 'I'm all right.'

'I'm not askin you, matey. You stink.'

'Your opinion. Ain't mine.'

'Jack?'

'Can smell him from here. I reckon he's forcin our hand, eh.'

'Like hell,' John muttered. He turned from their stare and knocked out the pipe and began unbuttoning his shirt.

.

The shirts and trousers they wore were sadly wrinkled from being in saddlebags. Spread to dry on rocks were the clothes they'd arrived in, except that the sun had clouded over and there was the rumble of thunder, still distant, but approaching. The thickening air held the smell of hot pebbles and the algaed water trapped in basins. Storm light had varnished the she-oaks to a lustrous golden green. None of the three was consciously sniffing the air or admiring the light. Jack had a stone jammed in his boot and was using another as a hammer. He pounded the heel, then felt inside and muttered 'bastard' and once more positioned the stone inside the boot and brought down the hammer stone. Ben was seated cross-legged on his poncho. He'd used the tommy axe to rough out a blank from a stringybark joint and was working now with his pocketknife. Propped against a dead limb in front of him was a Colt Navy. John had finished sewing up a rip in the sleeve of his coat. He inspected the job, then bit off the thread and turned the coat to the front, looking for more of the snags their clothes constantly suffered in the scrub.

There came the crackle of twigs followed by the clatter of shod hooves on a loose log. They dropped like hot things what their hands held and snatched up revolvers and each sprinted in bare feet to the cover of a trunk. John kept going into the she-oaks. A voice called, 'Ben? It's Jos!'

He and Jack lowered but didn't uncock the revolvers. Minutes later Strickland emerged on foot from the gloom of the oaks leading a heavily loaded pack mare. He looked to find them, then quickly towards the gravel slope to the ford. So, Ben thought, you've heard about Jugiong. He uncocked the revolver and pushed it into his belt and walked back to the spread poncho and picked up the pannikin there. Strickland led the animal down to the ford and crossed. When he came onto the narrow beach Ben lobbed the pannikin. The man caught it and dropped the animal's reins. He walked to the pool and dipped the pannikin and stood drinking, his back to them. Jack nodded towards the man and pulled a sour face. He continued on to the mare and began untying the ropes holding the bulging corn sacks across her flanks.

'Talkin about us in town, are they?' Ben said.

Strickland spoke at the pool. 'You could've told me yous killed a trap.'

John stepped from the gap in the she-oaks through which Strickland had come. His revolvers were in his belt. He nodded, just him.

'Nothin to tell, Jos. She was a fair fight.' He waited. Strickland stood staring across the pool, fingers drumming on the pannikin. 'So where they reckon we are?'

The heels of Strickland's boots crunched in the gravel as he spun. 'They dunno. But I been leadin that nag all over town loaded up with grub, caps, powder. The traps know me, they know there's only me and her out here.'

'We told you to buy at different stores.'

'It's still all gotta go on the nag! Can't hide a bloody pack mare!'

Jack had opened the sacks. He said over his shoulder, 'You get them papers?'

Strickland broke off his half-angry, half-pleading gaze at Ben and went to the pack animal and pulled a rolled and tied bundle of newspapers from the near saddlebag and slapped the roll into Jack's hand. Jack ignored the anger. He snapped the string and flattened the bundle. On top was the *Yass Courier*, which, during one absence in Victoria, had declared him dead of blood poisoning from a bullet wound. He skimmed the front page, then halfway down began to read. The others watched the movement of his lips. He grunted and looked up.

'You'd wager this bastard was there.' He dipped his head again and read aloud. '*The bushrangers, three in number—Hall, Gilbert and Dunn—then charged them in a body down the hill, with a revolver in each hand. They worked their horses with their bodies, yelled, and tossed themselves about in the saddle, never for a second maintaining the same position.*'

John was grinning in recognition. 'That'd be in the Sydney ones too, eh?'

'Thinkin of makin a splash down there, are you?' Ben said.

'No harm in thinkin.' He looked his excitement at Jack, but he'd returned to reading. 'What else he say?'

A clap of thunder broke overhead. The pool had turned from tea-brown to purple, the she-oaks to grey. Strickland strode to the mare and began unlashing the remaining sacks and lowering them to the gravel. Ben hooked his head at John and started towards the animal. Jack read a few more lines, then folded the flimsy pages and tucked them into the waistband of his trousers.

'The other thing, Ben,' Strickland said, 'I seen the black bloodhounds in town.'

Ben lifted a finger to the approaching mountains of cloud. 'That'll be here a sight quicker.'

As the man glanced up Ben tucked a fiver into the breast pocket of his coat. It was so smoothly done the man had to peer at the note poking from the pocket like a kerchief to be sure it had happened. Ben was already working at a knot.

·

Each gust of cold wind set the cypresses thrashing. Now wearing coat and boots, Ben was weaving between the trunks, pushing branches from his face. He met the first of the grey box the cypress had invaded and spotted the one with the small blaze he'd made a year back. Fifty yards beyond it was the giant box with the clump of boulders at its base. He stopped at the blazed tree and removed his boots. Socked feet wouldn't fool a tracker but no eye but a black's would see that anyone had ever walked here. He stepped on leaves, avoiding twigs and bare ground. Beyond the tree the scrub thinned but the light didn't alter. He looked up at the sky. The clouds were boiling. There was hail for sure in the big-bellied bastards. Thank Christ they weren't camped in the open. He lengthened stride. From ten yards off he saw that the stones were undisturbed. He halted and, from old habit, looked a slow circle, then moved to the boulders and crouched at the mouthed one, a slab closing the mouth and a round rock keeping it in place. He rolled the rock and with both hands lifted the slab aside to expose a cavity stacked with lidded tobacco tins. He glanced again at the sky. There was no time to waste on gloating. From his coat's inside pockets he took two bulging shammies and placed them on the ground and from the hip pockets five new tins. He unlidded each and tapped out its crumbs, then reached into the cavity and began picking up tins and shaking them, taking out those that rattled and dropping them beside his right sock. When he judged he had enough he broke the bows on the drawstrings of the shammies and began transferring notes to the tins, not bothering to sort but simply stuffing as many notes into a tin as it would hold and jamming the lid back on.

When the bags were empty skins and the tins back in the cavity he sat on his heels and studied the five neat stacks. He'd never done a count but judged the bank held a couple of thousand. He had two more banks, the three making a triangle with sides of a hundred miles. Jack knew his and he knew Jack's. Will had a sketch map and description, in case. He reached in and fingered the dust on the cavity floor. It was dry as flour. The coming storm wouldn't be the first the bank had weathered. He nodded to the stacked tins and took up the slab and doored the cavity and rolled the round rock against its base. He walked five yards, then turned and gave the bank a stare, head still but eyes flicking to all parts of the arrangement. A person would have to be really looking to see the rocks were placed. And why would anyone come here? It was a small piece of nowhere. Still, caution was now ingrained in him. He looked up again and, as if awaiting his audience, lightning pulsed white in the belly of the clouds and the clap went through him and shook the ground. Caution be damned, he sprinted for his boots.

·

By late afternoon it was nightfall. The hail had mostly melted but the pool was gone beneath a brown torrent and the rain was a roaring wall a foot beyond the cave mouth. They could thumb their noses. They had a dry floor and a fire, a pile of wood, and a half-dozen bottles of port. They were snug as roaches.

John was dozing, his face to the cave wall, ear pillowed on his hand. Jack was stretched out on his blankets, head propped on his saddle, socked feet toasting at the fire, the *Courier* open in front of his face. Ben was seated on his poncho on the other side of the fire working on the wooden Navy. The butt was shaped, he was carving the tricky section around the base of the cylinder. He laid down the pocketknife and picked up a nest of shavings and placed them at the edge of the coals and watched them blacken and flame trickle across them. He took a swig from the pannikin at his hip, then leaned and put the backs of his fingers to the bottle propped against a cypress log. The glass was hot. Boiled port wasn't much cop as a drink. He swirled the liquor to cool it and moved the log and propped the bottle again. He wasn't sure that Jack hadn't fallen asleep behind the newspaper. He picked up a pebble and fired it against the sheet. The paper was moved aside and Jack looked at him.

'What?'

'Just wonderin if you was still here. John's left us.'

They were almost shouting to be heard above the creek and the rain.

Jack glanced at the youngster. 'Gone to Sydney.' He grinned.

Ben picked up the pocketknife and gestured with the blade towards the newspaper.

'We should get that fella along with us. Bit more bloody honest than most.'

'Traps've give him a *Description of Offenders*. This sound like anyone you know? *About twenty-eight years of age, five feet nine inches high, stout build, figure erect, respectable appearance, light brown wavy hair, short light beard thicker and darker near the throat and jaws, grey eyes, nose inclined to be hooked, and thin compressed lips with a curl to one corner.*'

Jack drew the sheets half aside like a curtain and looked at him.

'The height, and the hair. Dunno who the rest is.'

'Respectable! That's all right.'

'What's it got for you?'

'Not bloody tellin you, but not "stout".'

'I don't mind em lookin out for a stout fella, bastards'll walk right by me.'

Jack had gone back behind the newspaper. Ben picked up the wooden revolver and found the edge he'd been working. Jack said quietly, 'He's also callin us "Ben Hall's gang".'

Ben paused the blade with a curl half made.

'Well he's got that wrong, ain't he.'

Jack lowered the paper to his waist. 'Don't bother me. Means you get the longest drop.'

There was a bad moment as they stared at one another. Then Jack jabbed a finger. 'You should see your bloody face!'

'Well yours don't look too good neither.'

The sudden howls of laughter woke John. He stirred and turned over, rose onto one elbow. The two were rocking now from the hip and wiping away tears.

'What's bit yous?'

Incapable of answering, Ben could only point an accusing finger at the newspaper.

4

The indentations of boot heels and a littering of dry chewed grass stems had informed Will he'd chosen the same patch of boulders to sit in as Ben used. He'd been camped for two days on the ridge, coming down to the boulders at first light and staying till dusk. Now, late morning of the third day, he had his answer.

The troubling moment, the whole three days of waiting in hazard, had been when Taylor walked to the barn. Would he emerge leading two horses or three? But he'd led out only the two, saddled and bridled, and walked them round to the steps and tied the reins to the rail. He'd gone inside the hut and come out with valises and strapped them on the flanks of the animals. The boy had sidled out and sat on the bench at the verandah wall.

Biddy had then emerged dressed in riding habit and carrying a hatbox which she handed to the man, standing then to watch as he lashed it behind her saddle. They were too distant to hear but Will could see her mouth moving and knew what she'd be saying, he'd heard it from Ann, tie it flat, I don't want it jouncing around. Her best bonnet would be inside. Since Taylor left the barn the air had been filled with the half-mad bellowing of a cow newly separated from her calf.

She was still bellowing now as Taylor rode along the track, nearly to the sliprails. Biddy was sitting her horse at the hut steps giving to the boy, standing on the top step, what Will supposed was a list of last instructions. He saw the boy nod. His arms hung at his sides and he didn't look at his mother's face. Biddy swivelled in the saddle to see where Taylor was, and Will too looked. The man was leaning from his horse, sliding open the top rail. She turned back to the boy and whatever she said caused him to raise his face to her and open his mouth. She threw back her head and slapped a hand on her thigh in exasperation. She stabbed a finger towards his chest, then took the reins in both hands and wheeled the horse and heeled it into a canter. The boy gave the geraniums growing beside the steps a kick that sent flowers and leaves flying.

He was bound to the boy by more than blood. He had passed him wailing across the font to Father Brennan, spoken the name he was to bear, then the words that sealed their bond. It was a commitment to the grave. In the eyes of God, Harry was as much his as Ben's. Ann too understood that, why she'd agreed without argument to his coming here. The boy neither liked nor trusted him, that he knew. He was his father's brother. He didn't anticipate that the boy's feelings would have changed in the months, or was it already nearly a year, since he'd last seen him, at McGuire's, the wedding of Ann's and Biddy's cousin Ellen. He'd forced the boy to shake hands, but thereafter Harry had avoided him. As had Biddy. That he hadn't minded. She wasn't the only reason Ben had gone bad—Gardiner was already hanging round honeying the bent life—but taking the boy and going to live with Taylor had, he believed, made up Ben's mind to go to Eugowra. Ann didn't share that belief. A man chose right or wrong, that was hers. He respected and deeply needed his wife, she'd kept him on the straight when easier money beckoned. But like most people strong in their beliefs, she was short with the weaknesses of others. Biddy she'd long thought a fool for going with a man like Taylor, a known gin-soak. She would never have said such a thing about his mother to the boy, but Will believed she'd given him her opinion of Taylor in the talk she'd managed to have with him at the wedding, because she'd told him on the way home in the sulky, her voice lowered even though the children were asleep, what the boy felt about the man, that he hated him. 'What? You guessin, or he told you?' he'd asked her. 'We had a quiet talk.' He'd burned with curiosity to know if she'd asked the boy about his father. 'Who else you talk about?' He well remembered her answer, because it still rankled. 'That's between Harry and me.' He'd thought she was joshing with him, but the silence that grew had made clear she wasn't. 'Damn it, Ann, I'm godfather to him!' She'd punched his arm, not hard but meant. 'Don't swear, and don't carry on. Because he's a child doesn't mean I don't respect his confidings. As much as I would yours. That's an end to it, please.'

He'd gone on watching as his mind worked. The man and woman were no longer visible, but he knew where they were in the gully the track took. He was waiting for them to ride up from the trees onto the white ribbon of the rise before the track fell to join the Burrowa road, after which he could safely tell himself they were gone. He returned his gaze to the hut. He'd seen the boy go inside and seen then heard the slam of the door. If he was like Charlie he'd be on his bed in a sulk. With nothing else to watch he pulled his hat brim lower and cupped his hands round his eyes and searched the barn, sheds and yards for any hint of colour that might be the cow, her voice now hoarse from the bellowing she'd been making since the man had led the horses out. Chose today, didn't you, you bastard, he said silently, so you wouldn't have to hear her bawlin. She was further reason the boy might be willing to leave with him. Wait, no, he'd have been told to keep her milked. Another thing he'd have to work into the story he spun him. He lowered his hands and straightway caught movement at the edge of his gaze and turned his head and cupped his eyes again. The two were climbing the rise. The blue on the figure in front made it him. He topped the rise and began to sink. She stopped. He saw the faint blob of her face as she looked back towards the hut. 'Did you reckon he'd be waitin to wave, Biddy?' he said aloud. It would take him a half-hour to ride along the ridge and down to where he could join the farm track. He didn't think the boy would be watching but went in a crouch up through the boulders till he reached the treeline, then straightened and walked to his camp. The mare heard him coming and gave a low whinny.

'Hello, girl—yeah, we're both bloody glad.'

From the sliprails he saw that the boy was out of the hut, but it was too far to make out what he was doing. When he drew closer he saw he was at the woodheap standing cut blocks on each other. He put his hand to the brim of his hat to shade the sun but still couldn't make sense of what the boy was engaged in. He waited for the pause when the bellowing cow drew breath and put fingers to his lips and blew the two-note whistle that carried sharper than a shout. The boy spun but didn't stand gawking, he sprinted for the verandah. 'Good man,' Will muttered. The gun would be leaning just inside the door. He took off his hat and placed it in his lap.

When he rode round the end of the hut he saw the boy standing with his right hand resting on the jamb. The boy recognised him and moved his hand to the latch and pulled the door quietly to.

'You won't need it for me, Harry.'

The boy didn't answer. His stance was anything but welcoming. He was watching his uncle through narrowed eyes for, Will thought, any sign that might explain what he was doing there. Will rode up to the steps. The boy had grown by some inches and filled out. The hard eyes and mouth were pure Ben.

'Mug of water'd be good though, mate.'

Still without a word or nod, the boy turned and went into the hut. The insulting muteness was Ben too. He placed the hat back on his head and dismounted and tied the reins to the post directly behind the geraniums. The mare wouldn't eat the smelly things. He looked over at the piled blocks at the woodheap. He still couldn't work out what the boy had been doing. At least with the hut now in the way the cow wasn't so loud. But she'd been at it since before they left and her throat was raw, her bellow breaking. It made him thirsty to hear her. Harry came back onto the verandah with a pannikin. Will mounted the steps to the shade and took off his hat and drew the sweat rag from his trouser pocket and wiped his forehead and hair before accepting the pannikin.

'You been musterin?' Harry said.

Will pretended he hadn't heard, too busy drinking. He handed back the empty pannikin.

'By crikey—every time I see you y've grown another two inches.' He read in the boy's face his uncertainty as to what good manners obliged him to offer. 'We don't need to go in, we can stay out here.' He lifted a hand towards the sliprails. Now that he had to start on the lies his throat was suddenly as dry as if he hadn't drunk. 'I met your mother and Taylor on the track. Headed in for the shindy at the Royal, they said.'

The boy narrowed his eyes again and the man had to force himself to meet their gaze, his own wide and, he hoped, not betraying the dissembling he felt. To his great inner relief he saw that the boy couldn't explain how else his uncle knew where the two were going and why. He gently pressed the advantage.

'Your aunt and me, we been thinkin, since we seen you at McGuire's, we should have you over and stay for a bit with your cousins. So I fluked the right day, didn't I. Your mother was pleased I come.'

He saw instantly in the boy's face that he might have gone too far, the boy would know his mother's opinion of anyone bearing the name Hall. He was saving his best card but he'd outplayed himself, he'd have to lay it down.

'Charlie was pleased too I was comin. He's asked pretty near every week when he might be seein you again.'

At McGuire's the two had met for the first time as boys, not infants. They'd taken a fast liking to one another, which grew so strong over the three days the wedding spread into that both had got weepy at parting. He didn't think Harry would have forgotten.

The boy looked away along the verandah. Not at anything, Will didn't think, just away from him. He looked back at him and flicked his head towards the end of the hut.

'What about her?'

'Eh?'

'Her, bawlin. I have to keep her milked.'

'Ah!—Yeah, that was the other thing to tell you—he said put the calf back in with her. Couple more days won't hurt.'

Harry stared at him.

'*He* said.'

Will met his stare.

'The exact words.'

A half-hour later they were riding away from the hut, Harry sitting behind him, his arms lightly encircling his waist, a small valise tied to the straps of his bedroll. The bellowing had stopped.

•

Ann Hall stood on the verandah with Charlie and Lizzie, now four, and watched the horse with its two riders come the last quarter-mile of track. She kept a hand on a shoulder of each of her children. The girl stood patiently but through the cloth of her son's shirt she could feel in the twitch of muscle his nervy eagerness. He'd wanted to go to meet the horse but she'd told him no, they would welcome his cousin properly at the steps, all of them together. She didn't want Harry distracted. She wanted the first words he spoke to be to her, and from hers to understand that the trust he'd invested in her behind the hayshed at McGuire's held good for this place too.

When the horse entered the house yard she saw that she and Lizzie didn't exist, that peering from round Will's shoulder Harry had eyes only for Charlie. That was fine, she knew her son was more the lure than she. She lifted her hands and gave the children a gentle shove between the shoulderblades to start them down the steps. Will brought the horse to a halt, took Harry's arm and swung him to the ground. The boy knew his manners and walked to his aunt. When he came close she saw him frown—he was now almost as tall as she. Then he masked his shock and put out his hand.

'Hello, Aunt Ann.'

His hand was dry and hot.

'Hello, Harry. I've been very much looking forward to seeing you again. My word, though, haven't you grown! It's lucky you came with your uncle or I mightn't have known you.'

The boy looked his embarrassed pleasure at the ground.

'You remember Charlie, don't you.'

Charlie stepped round her and the boys shyly shook hands, trying not to grin.

'And Lizzie—not a baby any more.'

He put out his hand but the girl clung to her mother's skirt.

'Never mind. Are you hungry?'

'Yes, Aunt.'

'Come in, then. Leave your port, your uncle'll bring it. You can all have a bread and meat, dinner will be a while.'

She ushered the children ahead of her up the steps. At the top she stopped and looked back at Will and nodded, well done. He returned the nod, thank you, madam.

She made them cold mutton and pickle and ordered them outside again. The mare was unsaddled and waiting to be led to the water trough. The saddle was over the verandah rail and Will was standing at the outside of the rail tugging wrinkles from the sweat-dark circle in the rug. Charlie took the mare's reins in one hand and, balancing his slab of bread on the other, began leading her towards the trough, Harry at his shoulder. Lizzie had stopped on the verandah to chew at the corner of her bread but started towards the steps to follow.

'Lizzie, darling, no—here, to me.'

The girl halted and began to whine.

'I know, but you'll spill your meat and it's fit then only for the ants.' She hoisted the girl and sat her on the verandah bench.

'I'll be up in a tick, Lizzie-lou,' Will said, 'and you sit on my knee.'

'But I'll tell you this first,' Ann said. She glanced to see that the boys were gone out of hearing. 'We had the traps here.'

She saw him stiffen, but he went on tugging the wrinkles from the rug and picking off grass seed.

'I gave them to think it was all news to me.'

He said without looking at her, 'Charlie hear?'

'No—I sent him over to the poddies when I saw them coming. There were five of them and a black. From Forbes. None I knew. They were cold but fierce, Will. Most I think at being on the property of a Hall.'

He glanced at her, then went back to the rug, his fingers now working mechanically.

'They wanted to know where you were. I told them you'd gone over the river after strays.'

'They believe you?'

'Who would know? I certainly got no thank you.'

'Didn't see no sign of em but I come cross country. He didn't say nothin so I reckoned he knew why.'

'How long were they planning to stay in Burrowa—did he know that?'

'Long as the grog lasts'd be my guess.' His mind was still on the troopers. 'Them five just speckin, or workin from an information you reckon?'

She shook her head. 'Ben's many things, but not careless.'

Will looked over at the trough. The boys were either side of the mare's neck as she drank, Charlie talking, Harry leaning against the bottom rail of the yard in the diffident slouch of his father at the same age. He gave the rug a last swipe-down with his hand and walked to the steps and up onto the verandah.

He put his hand to his wife's cheek, she lay her hand on his. He went to the girl and took the bread from her and placed it on the bench and picked her up round the waist and kissed her, then, pulling a sour pout, held her at arm's length and gave her an admonishing shake. 'Where's my little poppycake? You smell of pickle!' He grabbed her again to his face and ran his beard up and down her neck which sent her into a fit of giggling.

'Don't, Will, she'll choke.'

He stopped his tickling and sat on the bench with the girl on his lap, his hands cupping her hips. He leaned his head against the wall and closed his eyes against the past three days of sun and glare.

'Do you want a meat and pickle? Or cheese?'

'Cheese.' He spoke without opening his eyes. 'There anythin left in that bottle?'

'There's whatever you left.'

5

The creek had fallen as quickly as it rose, but was still running brown. Seated beneath the solitary she-oak growing between cave and pool the three were tucking into slices of fresh bread and dark plum jam. The half-destroyed loaf and another were on a clean flour sack, beside them John's open pocketknife and a spoon and the jar, its muslin back in place against the black bees. Seated a few yards off, watching them eat but not herself eating, was Susan Strickland.

Ben looked up and once more saw her eyes flick away. It was the third time he'd caught her. She was pretending to watch all of them, but whenever he bent his head to take a bite her eyes slid back to him. He stopped chewing and gave her a quizzical smile. She answered with a shrug of apology.

'I wanted you to at least taste it before I told you.' She pointed with her chin at the jar. 'That's your sister-in-law's, not mine. He's there.'

He lowered the half-devoured slice to his lap. His heart had begun to thud the way it did in the final minutes of waiting for a coach, hearing the rumble of the wheels then the jingle of the traces. Jack was turned and watching him. When their eyes met Jack gave him a wink, off you go then. He didn't know if his legs would work. But when he pushed himself up they held him. He came to her, brushing oak needles from his palm on his trouser leg, and rested his hand for a moment on her shoulder—thank you—then walked on to the lapping edge of the pool and halted with his back to them, the bread in his other hand forgotten, jam sliding from its corner to fall in thick ruby blobs onto the stones.

6

A docile mare, grey round the muzzle, stood in the creek. The boys, wearing just drawers, were sluicing her down at the end of a hot day using empty five-pound biscuit tins. Harry glanced under her belly to see where his cousin was, then, pretending innocence, hurled a dipper of water clean over the mare's back and all over Charlie. Charlie yelled and the fight was on! Soon both were shiny as eels. As if water fights erupted around her every day the mare didn't move except to flick her ears or blink when stray drops struck her face.

Ben watched from behind a curtain of stringybark streamers, grinning when either boy succeeded in giving the other an especially good drenching, but his arms involuntarily lifting in a silent signal to Harry to throw, throw now! each time his son possessed the advantage.

•

Will and Ann stayed up later that night than was their habit, he reading an old *Illustrated News*, she mending the snagged hem of one of Lizzie's dresses. Before taking his seat at the table Will had pushed a large wattle root down into the ember. The odd smell they gave that bit in the back of the nose like inhaled vinegar had crept to where they sat. The children were asleep, Lizzie returned to the box cradle in the main room, the boys behind a curtain in the bed Charlie usually shared with his sister. Will turned the folded newspaper over from the wondrously detailed etching of the wharves at Sydney Cove he'd been staring at for near ten minutes to a series of blocks of the Icely family and their station Coombing near Carcoar. He'd barely begun to read the first caption when a long low whistle came out of the night. He met Ann's eye, then placed the newspaper on the table and stood and lifted down the lantern from its hook. Ann drew a stitch tight then pushed the needle into the hem and lay the dress on the bench, then she too stood and walked to the second lantern on the dresser and turned up its wick. Will was already at the door. He opened it and stood in the doorway, seeing little but his own shadow thrown enormous, and raised and lowered the lantern, then brought it down beside his knee. Soon he heard the soft clop of hooves in the dust and Ben rode into the pool of yellow light.

The brothers embraced, then Will stepped aside and Ben entered carrying a small flour sack and a port bottle. Ann was busy at the fire, first moving the stewpot to hang over the flames she'd blown to life, then the kettle, and lifting a plate from the hob to the rails to warm. He knew she was aware he was standing there. This small woman with the stab wound of a mouth and bat ears always put him on his guard. She had the severity of a nun. But family she gave her fierce protection, and he was family. She shook fly ash from her apron and looked round.

'Ben.'

'Ann. An extra mouth to feed, I hear.'

'And welcome.'

'Where is he?'

She nodded towards the curtain. He stood the bottle on the table but kept the flour sack in his hand. He parted the curtain and looked on the sleeping boys. Harry had his face buried in the chaff pillow. The slow rise and fall of his shoulder offered no hope that he might wake. Ben let the curtain fall and turned to the crib and stroked with the backs of his fingers his niece's fiery cheek. She didn't stir. He walked to the sideboard and opened the flour sack and took out two wooden Colt Navys and placed them as he'd seen mint Navys propped once in a gunsmith's window, barrel to barrel.

'I dare say they'll spot these in the mornin.'

Will had rehung the lantern. He stared for a second in wonderment, then walked to the dresser and took up the darker of the Navys in both hands, turning it to the lantern to study the carving, then gripping the butt and sighting along the barrel at the flame, before lowering the revolver and cradling it once more in both hands.

'Where'd you get em?'

Ben held up his hands and waggled the fingers. Will had once again gripped the revolver by the butt. He caught the warning look Ann threw him and stood the revolver back on the sideboard. She walked to the table and placed three pannikins. Ben uncorked the bottle with his teeth and poured generous measures. It was a good sign that she was taking a drink. He lifted his pannikin and waited. Will came and took up his. Ann was ladling stew onto the warmed plate. She set a spoon into the piled mutton and carried the plate to the table, then did what the two were waiting for and took up her pannikin. Ben made the toast.

'To him bein with true family.'

They clinked rims and drank.

'I suppose Will's told you why he's got urgent.'

'No, Ben, a passing crow.' She waved her other hand towards the plate. 'The man's dead, you're not, sit and eat.'

Meekly, he did as ordered. He spooned a dripping chunk of mutton to his lips and blew on it, then shoved it in and began chewing hungrily. Ann stood her pannikin and went to the stove bench and returned to the table with a loaf and slices on a board and a bowl of butter with its knife. The butter was a deep clean yellow, made that day, its surface shining. Ben looked up at her and nodded his thanks. He lay the spoon along the rim of the plate and took a slice of the bread and began slathering it with butter. He cleared his throat and, still working the knife from head to toe of the slice, spoke over his shoulder to Will standing stiffly with his pannikin. His brother suffered whenever he came, caught between two people he loved.

'She was a grizzly old thing the boys was slooshin down this afternoon at the creek.'

He bit into the slice. They would know he'd been around without showing himself.

'Plough mare I bought off Laidlaw for three quid. She does.'

'I could fix him up with somethin better,' he said between chews. 'Work yous a receipt.'

'She's a nice even-tempered thing,' Will said quietly.

Ben knew better than to debate this tone in his brother's voice. He picked up the spoon and lifted a gravied chunk of mutton onto the bread.

'Yous heard anythin from up Murrurundi?'

'They're both on charges—her drunk and assault, him nags again.'

'Slow to learn, ain't he, the laggins he's had. Any nag goes missin, they come straight to him. This in the paper or yous got word?' He swallowed the mutton and bread and picked up his pannikin.

'You want tea?' Ann said.

He shook his head. 'No, Ann, thanks—the grog's warmin me.' He looked back to Will.

'Edward wrote Poll. We seen her in Forbes month or so back. She's carryin.'

'By the new fella? What's his name again?'

'George Huddy.'

'Saddler, yeah? He all right?'

Will glanced at Ann before giving him a wink. 'Dunno yet—till I need a saddle.'

Ann leaned into his vision. 'And Jack? How is he?'

He had been awaiting the question. She liked and worried about Jack more than she did him. He turned to face her.

'He went glum for a bit, but he's come back. We told him, could've been John or me done for us, just our fella bailed and his didn't.'

'The "fellow" had a name, I believe.'

'I'm not afraid to speak it, Ann. Parry. He don't keep me awake, or Jack.'

'God's blessing there was no Mrs Parry. She would not be so fortunate.'

Will placed a hand on her wrist.

.

He never slept in the hut or barn. After looking again on Harry he said goodnight and rode away towards the belt of scrub he used, bearing on his lap a raisin duff wrapped in its muslin and a small bag of plums.

The two changed into their nightshirts and got into bed. Will blew out the lantern. The bed was curtained off but the glow of the fire came through the thin stuff and was reflected on the glazed undersides of the bark of the roof. They lay still, not touching. Will knew what was coming. She started on the offer to supply a lifted horse, followed by the whittled revolvers and the games in which they'd figure. It wasn't long, though, before she moved on to larger home truths.

'He keeps on repeating that it was a fair fight as if that excuses the fact the man's dead. He forgets, or he chooses to, that the man wouldn't be dead if they'd not been there in the first place to bail the coach. You heard him. Nothing's his fault any more. It was the poor man's fault he was a trooper and that it was his job to guard the coach. Get in my way and it's your lookout—that's how he now sees it. I'm Ben Hall and look out!' Hearing Lizzie stir, she paused. When there was silence again on the other side of the curtain she added in a lowered voice, 'He's got hard, Will. Much harder than he was.'

'He's been made hard.'

'Lately, perhaps. I know it's not a gentle life he's leading. But he made choices. Two years back he made choices, remember. He chose to go to Eugowra with Gardiner and them. You were asked and said no. And you were still arrested!'

'That weren't his fault. And I weren't the only one they took and then had to let go.'

'Yes—after three weeks! And me with Lizzie a baby and Charlie so frightened he wouldn't leave go my dress and the farm to run! But let's not lose the real point shall we, please. He *chose* to be there after easy money. He *chose* to give up Sandy Creek. No one forced him, not even Biddy, though I'm sure he likes to tell himself it was her fault—which goes to what I was saying about blaming everyone but himself. He's not the first man to be left by his wife. If they all used that as a reason to take to bushranging there wouldn't be a road safe to travel.' She paused to allow him to reply. There came the distant lowing of a beast. Both fell still and listened. When it came again they heard that it wasn't in distress, it was just answering the urge.

'Are you wantin me to say these things to him?'

'If I thought it would change matters I'd say them myself. And if I believed him more thick-headed than he is.'

'He knows, you're sayin.'

'Of course he knows.' She found his hand. He didn't return her grip. 'None of this is about Harry. I'm very glad to have him here and I very much hope she's willing to let him stay. She must know his feelings about Taylor. But it's my bet she'll want him back, if only to spite us. The answer to the horse remains no but we'll give them the revolvers, which is why I left them out. But what worries me, William—and what I will not have—is them thinking because Ben's bailing up coaches and fighting troopers and can hand out quids he's a better man than you.' More gently she added, 'And I won't have *you* thinking it.'

'Ann, he's facin goin the way of that trap or else a rope. You reckon I judge that's better than this?' He waved his loose arm over the bed, then towards the room beyond where the children lay.

'Shh. No. But I wished to hear you say it.'

She squeezed his hand but he slid his from hers and turned on his side.

'Are you sulking?'

'No,' he said at the dead lantern. 'I perceive truth when I hear it.'

'Good.'

•

When he woke they were already awake and whispering. He could distinguish the two voices, Harry's softer, more guarded, than Charlie's. He lay still so as not to cause the bedframe to creak and tried to make out what they were saying, but couldn't. After a silence when he feared they might be consciously listening for his changed breathing, Harry whispered a few words and Charlie giggled and quickly smothered it and then both were smothering giggles. Despite his lingering mood he smiled at the memory of similar early-morning whisperings, firstly with Edward and later Ben when he began to suffer nightmares and was put to share the bed with him. A day had been enough it seemed for these two to have taken up their friendship where they'd left off. He was glad for both. Lizzie was no company for Charlie and at Taylor's Harry had no one. The question now was

Biddy. Surely what Ben was willing to offer would swing it for the boy to stay. Taylor would damn sure push her. They could stop leasing and buy the whole run, then lease out what he didn't want to work. Grog money for life. From what he'd heard and seen of Biddy, that would be a prospect hard for her as well to turn her back on. The labour the boy represented wouldn't amount to a few quid a year. They could employ hands. That would appeal to Taylor, having men he could boss rather than a boy. The giggling died down, then one of them farted, probably deliberately, and it restarted, both of them snorting from holding their noses. They wouldn't expect him to sleep through this. Nor Ann, who he felt stir. He groped on the plank for his watch. Eighteen minutes past six.

'Boys,' he called, 'up and dressed.'

Last night after Ann had dropped off he'd been too angry to sleep. He'd diverted himself by inventing the story needed for morning. Now, as he dressed, he rehearsed it a last time. That a month back he'd found the revolvers in a flour sack hanging from a nail in the barn. Maybe both were intended for Charlie, or maybe whoever left them had guessed what was in his mind about fetching Harry to come and visit. He thought the second the likely answer. He might have mentioned to the man that it was what he was thinking. So it was one each. They could draw straws for first pick. Not part of the story, but which had needed saying to Charlie, was that if Ben came up in talk between them it was all right to tell Harry that he'd seen his father. To have Charlie believing he must keep silent was to expect the boy to carry off a deception he wasn't up to. Charlie had been relieved. The poor kid had been worried about the same thing. He hoped in the minds of both boys a month would put the leaver of the guns, in the song's words, 'over the hills and far away', not, as he was, a mere hill.

When he parted the curtain the two were standing at the sideboard staring, but their hands resolutely at their sides.

'They're a couple of beauties, ain't they?'

'Where'd they come from?' Charlie said softly. The glance they gave one another told Will that Harry knew about their visitor to the creek flat.

'Your ma's asleep, come outside.'

He picked up the revolvers. Charlie opened the door for him.

He told them of finding the flour sack in the barn and what he'd concluded. Then he bent and picked up a dry grass stem from the verandah stones. Charlie drew the shorter half. Harry chose the Navy with the dark butt. It was the one he too would have chosen. He allowed them the revolvers for the few minutes it took to go back in for his coat and the gun and four shells.

Then he told them to leave them on their bed and go over to the barn and fetch the traps and sack.

As they walked up the ridge overlooking the farm the boys began skylarking at being a rabbit caught by the foot, each trying to outdo the other. He ignored them and returned to the conversation in bed. Who was Ann to be saying Ben had grown hard? Couldn't she hear herself? If a trap shot at you what choice was there but shoot back? Yes, they were doing coaches. But what did she expect them to do, go round farms begging grub and shillings? The acting around him was growing louder and more grotesque. He was about to tell them to pipe down and walk sensible when Ben stepped from behind the trunk of an ironbark some forty yards above and stood staring down the slope at Harry, a half-grin playing round his lips. Charlie saw him first and froze. Harry followed where his cousin was looking and he too froze. Fearing he might bolt when he overcame his shock, Will stepped to the boy and put a hand to the middle of his back. When the boy still didn't move he leaned down close to his ear. 'Come, Harry, someone to meet you.'

Ben couldn't wait, he strode down through the dewed grass. He'd got himself up for the occasion in knee boots and corduroys, a cream linen shirt with a red neckerchief, and a waistcoat of royal blue under a brown frock coat. Except for the bulge of the revolvers about the line of his waist he might have stepped from the gentry pages of the *Illustrated News*.

'Took a visit to the Syrian's, did you?'

Ben grinned but his eyes didn't leave Harry.

'In a roundabout way.' He halted before the boy. 'You remember me?'

Harry nodded.

Will tapped Charlie on the shoulder to bring him out of his stare at the revolver butts moulded in the cloth. 'Get them traps off your cousin.'

As Charlie lifted the chains from his hand Harry looked the question, did you know about this? Charlie gave a small shake of the head.

Ben walked the boy up to the clearing on the ridgetop that looked down on the creek flat. In the slanted morning light the remaining stumps and their shadows made thirty different sizes of the letter L. He thought to point this out to the boy then saw he ran the risk of embarrassing him. He had no idea if he knew his letters. He took off and folded the frock coat and draped it over the portion of log from which the dew had dried, then drew the revolvers from the heavy leather belt in pairs and lay them on the coat. He sat beside the coat and looked at Harry and patted the log. The boy sat not where he'd patted but leaving a good gap between them. Neither had spoken on the way up, he too shy and the boy, he suspected, too confused. He gave no sense of being frightened of him. Since first light, when he'd woken, he'd spent much of the time thinking what to say and how to begin. He should start with Biddy, he'd decided, ask the boy how she was. He didn't give a fig but the boy didn't have to know. Now, though, in the presence of the real boy, not a sleeping form or a distant figure at a woodheap, he was lost. He scratched at a half-healed nick at the base of his thumb. The boy glanced to see what he was doing then looked back down at the ground between his boots. You're a fool, Ben thought. The answer was lying on his coat. They'd have the revolvers, he and Charlie.

'So, you find somethin waitin for you down there?'

The boy nodded.

'Your uncle give you first pick?'

'I won at straws.'

'Did you? So which one you pick, the dark butt or the light one?'

'Dark.'

'Good man. I did the light one first. Mucked up the line of the barrel a bit. I got yours right.'

He risked a grin at the boy, who'd sat erect and turned and was staring at him.

'You made em?'

The wonder in his voice set Ben's heart singing.

'Carved em with me thumbnail.'

He displayed to the boy the hard horny nail, saw the eyes narrow. Too soon to be making jokes.

'I'm chaffin you. Done em with a tommy axe and pocketknife.' He let the boy see his face grow serious. 'I made it for playin with here, you can't take her nowhere else. You know what other place I mean.'

The boy nodded. He could ask now and it would sound natural.

'So, how's she keepin—your mother?'

'All right. Sometimes her arm hurts.'

Ben waited for him to go on. The boy had returned to staring at the ground between his boots.

'What she do to it?'

'Centipede bit it. And it swelled up.' Harry drew fingers down his left forearm. 'All this part went nearly black.'

The coldness that slid into his gut like a morning drink of water told him he might regret the next question. He had to ask it.

'What about him and you?'

The boy gave a quick shrug.

'What do you call him?'

'Don't call him nothin.'

'Who whacks you?'

'Her.'

'So he ain't game to touch you.'

Again the boy's answer was a shrug. Ben turned from him and gave the trees a fierce, pleased smile.

'The police burned down our house he said. Sandy Creek.'

'Yeah. Made em feel better.' He'd ridden there the day after with Susan Prior's ten-year-old brother. She and Ellen McGuire had been living in the hut, Ellen entertaining all and sundry, Susan him. The traps had evicted them and the furniture, fired the place. He saw again the blackened chimney, the stone footings enclosing a hump of ashes, stones he'd carried and mortared himself. He said quickly, 'So what you reckon about Charlie? You looked more like brothers than cousins, comin up the hill.'

'I met him before.'

'I know, I'm asking what you reckon about him.'

The boy grinned and hid the grin with his hand.

'What?'

The boy made him wait until he could speak without the grin breaking out.

'He likes to lark about.'

'Well that's all right, eh. I got a mate likes that. Jack Gilbert. You heard of him?'

Harry nodded but kept his head down. 'He reads about yous from the newspaper.'

'Who? Taylor?'

'Yeah.'

He went cold. But he'd been given no sense that the boy knew about Jugiong. Still, it was better to steer away from newspapers.

'So what larks does your cousin like playin at? Apart from chuckin water on you.'

That made the boy look.

'She's a brum old nag yous was slooshing down. Better than no nag, though, eh. Your uncle tells me you ain't got nothin. What you told him. That right?'

The boy was still staring at him.

'I would've thought Taylor'd spare a few quid from the grog to get you somethin.'

He saw the eyes hood.

'Yeah, I know him, mate. From before. Don't reckon he's changed much if he leaves you out there with no nag.'

The boy had found a loose thread in his trousers. 'I ride hers.'

'Not the same as havin your own, though. I said to your aunt and uncle that could maybe happen here.'

He almost heard the mind debating whether or not to ask.

'How?'

'Lots of nags in the world.'

'I don't live here.'

You could. The words were in his mouth to speak. But like fishing for cod, strike too soon and you missed. The boy was angry. Not at Taylor, at him.

'I didn't clear out, son, your mother did. She ever tell you?'

'Aunt did.'

'Your Aunt Ann?'

The boy nodded. Ben was amazed and pleased. She was a dark horse, his sister-in-law.

'What else she tell you?'

'I can't. She said not to.'

'You just told me what she said about your mother.'

'It come out cause you asked me. She and me promised.'

'Well, promises you make to her you keep.' And, he thought, if anyone is to be telling him about you, best that person is you. 'Goin back to your mother. I don't say I didn't give her reason. I was drinkin—' and going with shanty harlots, his mind added— 'lot of the time with a man named Gardiner. I done the gold escort with him and the Jack Gilbert I just said and some other fellas. Traps couldn't get no one to swear I was there, so they had to let me go. But I couldn't go back to bein a cocky, back to an empty hut. You followin me?'

He'd gilded the story, badly wanting the boy to warm to him. He had to gamble that Ann hadn't told him the truth, that he'd already turned before Eugowra, hadn't set foot in that 'empty hut' for months. The boy nodded.

'I'd had the taste, eh. How she felt to have a saddlebag full of quids. I hope you have her too, eh, one day, that feelin. But not like how I done.'

His hope was that the boy might smile. The crack of a twig ended the hope. He snatched up a revolver and cocked it, knowing it would be Will but a part of his mind always whispering 'traps'. Will and Charlie emerged from bracken at the head of the gully and walked out into the sunlight, Will now carrying the sack as well as the shotgun. The bumps of bodies showed through the hessian. Charlie was down to three traps. Will halted, lifted the barrel to point down the hill. 'We'll get back.'

Harry jumped to his feet.

'Not you, mate. Charlie and me.'

'I want to come.'

He half ran towards his cousin. Ben stood and looked at Will, what do I bloody do? Will gave Charlie a light shove between the shoulderblades.

'Both of yous go see whether she's worth settin them last traps at the split boulder.' The boys hared off as if sprung for dogs. Will yelled, 'Hey—just a look!'

Charlie dropped the traps in a clanking heap and they continued their sprint down the slope towards the creek flat. The men watched until they vanished into wattles. Will came to the log and leaned the gun and snagged the sack and sat. He patted the log to say sit. Ben remembered doing the same to the boy. That seemed hours ago. He saw he still held the revolver, and that it was still cocked. He lowered the hammer and lay the revolver with the others on the coat. Where had his mind been, that he hadn't straightway uncocked it?

'How long's it been?' Will said. 'Over three year? Needs more than half a mornin. Don't rush him.'

'I was tryin. But he makes you do all the talkin, he hardly opens his gob.'

'Not just with you. Before this mornin he trusted me about this much.' He opened finger and thumb a half-inch. 'Now she'd be this.' He closed them, let his hand fall to his thigh. 'What his gob'll be too.'

'He talks to Ann he reckons.'

'So she tells me. They had a talk at Ellen's weddin. She won't tell me what about, and you know how far I'd get with pushin. Only thing she passed on is he hates Taylor.'

'He ain't on his pat there.'

They exchanged grim smiles, Ben's quickly fading.

'I didn't get to ask him about dossin with me. I was workin up to it just as yous come.'

'Ann'll have a word. I reckon he'll say yes if it's her puttin it. About Ann, Ben. She talks straight to you, I know, more straight than you'd like or you're used to coppin these days. But don't think that means she don't want him here. Or you. You're blood, both of yous.'

'So's Biddy.'

'What stops her out loud callin her a fool. She don't hold back on Taylor, but.'

'How about the three hundred? When'll they hear about that?'

'When whoever comes. Him on his own'd be good, send him packin with the quids in his eyes. If it's her, but, and she's demandin him back, he'll have to go with her, Ben.'

'What if he don't want to?'

Will shook his head. 'Law don't give him no say. Or us. You know that.'

Half an hour later he stood at the same ironbark watching the three figures descend the hillside. He willed the boy to turn for a last look at him. But Harry was listening to his creek mouth of a cousin, who had his arm lifted and was pointing. The two stopped. They didn't call to include Will in whatever it was had caught their eyes. Curiosity replacing the habitual jolt of alarm, Ben followed his nephew's arm. Nothing obvious hooked his gaze. It was just the familiar hawk's view of his brother's farm—the stitching of fence lines, the green square of the kitchen garden and the larger square of the orchard with green blobs of trees, the smoke trickling from the chimney and fraying to nothing over the barn and yards. All the things he gave up and would never have again. He breathed in and lifted his gaze above the ringbarked creek paddock to the granite hills that would take him, if he wanted, to the Fish river and Fogg's and oblivion. If he wanted.

·

He woke at first light. He lay unmoving and scanned the bush for sounds. Birdcalls. The light rubbing of a branch. A beast lowing down on the flat.

By sunrise he was at the ironbark he'd stood vigil behind yesterday. He was watching the door of the hut and eating bread and cheese and limp shallots from the cloth Ann had tied them in. From the Jugiong loot he'd chosen the silver watch with a chased horse's head the surveyor had carried. By its hands twenty-three minutes had passed. He pressed the lid shut and as he did the hut door opened and Harry came out. He had on different trousers from yesterday and a coat too big for him with the sleeve cuffs rolled. Hanging from one hand was a blanket tied into a swag and from the other a filled sack. Ann had been persuasive then. He worked the rope of the swag up his arm to lie on his shoulder and walked to the steps and looked up the hillside. Ben lifted a hand. He saw that the boy had seen, but the gesture wasn't returned. Because of the sack, he told himself. Out of sight of the hut the boy hung the sack on a nail and pissed against a fence post, then took it up again and came on.

They were seated on Ben's poncho. Billy and sugar tin and two pannikins stood on a bark tray. The fire, no longer needed and in daylight dangerous, was burned down to clean white ash. Harry's wooden Navy lay on the poncho before his crossed boots, beside it in a line the percussion caps from the real Navy he held in both hands. He'd already tried to lift the revolver with one hand and aim as he and Charlie did with the wooden ones and discovered the real thing was far heavier. Now he was working at the hammer.

'What you tryin to do, cock her? You gotta pull straight back.'

The boy changed his grip as if to pull a shanghai.

'Not like that! With just your thumb.'

The boy juggled the revolver so as to rest the butt on his thigh and use one thumb on top of the other. He pulled back the hammer until it made a click.

'That's half, you've locked her. Full cock's right back.'

The click of full cock was authoritative.

'Now get both your fingers on the trigger and aim her at that ironbark and squeeze.'

The boy did as instructed, his lips tightening in expectation. With a suddenness that made him jump, the hammer struck the firing pan with a loud metallic clap.

'You just nailed a trap.'

Harry kept his face towards the tree but couldn't hide a tight grin. His father saw it with a mix of pride and misgiving.

'Can I do it again?'

'If you want. But hold her like you are and try gettin your thumbs on the hammer.'

He coached the boy through another three cockings and firings, then lifted the revolver from his hands. He wasn't intending they sat all day fiddling with guns, he told him, and directed his attention to the mare and the packhorse saddled and waiting in the shade. But before they went, he said, there was one more thing he'd show him. He asked the boy to pass him a cap. He thumbed it onto one of the nipples, displayed how it sat, then removed it.

'You reckon you can do that?'

The boy took the cap from his fingers and motioned to be given the revolver. Ben nodded down at the caps lying on the poncho.

'Do em all. And while you are, you're thinking this—stayin alive might depend on you done em right.'

'Why's there only five?'

'What? Oh—yeah—you load six, cap five, the hammer goes on the uncapped one. You cap her when you mean business. Don't want to blow your balls off, never know, you might need em.'

He stood, not waiting for the boy's reaction, and started towards the trees to take the stirrup straps on the pack mare up another hole.

.

They spent the day on horseback, stopping only to water the animals and to eat the slabs of bread and mutton Ann had wrapped in a cheesecloth. The boy rode well. Ben didn't ask who'd taught him and Harry didn't volunteer. They rode the hillsides as well as the cleared land but he chose the lighter-timbered rises where he could see well ahead through the trees, and took care to keep within the farm's boundaries. They didn't meet with a soul.

When they returned to the camp ridge their things and every stick, leaf and stone were bathed in the bloody light of the setting sun. He gave the boy the job of unsaddling and hobbling out the horses while he got the fire going. Both animals were racers, taller than any stockhorse. As he broke sticks and placed leaves he watched from the corner of his eye. The boy was no fool. He led the animals to a boulder. When the saddles were off and both mares hobbled on a patch of pick Ben called to him to leave the saddles, he'd fetch them. Harry walked to the fire with the bridles. He lay them neatly separate on the log, then sat and pulled off his boots and leaned the mouths towards the growing flames.

'You worked that out, eh.'

He tried to ruffle the boy's hair but he ducked beneath his hand.

'Hers is tall like them.'

'Ah.' He tried to call up a memory of his wife on horseback and couldn't. When his gaze returned to the clearing the boy was staring at him. He pointed down at the bark tray they'd used at breakfast and lobbed his pocketknife beside it. 'Do us a bread and cheese while I start on the grub.'

He fried the mutton chops, onions and potatoes Ann had put also in the sack. Her green beans they ate raw. He asked the boy no questions while they ate, they talked only of the day. The mob of roos they'd come on in a gully and that scattered

in all directions like giant fleas. The spill the boy had nearly
taken when a goanna shot from a log the pack mare was
stepping over.

The water in the billy began rolling. He made tea and cut
slices from the cold duff, plum this time, Ann had put in for
dessert, remarking on what a fine cook his aunt was. He asked
did they have plum trees at Taylor's. What crops the man was
growing. How much work Harry must be doing on the place
with him the only farmhand. Didn't he get lonely some days
with no brothers and sisters. By such questions he worked the
conversation round to how Harry might feel about living with
his aunt and uncle.

'They're family to you too, son. Not just your uncle and
cousins—your Aunt Ann's your mother's cousin. She tell you
that—your mother?'

Night had come down, their faces were lit now by the fire.
Harry shook his head. 'Aunt.'

'This at the weddin too?'

'Yeah.'

'So you can see what I'm sayin. *All* them down there are
blood to you! I already said how like brothers you look, you and
Charlie, and he sure as hell feels yous are more than cousins.
Don't he. I can see you here, mate. I can't at Taylor's.'

'I go bunnyin on me own.'

'What? Yeah, well . . . Wouldn't be able to do this but, would we.' He swept his hand above the pannikins, the plates crumbed with duff, then wider to take in the firelit clearing, the horses hobbled and cropping among the trees.

Harry said softly, 'What's at Jugiong?'

The name landed between them like a stone from the sky.

'Eh? Nothin. It's just a place.'

'I heard Uncle Will. They was talkin in bed.'

Ben picked at the half-healed nick on his thumb. He'd been given since morning the evidence that the boy was no fool. He lifted his nail from the scab and drew in a breath.

'A trap's got shot.'

The boy was staring at a spill of ember inches from his socked feet but looked up instantly at his face.

'Not by me—Jack Gilbert shot him.'

The boy's head slumped again.

'What, you'd rather I done it?'

Harry shook his head. But when he spoke he'd returned to the flat tone of his replies to the questions about family. 'They come here. Five of em and a black. Charlie saw em. They'll start watchin if I'm livin here.'

'They already do. But they can't watch all the bloody time, can they. Gotta be other places. Anyhow, they ain't the only ones good at watchin.'

The boy was staring again at the spill of ember.

'How come he got shot?' He looked up. 'Were they after yous?'

'He was an escort trap. We was bailin the Gundagai mail coach. He took us on. Should've just chucked his pieces down.'

'Was he shootin at yous?'

'Course he bloody was, why Jack nailed him! Why you askin if you reckon you heard?'

'I didn't. Cause I don't know what happens. When you're bailin a coach.'

He told him. Selecting the spot, closing the road both ways and impounding travellers, waiting for the rumble of wheels. The boy listened with a dangerous intentness, barely breathing. He cut short the account.

'But we ain't never had em take us on before—not like that, ridin at us.'

'Why did they?'

'I ain't sure they even give it thought. Like you just hook in if someone's takin somethin from you. Or they reckoned they could have us—drop one and she's equal peggin. But I'd reckon she's to do more with bein able to hold up your head, even as a trap.

In people's eyes. You know what I'm sayin?' The boy nodded. 'All them people watchin, yeah, but your fellow traps, people in town back where they come from. We all got a streak of it. Not just blokes, women too.' He lifted a hand to forestall the boy. 'We've had enough on bailin coaches. Gettin late.' He pointed at their woodpile. 'Lay that big one on, and the one under her.'

The boy needed two hands to lift the ironbark bough. He placed it on the embers and sawed it back and forth to bed it, sending up sparks. The second bough he laid across.

'A few hours in them,' Ben said. He rose to a crouch. 'Do a piss and have a last drink and get in your blanket. I'm goin for a look at the horses.'

The saddle mare knew what was coming. She lifted her head and snickered. The boy had done a good job of her hobbles. He fed her the heel of bread and stood stroking her neck.

'Bit lighter load than me, weren't he, girl?'

The boy had ridden her from the flat up to camp. He'd also asked her name, and that of the pack mare, and been mystified when he could give neither. He'd had to tell him that they'd lifted both these, and Jack's, from the stables of a man named Rossi at two in the morning, leaving the groom tied to his bunk. They'd forgotten to ask him.

'Should give you one, though, girl, eh. You're a good'n.'

The mare knew she was being addressed and turned her head to nuzzle his hand.

'Maybe get him to.' He cupped her muzzle, rubbed. 'He'd stay I bet if I told him he could have you.' Have a bit of explaining to do to the first trap that seen you, though, wouldn't he. 'Must be somethin else he'd take to, just I bloody dunno what.'

•

He was filing a burr from one of the pack mare's stirrups with a stone when the low whistle came from the trees below. He replied with the same whistle. In a few minutes he spotted Will weaving between the trunks of the ironbarks. He was alone. Ben stood from the log and put stirrup and stone down on its grey smoothness, itself hard as stone, and lifted the billy and moved it onto the coals and picked up a pannikin and flicked the dregs from it.

When his brother reached the fire Ben saw the tiredness in his eyes and the pouched skin beneath them. His lips were a thin line. He filled the pannikin and handed it up to him. Will remained standing. He swigged a mouthful, running it noisily through his teeth before he swallowed, then wiped his other hand down his beard. He still hadn't looked at Ben.

'Where is he?'

'Waterin the nags.'

As Ben stood Will sank to his haunches. The timing was probably accident, but Ben didn't feel like playing at bobbing up and down and stayed on his feet. Will reached for the billy and topped up the pannikin but didn't drink, he stayed on his haunches cradling the pannikin in both hands and staring into the coals. Ben took up the stirrup and stone and perched on the log and began working again at the burr and at holding down his impatience. Finally Will cleared his throat and spat onto the coals.

'Taylor come last night demandin him back. I told him he was no blood to the boy to be makin demands. She won't come, though, she'll send the traps—with a summons. They'll move smart seeins the name Hall's on it. Be here by mid-afternoon I'd reckon.'

'What, you didn't offer him the money?'

'Course I bloody did! He reckoned she wouldn't take it.'

'Three hundred quid!'

'I'm givin you what he said.'

'How about him, but? He bloody would!'

'He ain't gonna cross her, Ben. Not over the boy.'

Ben slammed down stirrup and stone each side of him on the log and stalked round its root end and stood staring at the hills rising from the other side of the creek flat. Hazed blue and framed in the dip level with where he stood was the bare rock ridge with the painted blacks' cave he'd used before when the need arose to disappear. He and the boy could be there by nightfall. And then where? They'd charge Will with abduction. He spoke without turning.

'Go with em, will you? I don't want the bastards cheekin him about bein mine.'

'You reckon I weren't.'

•

They sat on a low boulder warmed by the sun and overlooking the farm. The blanket was tied again into a swag and the sack held only the wooden Colt and the cheesecloths the chops and the duff had been wrapped in. The boy had turned his head to stare at Ben, who'd just described Taylor's farm in detail sufficient for the boy to know that his father was not repeating a description given him by his brother but had seen with his own eyes the hut and outbuildings, the yards.

'So . . . you seen me cuttin wood.'

'And not cuttin it.'

Harry flushed and looked at his guilty hands.

'How many times you been there?'

'More than the once.'

'Where do you watch from?'

He'd begun to think it a hopeful sign for what he was leading to that the boy was asking questions. This question gave him pause.

'Ah . . . all different places. Depends on the sun.'

He watched the head beside him, trying to guess what was going on beneath the thatch of brown hair. The head nodded. At, he thought, the fact that because the answer made sense it was probably the truth.

'But mostly up in them boulders?'

'Listen, mate . . . No, look at me.' He waited till the boy turned and was watching his face. 'I'm tellin you because I trust you to keep your gob shut.'

Again the boy nodded.

'No, noddin ain't enough for this, I need your word. Your solemn word.'

The boy frowned. 'How?'

'You say it!'

'Just, I give my word?'

'Your solemn word. Which says you mean it.'

He saw the boy absorb the import of what he was being asked.

'I give my solemn word.'

'And I accept.'

He lifted his hand from his lap and held it between them. The boy hesitated, then lifted his hand, having to lean away, the angle awkward. Ben gripped but when the boy didn't return the grip he let him go. The boy pushed his hands between his knees and looked down at them.

'So, back to the boulders. You know them four or five a bit apart, over near a big dead wattle?'

'I been there,' the boy said at his hands.

'You just need your eyes. One mornin there'll be two little ones sittin on the highest one. Give you somethin to look for while you're doin a first piss.'

He'd calculated that would elicit a glance and when it came he was waiting with a grin. It wasn't returned, the boy went back to staring at his clamped hands.

'My wit ain't funny, just your cousin's? Never mind. You see what I told you, don't say nothin, just grab your sack and traps and come up. Past the boulders, come to the trees.'

'What if him or her's up and around?'

'You hopin are you?'

'No. Just askin.'

'What'd be the go, you reckon?'

The boy was crushing his hands then cupping them to force his knees apart.

'If later the little rocks are missin, next mornin I get up before em and see if you put em back?'

'Our minds work the same, Harry. Wonder how that come about, eh?'

Again he didn't get the grin he was fishing for. The boy took the swag in one hand and the neck of the sack in the other and slid from the boulder. He spoke looking down at the farm.

'Aunt said I need to be at the house when the traps come.'

Ben thought to tell him to sit down, from up here they'd see them two mile off, where they broke from the trees at the ford. But if they believed him the reason the boy was here it was possible they'd be armed with a scoping glass as well as carbines. He put his hands on his knees and pushed himself to his feet.

'Yeah.'

The boy dropped the sack against his ankle and thrust out his hand. The rigidly straight arm precluded any invitation to come closer.

.

He stayed in the boulders, draped in his poncho. At around what he judged to be noon he took out and opened the silver watch, slipped it back into his vest pocket. When he looked up two mounted figures wearing blue had ridden out from the trees at the ford. He removed his hat.

The two kicked their mounts into a trot to come the last half-mile. The gleam on the horses when the sunlight caught their withers or flanks testified to how hard they'd been ridden. As the troopers came past the orchard he saw one of them point out to the other the plum-laden trees. 'Fat chance, matey,' he said to the pointer. They rode round to the verandah. The door remained closed, forcing them to dismount. One turned towards the hillside and spoke to the other and both studied the trees along the ridge above where he sat. He kept stone still. Then the door opened and Will came out onto the verandah and clearly asked them to state their business, as one got busy with unfastening the pouch on his belt.

They were not invited in, nor to water their mounts, and were back in the saddle in less than twenty minutes, one in front of Will's horse, the other behind. Harry's red shirt showed plain against the back of Will's brown coat. A small valise was tied by its handle to a packstrap. He hoped the boy had done as he'd warned him and the wooden Colt was with his cousin and not in the valise. But he judged him too smart a little devil to have packed it. Anyway, Will would have made sure.

He had nowhere else to be. He watched until the heat haze blurred his son and his brother and each trooper into one shape with his mount and the three shapes rode into the air to float above the track. Then he stood and lifted the poncho over his head and started up the hillside, folding and rolling the hot soft oilcloth as he climbed.

7

They sat at the table sipping port and eating with spoons and
fingers from an iron dish which held a large peach pie. Jos
Strickland sat with them drinking but not eating. In the corner
of the room near the starred curtain a white linen dress, dipping
low across the shoulders and bosom, was mounted on a makeshift
dummy formed of a broom with a wattle wand lashed crosswise
for arms. On a stool beside the dress was an open sewing basket.
Scallops of new ribbon were pinned to the bodice awaiting needle
and thread. Between mouthfuls Jack was taking speculative glances
at the dress. Ben read the imaginings behind them. He pretended
to pick a piece of skin from his teeth and looked at Strickland.
The man too had read the glances and needed distracting.

'So, Jos, prices in Forbes still holdin up?'

The man vacillated, then turned to him. 'Yeah. When they got a couple of hundred head they drive em down to the Flat. Bastards get double for em there.'

'Why don't you make that your lark?'

Strickland shook his head. 'Even if I had the beasts I don't have the blokes.'

Jack sat forward, licked his fingers. 'We'll do it. What do you pay?' He winked at Ben.

Strickland smiled. The strain had eased. At least, Ben thought, till Susan came back. As he had the thought the door opened and she came in. The chipped crockery bowl was filled now with eggs and in her other hand she carried young green bracken fronds. She crossed to the benchtop where Ben's blackened billy stood and set down the bowl and began to line the billy with fronds, folding and pushing them inside. Jack took a sip of port and wiped his lips with the heel of his hand.

'She's a good pie, Susan.'

'Thank you.'

She began to pack eggs into the billy, pushing fronds between and around them.

'And you'll be belle of the ball too, I reckon. Where's she on?'

'Binda. Boxing Day.' She placed two more eggs into the billy, picked up another frond and bent it into a bow.

At the name Jack's eyes had swung instantly to meet Ben's. The Monks sisters and their cousin Christina McKinnon had entertained him and Jack for two days in the hut at Long Nose Creek where the sisters had moved to, no longer willing to live in the farmhouse. They'd joked about the ghost of their father making noises in the fireplace up at the house, but when Jack suggested they all go there for a listen the three women had fallen silent and taken long pulls from the gin bottle. Ben remembered clearly Christina McKinnon's foxy face, and her black hair. She'd trickled it over his eyes as she sat astride him.

'You go a long way for a dance, Susan.'

She didn't note the huskiness in his voice, too busy with her hands. 'We go every year and take my mother. I'm from there. I think I told you.'

Jack gave a light cough but kept his eyes on the pannikin standing between his hands on the table.

'I wonder are the Monks girls still livin at Long Nose? You know em? Ellen and Maggie?'

Ben pressed fingertips to his lips but before he could look away was caught by the frowning question on John's face, what the hell's goin on? He shook his head and turned and stared at the kettle on the fire rails, but kept Susan in the corner of his eye. Jack could do this sort of thing with a straight face but if their glances met he'd have to stand and leave the hut.

'I imagine so,' Susan said curtly.

'And . . . they have regular beaus—do you know?'

She flashed him a look of disbelief. 'Would you go with girls whose mother was hanged!'

'Might think twice about marryin one.'

Ben snorted. Her gaze shifted. He nodded an apology. But she'd guessed what was afoot. Her mouth became prim and she turned back to the benchtop and picked two more eggs out of the bowl.

Jack said smoothly, 'And if a fella was to go to Binda, would he find that slimy piece of work Morriss still runnin the store?'

The waiting filled with the soft clack of eggs being settled against one another then the scratch of a stem sliding down the metal. When it was plain she wasn't going to answer Strickland said, 'Yeah. And half the bloody town.'

'Got a book has he?'

'So we're told.'

Ben turned again to the table. He'd heard in the voice and saw now in the eyes that there was no longer any smirk to Jack, he was all hard purpose. His tone, though, when he spoke, belied it.

'And do yous dance the Lancers?'

Strickland shrugged. 'If they got the same players. Had em for each of the last three.'

Jack kicked his boot heels together under the table and whistled.

'She ain't a ball without the Lancers!'

•

Susan put the remainder of the pie in a clean flour sack and very deliberately chose John to hand it to. Ben paid Strickland for a bottle of Old Tom.

When they rode away from the hut the sun was a hand's width above the low range that bordered the run to the west. Jack set an ambling pace. The pool was a mile, but flat going. There was always wood to be found even in the dark. He called back over his shoulder, 'You got a good grip on that pie?'

'Yeah.'

'I hope she ain't give you the idea the rest's yours.'

'You don't tell me what yous was playin at I'll eat the bastard ridin.'

Jack grinned back at the youngster. 'We're goin to a ball! You can dance can't you?'

'I dance as good as I ride.'

'Well there's ridin and ridin, my man. What ridin we talkin?'

'I know what you're gettin at,' John said quietly.

'And you done that kind?'

When the youngster didn't answer Jack swivelled in the saddle. 'Eh? Have you?'

Ben was riding abreast of the two and some ten yards off. He didn't like that the names had been brought up in front of Susan. Nor that she'd guessed how well he too knew the Monks girls.

'Leave him be, Jack.'

'I can answer. Yeah, I have.'

'There you go, Ben, that smooth face is a liar, he's rid bare-arsed, he reckons.' He swung his attention again to the youngster. 'There's one apiece—they got a cousin, Christina. But she's Ben's. Ellen's mine. Leaves you Maggie. She's far from leavins, but. Except I reckon she'll leave you behind.' He broke into his high wicked giggle.

Ben glanced at the youngster. He was giving Jack a calculating look. Ben didn't think he'd resort to a revolver even to bluff, but he might hurl the pie. His left hand remained couched on his thigh.

'I heard about a woman up that way bein hanged.' He aimed the words into the air between the two of them. 'What'd she do?'

'What didn't she!' Jack threw over his shoulder.

Ben waited. Jack chose not to elaborate.

'The old man give em all beltins for years, her and the girls. She couldn't take it no more. Bashed in his head with a hammer and burned him in the fireplace.'

'Jesus.'

They rode in silence for a few paces, the smell in their nostrils. They'd all worked stock, dragged dead animals onto a fire or built one over them.

'And they're still livin there? These girls you're talkin?'

'Were livin, not now,' Jack said, again without turning. 'You won't have to go near the place.'

Ben watched the tails of hair rising and lowering on Jack's coat collar. Ellen Monks wasn't the only thing going around in that head.

'So what's between you and this Morriss?'

Jack glanced at him over his shoulder but spoke into the air above his horse's ears.

'You never been into Binda?'

Ben kneed the grey into a canter and caught him up, reined her back to a walk.

'Long Nose that time's the closest I been.'

'Bastard owns the store.'

'We already heard that. No odds in it. We're with the women, we can't do his bloody store, they'll have em for aidin.'

'Might anyway if he's got any say. Bastard used to be a trap himself.'

'Where?'

'There—Binda.'

'And what business you have with him?'

'None there—Marengo. Fell out with my uncle and moved up there, workin for a fella named Price. Before I ever met Frank. Morriss come there wantin to have me for liftin. No warrant, not even an information. I done a few by then but I never heard of the nag he wanted me for. I refused to go with the bastard so he tried gettin me the sack. Well past time him and me had a chat.'

There was no grin, his gaze remained fixed on the belt of cypress marking the creek.

•

They carried their saddles, bridles and rugs up to the cave to be out of the dew but made camp on the gravel. John had dragged in an entire dead she-oak sapling and they sat at a fire of box and oak drinking gin and finishing the pie. Then John cut bread and Ben fried eggs and they ate them on the bread with the half-ripe tomatoes Strickland had given them from the sill in the barn. Egg shells on a fire made a foul smell but tossed they'd bring a goanna. Ben buried them and placed a slab of rock on the disturbed gravel. The greasy pan he hung from a branch of the solitary she-oak to await the rest of the eggs in the morning.

When he returned to the fire John and Jack had pouches out and were filling their pipes. Jack topped up their pannikins. Ben sat and took out his pouch. John reached first to the fire for a twig and a moment later the air filled with the blue smoke and smell of shag. Ben lit his, got it drawing, then reclined on his elbow. The creek was a constant low gurgle where it ran through the dam of jammed timber at the tail of the pool. Wind moved in the she-oaks but didn't reach them on the gravel. The channel of sky overhead was clear, the stars not yet at full brightness.

'A fella could do worse than live here.'

Ben was startled to hear the thought in his own head put into words, and by the youngster.

'He could that, John.'

Jack made a derisive snort. 'Build a hut and fence and nail up a sign will we—Traps Keep Out.'

They laughed.

Then, not looking at Ben, he said, 'More water and less oaks, she could be Sandy Creek. What'd the boy say to seein you? He know you?'

'Yeah.'

'Which Navy you give him?'

'Will had him and Charlie—his boy—pick straws. He got the dark-butt one.'

Jack grinned. 'That was clever. How'd you swing that?'

Ben fired the pebble he'd been rolling between his fingers. It struck the stem of Jack's pipe and bounced into his chest.

'Hey—careful—only got the one.' He angled the pipe into the firelight. 'So, he stickin there?'

'He might have, except she sent the bloody traps.'

The pipe stem was not chipped. Jack looked at him and shrugged. 'What I told you. She's a bloody Walsh. Rather spite you than pocket a quid.' He hawked softly and dribbled spit onto the gravel beside his hip. 'She won't let you pull that caper again. You arrange somethin with him?'

'He goes bunnyin.'

Jack turned to John. 'When was the last time you seen your people?'

John cleared his throat. 'I been hidin out a month when I met you. Seen my mother and younger sister about two week before that.'

'So you plannin to go off visitin too?'

'You bloody went off visitin for five bloody months!' Ben said.

'Bloody Vic traps don't know me! Different story with both of yous.'

'Your uncle ain't in Vic.'

'I didn't take yous there cause I like the bastard! Before Jugiong was the first time I seen him in years!'

'I don't need to see my lot,' John said quietly. 'Papers'll tell em where I am.'

Jack and Ben were glaring at one another and ignored him.

'I'm not sayin he ain't shirty at me, but he ain't gonna shop me neither, Jack.'

'He know what you're worth?'

'I never asked. But he's smart enough to know who'd get it, and that it ain't him.'

They stared for a few seconds longer into one another's eyes. Then Jack nodded. He dropped a hand of apology onto John's knee and stood and walked towards the small bay in the oaks where it was their custom to piss.

'Your old man still livin, John?'

'Yeah.'

'Just you ain't never mentioned him.'

'Ain't worth mentionin.'

'I got one of them.' Ben took a swallow of gin, swilling it first to scour his mouth. He'd not seen his father or mother in the fourteen years since the man had moved back to Murrurundi to rejoin her. Nor would he, now. If Will's news was right, even at sixty-one the old man couldn't walk past a nag without looking around to see if it had an owner. 'What'd he get sent out for?'

'Killin a horse. Rode the bloody thing to death.'

'Jesus.'

'He reckons it had a crook heart but I got my own ideas. He's rough on nags ain't his. He done some jockeyin too, he's the one learned me to it.'

Jack was walking back to the fire buttoning his flies.

'Who?'

'John's old man.' He leaned and flicked into the fire the biggest of the fringe of glowing stick-ends lying on the gravel. 'So what was on the dray you done? I ain't never asked. You bail her on your own?'

Jack folded his legs under him and picked up his pannikin. He spoke at the fire, a grin hovering.

'He's a bit shy on this topic.'

'Back then. Don't matter now.' But the youngster's gaze rose only as high as Ben's chest. 'A mate and me done her. We been told they was goin to the Flat carryin grog and three dozen Navys and the bullets and caps to go with em.'

'So what were yous carryin?'

'A shotgun.'

'Between yous! No wonder you're bloody shy.'

Jack chuckled. 'That ain't it.'

'The shanty bastard put us up to it had her wrong. They was goin to the Flat but the fella whose load she were was goin there to set up a baker's. The barrels was all molasses and flour.'

'So what did yous get, nothin?'

'Their wallets, and a Navy off the driver.'

'Well you come a long way since in a short bloody time. Every trap in New South after you.'

'Still better than rottin on that farm.'

Jack grinned. 'Those are words a certain Mr Hall might've spoke after Eugowra.'

'No bloody might about it.'

8

The day after Christmas had been a scorcher, the air at dusk little cooler than at noon.

A man about forty named Edward Morriss was walking coatless and with sleeves rolled in the paddock behind his house and store and smoking a briar. With the ball that night he and Mrs Morriss had been run off their feet and it was the first time since just after breakfast he'd managed to step outside. The building was palely outlined by the lanterns he'd lit and hung along the verandah. He couldn't see the flag which signalled the store was open, but it would not be flying, the air as thick to breathe, it felt, as air in a mill. He'd have to go back in soon and relieve her at the counter so she could bathe and begin dressing. But not for a few minutes yet. He would finish his briar.

He drew a mouthful of sweet smoke, then halted dead when he heard the clop of hooves, his old policeman's instinct, and expelled the smoke into his hand. Three riders were coming slowly along the road which ran just outside the paddock fence. He was in plain view but if he stood still would not, he knew, catch their attention. He didn't know why the thought had come but he obeyed it. He enclosed the warm bowl of the briar in his hand and by degrees put his hand behind his back. He saw now why they were coming so slowly, they were not alone, three figures were walking beside the horses. From the spread below each waist they were women, dressed for the ball yet bearing side saddles on their arms and carrying what looked like small valises. He wondered why they were on foot and where they'd left their mounts. In ten yards all would reach the stretch of road where light was still falling through a gap in the trees. When they did he recognised immediately from her gait and her hair the woman walking beside the lead horse, Ellen Monks, who had worked for him in the store for a year but had left two months back after an argument with his wife over a missing brooch left as a surety. He didn't believe Ellen a thief but Mary had other ideas. He'd had to let her go, but had known what would happen.

And the thing had turned out as he'd known it would, men
came less often into the store now that Ellen wasn't behind the
counter. She was talking up at the rider. The other two women
walking, he saw now, with arms linked would be Maggie Monks
and Christina McKinnon. They were talking with the middle
rider. The fellow bringing up the rear was alone. All three riders
wore well-cut coats but their hats and the failing light made it
impossible to make out faces. Single men came in from miles
around for the Boxing Day ball, stockmen, station clerks, the
occasional squatter's son. Whoever they were, labour, trade or
gentry, if the Monks girls and their cousin had talons into them
the fellows had notes in their shammies.

He watched until the six disappeared behind the corner of
the house. Then, walking as quickly as the need to keep an eye
peeled for snakes allowed, he crossed to the other side of the
paddock. They did not reappear. They'd halted at the store. Ellen
would see to it the mug she'd hooked wouldn't get out the door
for under ten quid. And he wouldn't get anything for his money
either. Morriss had tried and got nothing. He gave the memory
of those attempts a sour grin and lifted his foot and tapped out
his briar on his boot heel and ground the dottle thoroughly into
the parched dirt. He pocketed the pipe and started towards the
pale oblong of light that marked the back door, curious to see

who it was Ellen had collared, but in no great hurry. She would try on every bonnet and bracelet in the place.

He passed through the kitchen and living room to the curtain that led to the store and stopped to put on again the dustcoat hanging from its hook. He heard who he thought was Christina McKinnon ask about grog and a man's voice reply that grog could wait, there'd be plenty where they were going. He put a smile to his lips and parted the curtain. Their faces turned towards him, all but his wife's and that of the man standing over at the tack examining bridles. The two men at the counter he didn't know. His wife was adding up the figures she'd jotted on the pad. She flashed him a frightened warning look then put her head back down. The look puzzled him. The men were scrubbed-up stockmen, clean-shaven and with fresh pomade in their hair. The man beside Christina was in his late twenties. He had his shammy out and untied. The young fellow standing with Maggie held two clean fivers in his hand. Oddly, both had their coats tightly buttoned despite the baked air. Morriss nodded to the men, 'Gents,' then to the women, 'And ladies,' allowing a hint of sarcasm into his voice. He ran his practised eye over the three piles on the waxed deal of the counter, bonnets on top, ribbons, two each of the silk chemises new in that week, and, at the bottom of each pile, a crinoline. He looked at Ellen and gave her a knowing pout. 'Crinolines, my goodness. It's to be quite a night.'

From over at the tack Jack said, 'Still the oily bastard, ain't you, *Constable* Morriss.'

Ben watched the feigned affability drain from the man's face along with the colour.

'Ah . . . Jack—Mr Gilbert.'

'Pity you ain't still a trap, Mr Morriss,' Ben said. 'He's worth a warrant now.'

'He can take me without one, I'm any man's. If he's game.' He walked to the counter. 'I suppose you've guessed who these two "gents" are.' He lobbed a roll of pound notes onto the countertop beside Mrs Morriss's busy pencil but kept his eyes on the man. 'Christmas. We're givin, not takin.'

He tipped Ellen Monks a wink. The women laughed. He was already swivelling his head theatrically to take in the high crowded shelves lining the back wall. His gaze stopped at a row of china Toby mugs.

'Could give each of them fat fellas somethin.'

'Might be a bit noisy, Jack,' Ben said.

'It's just I was thinkin, Ben, from the prosperin look of the place I'd reckon he'd have to be doin a fair bit of robbin himself.'

He turned from the counter and swept a hand towards the likewise crowded floor, with its crates of boots and soap, barrels of nails, salted fish, cheeses, a rack of miner's tools, rakes and brooms, an entire corner filled with saddles, rugs and other tack.

'He is,' Ellen Monks spat. 'Worse than a bloody bank. Both of em.'

Her last words were directed at the top of Mary Morriss's head. The woman went on pretending to add.

'Don't worry some to lie neither when they lose sureties.'

When the woman still refused to look at her Ellen reached out and rapped hard on the countertop. The woman jumped, the pencil veering across the columns of figures.

Ben had seen, at Long Nose Creek, what both Monks girls could do with their blood up. On the second night Ellen's answer to Jack baiting her was two hard punches to the face. Luckily Jack had been too drunk to stand. Her fist might not stop at a rap on the counter. He said quickly, 'So what do I owe you, Mrs Morriss? For Miss McKinnon's.'

The frightened woman had to go again to the piles of clothing to identify whose was which. Then she looked at the pad.

'Ah, nine pounds, three and eightpence, Mr Hall.'

He drew a ten-pound note from his shammy and dropped it on the counter beside the pad and pointed past her shoulder at a vase of cheroots. 'I'll take my change in them.' He turned to the man and unbuttoned his coat to reveal the revolvers. 'You'd better fetch your jacket and keys, Morriss, you're goin to a ball.' He lifted the counter hatch. 'I'll come with you and see it's all you fetch.'

●

By ten the ball was in full swing, tables and benches pushed to the walls, a haze of dust and tobacco smoke hanging suspended between the heads of the dancers and the hung lanterns. Some fifty couples were dancing the rowdy bush version of the schottische to the tune Keel Row being played by two men standing on upturned crates, one with a concertina, the other a fiddle. A few couples still danced with a stiffness that came from knowing they had armed guests and that no one was permitted to leave the hotel. But helped by the music and the flow of grog most had now let themselves go and were happily dancing out the workaday year, and bushrangers welcome. Even with every window and the double doors to the road open wide the room was daytime hot and the publican and his wife and the hired barkeeps were being run off their feet fetching beer or port or handing over glasses to be filled from the giant punchbowl standing on the counter.

At the finish of the last set Ben had sent John, and Maggie with him, to take a second turn on the door. He looked between the dancers and saw that again the youngster had obeyed to the letter, his back to the timber of the right-hand door and his coat open with its flaps tucked behind their butts to display the belted revolvers. He'd been excited on the walk to the hotel by the prospect of bailing up and keeping watch over so many people, but the job itself had given him an attack of nerves. His eyes were still darting everywhere but, helped by a few grogs, he'd unbent enough to have his left arm across Maggie's bare shoulders. As Ben watched he took a swig from the port bottle in his other hand, then handed it to Maggie, who turned to the wall to drink from the bottle neck. Ben grinned at this semblance of ladiness, and remembered he too had an arm about a woman. He hardened his grip and Christina McKinnon responded immediately, raising her face to him and parting her lips. Her tongue found his, then she turned again to the room, her eyes daring any to disapprove. Long Nose was too far, he told himself, when they left here they'd find a patch of scrub. Take a bottle. He glanced at the gin bottle standing on the windowsill. There were a few swallows left. She'd had more than he. With so many faces and hands to watch he'd kept the reins on his drinking. Even so he was feeling pleasantly tight. He looked out onto the floor to find

Jack and heard him before he saw him, plumb in the middle of course. He was flinging Ellen half off her feet with each turn at the end of the slip steps, then flapping whichever arm came free for the hop and crowing like a cock. He'd cleared a circle with his antics. Wild as he was being, though, he had his coat buttoned—more, Ben knew, to keep revolvers from hitting the floor than to spare his fellow dancers the sobering sight of them. He studied the faces of the couples circling about Jack and Ellen. Most were grinning or laughing outright, but a man in his fifties with heavy side-whiskers and his straight-backed wife were not. Ben nudged Christina.

'Who are them two—muttonchops and his missus?'

'That's bloody Hulett. Owns the produce and everythin else Morriss don't.'

'They look a bit sour on us bein here.'

'Not yous! They're sour on bein in the same room with girls named Monks.'

Ben began to ask where in the village was the produce, but broke off when he saw Jos Strickland dancing Susan towards his side of the room. They'd not acknowledged they knew one another. An exchange of looks at the doorway had made the tacit agreement. Now he and Susan were three yards away, doing the slip steps. Jos propped mid-step and lifted his left foot to inspect the heel of his boot. He placed his foot back on the floor and stamped the heel twice on the boards but Ben saw his gaze was not on his boot but was snaking through the dancers to the bar. He muttered to Susan and took her again in his arms and they danced the few more steps to where Ben and Christina stood. He propped again to inspect his boot heel and hissed at the floor, 'Ben—watch Morriss! Bastard's tryin to recruit some blokes to rush yous!' He cocked his ear to the music and danced Susan away.

Ben pushed Christina from him, already unbuttoning his coat. There were sixty, seventy men in the room. If a few moved the rest might get brave. They'd be swamped! He plunged into the dancers, the revolver above his head.

'Morriss! You bloody dog! Where are you? Jack—find Morriss!'

A ripple of panic swept across the floor. Lost in the tune the players were still squeezing and scraping. Ben changed direction and skidded to a halt at the crates and waved the barrel under their noses. A woman screeched as Jack, trying to get out of the hemming circle, elbowed her hard in the ribs. Ben yelled again, 'Morriss!', his voice amplified by the silencing of the instruments. As his mouth closed he glimpsed the man crouched and running a weave through the dancers like a hare through tussocks. He was almost at the middle window. He clambered onto the sill and jumped. Jack arrived seconds after him and fired two shots blind. The sound in the packed room was enormous. Women screamed, men swore, all clapping hands to their ears. Ben slid to the next window and peered cautiously out, revolver poised, not sure the man mightn't hurl a rock. Jack was doing the same.

'You see him?'

'Nah. Can't hear neither with this bloody racket. He's probably runnin for the store but, and a gun.'

Ben turned to the room.

'All of yous—listen! We treated him decent and this's what the mongrel's chose! So his damn store's burnin to the stumps!'

Jack was already moving towards the door, a path opening for the revolvers. Mary Morriss headed Ben off and clutched his arm.

'Please, Mr Hall. It's my place too!'

He shook her loose. 'He should have bloody thought of that.'

John was already outside. Jack halted in the doorway, leaning out to peer into the roadway, the revolver in his right hand aimed there, the other into the crowded room. Ben stopped beside him and lifted the revolver to point at the ceiling, finger on the trigger. Those who could see hushed those behind. He waited until he could be heard. 'No one leaves. Anyone tries he'll get his brains blown out.' He lowered the revolver and found Mary Morriss. Looking into her tearful pleading face he felt a terrible urge to pull the trigger. He turned quickly to Jack. 'You got John?'

'Thirty yards—the right edge of the road.'

'Watch em for a bit, then come.'

As soon as his heels left the verandah Mary Morriss was at the doorway.

'Please, Mr Gilbert, spare my clothes! And my wedding dress. Let Ellen bring them out. Please.'

He motioned with the revolver that she rejoin the crowd.

'They'll be all right.'

'Oh thank you, Mr Gilbert, thank you!'

Their three women had gathered before the doorway holding valises and bonnets. Ellen stepped to Mary Morriss, said into her face, 'I might find that bloody brooch too.'

Jack had marked his man, a burly six-footer. He singled him out with the revolver.

'You, matey—what's your name?'

'James Ferry.'

'Well, Mr Ferry, you're seein no one leaves. We're out, you shut and bar the doors. I catch em open I'll come back and deal with you.'

Ben halted in the roadway. There was no moon. The light from the hotel's windows and verandah was more hindrance than help, creating long shadows. John was visible only as a darker shape moving in shadow along the other side of the road, boots soundless in the selvage of dust.

'John.' He waited till the shape stopped moving. 'You seen him?'

'Nah. Ain't ahead of me I don't think, I come straight out. I reckon he's planted. He can probably hear us.'

Ben pushed both revolvers into his belt and cupped his hands round his mouth. 'Morriss, you mongrel! We're gonna burn your place to the ground!'

He heard Jack somewhere behind him mutter, 'Jesus,' and in a moment he was beside him. 'I thought we was keepin quiet.'

'Yeah, well that might get the bastard movin.'

They began to walk again. Ellen came up beside Jack and took his arm. Christina arrived at Ben's right side but didn't reach to touch him, his anger too potent. They rounded the bend in the road with canegrass growing from a ditch they'd passed earlier in the night in much merrier mood and came in sight of the store. A single lantern burned on a post at a safe remove from the verandah. They saw John veer to walk along the fringe of the pool of light. He ducked below the railing and moved along the wall to the double doors and reached and tested the padlock. The oval of his face turned towards them. He called in a stage whisper, 'He ain't been here.'

'He wouldn't open that,' Ellen hissed, 'he'd have gone round the back.' She turned her face up to Jack. 'I gotta go round there too and fetch her bloody dresses. If they ain't changed where they hide the spare.'

Jack lifted a revolver. 'Mr Colt makes a good key. Anyway, damn her dresses, bastard can buy her new ones.'

Ellen stopped. 'Really?' She giggled. 'Good!'

There was a sudden loud thud. John had given the doors a hard flat-foot kick. He raised his foot to give another.

'Hey—you won't, she's barred, we gotta go round the side!'

'I'll get our nags,' Maggie said to her sister.

John made to go with her. Ben told him to stay and keep an eye out for Morriss.

Ellen found the key in its place on a bearer stump and let them in through the store's side door. She went to the shelves beside the curtain leading into the house and pointed to a brass quart measure pushed into a high corner.

'Jack—fetch that down.'

She gave Ben a knowing wink. Jack upended the measure above the counter and notes fluttered down like butterflies.

'Bastards thought I was blind.'

'What other hides you know?' Jack said, reaching to flick her on the arse. She dodged his hand, poked out her tongue.

'I ain't done enough for yous?'

They lit two of the hung lanterns. The women gathered quick booty of bolts of silk, linen dresses, embroidered Chinese slippers and knee and ankle riding boots. Jack took down the bridle he'd examined earlier in the night and dropped it by the barred double doors, then skated on his gritty soles to the counter and vaulted it and grabbed by their necks six bottles of claret. Ben was filling a cotton drawstring bag with painted lead soldiers. He drew and tied the string and shoved the bag inside his shirt where it settled with a dull clank. He shook both lanterns, then lifted down the fuller one and unscrewed the lid of its tank and began backing to the door they'd entered by, pouring paraffin on the boards.

'Hey—go out the front.'

'You didn't see a bloody great padlock.'

Jack smacked himself on the forehead and went to the double doors, juggled the bottles, threw the bridle onto his shoulder. Ben stood while they all passed by him and out carrying their spoils. He looked about the crowded floor and shelves. With a gentle lob all this would pass from existence. He had never burned a building. It felt like a sin to rank almost with shooting a man, destroying him by destroying all he owned, the roof over his head. He wondered if the traps who'd burned Sandy Creek had entertained the same doubts before they struck a match. He would

never have lived there again, Biddy had stripped it of the best of
their stuff. Still, he'd built the place with his own hands, every
stone and timber. The man hadn't put a hand to this place. And
he was an ex-trap. 'Sorry, you bastard.' He turned the lantern
on its side so the glass would hit and lobbed it into the darkly
glistening pool.

The women wanted to stand and watch. He told them the
flames already filling the display windows made them too good
a target. John fetched the horses from the patch of scrub where
they'd left them, then all walked along the road they'd used to
enter Binda. They met Maggie a hundred yards along riding
hers and leading the other two. The women changed out of
their ball dresses, moving about in their undergarments while
they carefully packed away finery and spoils onto their mounts.
John leaned to Jack and whispered, slightly awed, 'They ain't
shy, are they.' When they wore riding habits Maggie took off
her old boots and flung them into the bushes and pulled on the
ankle boots her sister had taken for her. All mounted up. Ellen
walked her horse casually over to Jack. She swung a rein and
caught him a stinging lash on the thigh, then kicked her horse
into a gallop and tore off laughing. He sat stunned, then swore
and pulled his mount's head round and kicked after her.

When they were just the drumming of hooves Ben turned in the saddle to the other two women.

'I hope yous bloody know where she's takin him—he's got the grog.'

9

A month later the three were working the lucrative roads around Goulburn and Yass. Ben asked John did he want to visit his mother and sister and he said no. He wouldn't give a reason.

They made south from Gunning when an advance party of traps stumbled on them waiting on the hill up from the ford for the mail. They had to push their mounts hard to get away, one trap on a big bay pursuing them for miles before the bay too finally blew. So it was that an evening late in January saw them riding into the village of Collector, its only buildings of note a new sawn-timber Anglican church and the fieldstone-and-mortar inn, Kimberley's. They approached the inn from the south, that side having the fewest windows, all but one with blinds drawn.

Four horses were tied at a rail beside a stone trough. None was worth trading the animals they rode for. The smell of frying chops drifted on the air mingled with the stink of sullage. They watered the horses at the trough and examined the flanks of the four tied there. None bore the Crown brand. Ben sent John to stand at the corner of the building where he could observe the road in both directions and he and Jack went inside with coats buttoned and asked a girl going to the yard with empties for the publican. She stood the bottles on a table and went back into the bar. When a jowled paunchy man in his fifties came out and introduced himself, Thomas Kimberley, they bailed him and marched him into the bar and rounded up the drinkers, then proceeded through to the dining room and bailed the lodgers and travellers just sitting down to their dinners. Jack ordered three plates of chops and eggs and the spud and cabbage fry and then all in the inn aside from the serving girl and the cook were lined up at a doorway opening into a grassed and fenced yard adjoining the inn's side wall. The wives of two travellers, Mrs Kimberley and a boy of ten were pardoned through, but each man as he passed by Ben and his revolver emptied his pockets into a calico sack held by the publican. When the last was through and seated on the grass, Ben called to John to move to the opening in the paling fence where he could watch both the captures and the road.

'Jack and me'll do the upstairs.'

John counted the captures for his own satisfaction, seventeen, then beckoned the boy over and told him to go and untie their horses and lead them to the front steps of the inn and not let go the reins whatever happened or it would be the worse for him. Through the open upstairs windows began to come the screech of drawer runners and the crash of things hitting the floor. Ben appeared at a window. 'John!' He held a single-barrelled shotgun out over the sill. 'She's loaded with a green.' He waited for John to jam the revolvers into his belt then lobbed the gun flat. John caught it by barrel and stock. 'And here's more, and caps.' Ben lobbed a soft leather sack and vanished from the frame.

John checked to see there was already a cap on the nipple, then shoved the sack in his side coat pocket. Relieved to have a more intimidating weapon, he walked back to the gap in the fence and again did a head count. They were all there. But when he turned again to the road his belly performed a flip. A uniformed trooper carrying a carbine, bayonet fixed, had appeared on the road, coming from the direction of the village's few houses. Following was a younger man who, from having the same sandy hair, might have been his son. They were sixty, seventy yards off. The younger one appeared to be unarmed, but in the barred shade of the trees it was near impossible to decide. Keeping his eyes on the pair, John crabwalked to the inn's front doorway.

'Ben—traps comin!'

The sounds of ransacking stopped. Ben's voice came down the stairs. 'How many?'

'Two. Hang on—one, might be.'

'Well bail the bastard!'

He ran hunched and watching back to the gap in the fence and through and crouched behind the palings. 'Stay where yous are,' he called over his shoulder, 'and keep your gobs shut!' then lifted his head so his mouth was above the palings. 'Boy—let go of them reins and I'll blow your lid off!' He'd not had to face a trap before on his own. He touched a finger to the pulse in his throat. It was jumping like a small animal. He sucked in air and blew it out at the grey timber of the paling directly before his face, then, by feel, drew and half-cocked a revolver and with the tip of the barrel found the opening at the top of his boot and pushed the barrel in. He wasn't steady enough crouched, his thighs were shaking. He lowered his right knee to the ground and rested the barrel of the shotgun in the nock made by two palings. He thumbed the hammer to full cock and swung the bead to find the approaching uniform. The younger man was slowing, one arm extended as if to clutch at the sleeve of the man in front. John heard him say, 'There's one of them—behind the fence.' The trap answered without turning his head. 'I've got eyes, son.' The fellow was English-born. He cocked the carbine, the heavy click of its mechanism carrying so clearly in the drowsy air as to feel to John it was right beside his ear. He swallowed to break the tightness in his throat.

'You—trap—stand where you are!'

The younger one had already halted. The trap ignored the order. Maintaining a steady walk, he raised the carbine and settled the stock into his shoulder. He was now only thirty paces away. He had blue eyes, an apron of beard below his jaw that matched his pale blond hair. John centred the bead on his chest.

'You deaf?'

He heard the rising panic in his own voice. He had from the first hated and feared the police carbines, the roar of them and the shocking hole made by the .65 ball they threw. A paling wouldn't stop it, at this range the ball would smash clean through. 'No thanks!' he whispered and pulled the trigger.

Too close for spread, the heavy pellets and their wire struck the man in the breastbone. Dead on his feet he staggered, the carbine still levelled. John dropped the empty shotgun, snatched the revolver from his boot, cocking it, and fired, the bullet striking the man in the face. His body dropped to the roadway leaving the younger man standing exposed some twenty paces further back, his mouth agape. His mouth clapped shut and he turned and ran. Without thought, John snapped a shot after him. The man kept running, head into his neck as if to ward off a blow. He veered to the roadside and leaped the drain into a stand of rushes.

John rose unsteadily from his knee, half afraid the dead man, as in a dream, would climb to his feet and come at him again. He kept the revolver aimed. But the trap stayed on his back, right leg buckled under him in a way no living man could lie. He felt a grin start at his mouth, then spread across his face. He'd brought down a trap! On his own, and the bastard armed with a carbine! From far off, it seemed, he heard the clatter of boot heels on wooden stairs. He turned to his witnesses, who'd stayed sitting as ordered but were craning their necks trying to see over the palings.

'Well there's another of your bloody traps down.'

'Who is it?' the publican, Kimberley, said quietly.

'How would I know? A little sandy bastard.'

Jack and Ben burst through the doorway, revolvers levelled. They saw John standing unharmed, then the uniformed body lying in the road, the face staring up at a sky of mild blue streaked with pink. They uncocked the revolvers. John pointed with his at the prone figure.

'Bastard wouldn't stand. He damn-sure won't now.'

Ben looked at the boy with the horses. He still had a tight hold of the reins but was whimpering and had pissed in his trousers.

'It's all right, boy, no one's goin to hurt you, just keep hold of them reins.'

The boy seemed not to hear. The whimpering turned to a thin mewling and he began to shake. Ben pushed the revolvers into his belt and walked to him.

'Hey, look here at me, don't look there.'

Kimberley had stood and come to the fence.

'It's the boy's father.'

John heard, but was already stooping for the shotgun. It had brought down a trap, it was going with him. Ben glared at the publican.

'What in hell was he doin here?'

'Returning empties.'

Two other men had stood and come to stand beside Kimberley. Ben pointed to one in a striped miner's shirt. 'You—blue shirt— come here and hold these nags.' He looked at Kimberley and hooked his head towards the boy. 'Take him inside and get a brandy and milk down him.'

The publican made no attempt in coming through the gateway to avoid colliding with John's elbow.

'Hey!'

'Leave it, John,' Ben said.

The publican had to grip the boy's wrists and prise the fingers open. He held the reins out to the waiting man, then took the boy by the shoulder and wiped the slobber from his chin with his hand and turned him towards the inn door.

Jack had walked out to the dead man and was standing at his hip. Ben walked to the man's other side. He was short, not much taller than his son. He lay on his back, the eyes not yet glazed, the whites tinged pink by the sky. The left cheek was deformed yet strangely bloodless despite the red hole an inch below the eye. The chest was a mess.

'Game or a fool don't matter if you're killed twice,' Jack muttered. He crouched and unbuckled the brand-new cartridge belt the man was wearing, having to tug the tongue end from under the body.

'Hand me up his piece.'

Jack slung the belt over his shoulder and lifted the carbine from across the man's groin where it had come to rest and lowered the hammer.

'What was the bastard's name?' they heard John, behind them, say.

'Nelson.'

'Nelson! Well he wouldn't have made no admiral, just bloody walkin up like that. I'd reckon he was after the reward. Wonder how he'd like this caper—she's a dead trap's gun done for him.'

Ben glanced and saw he was displaying Parry's Colt to four men who'd decided no worse could happen and come to the fence.

He turned from the corpse and swung the carbine by the barrel and brought the stock down onto the brick-hard clay of the road and felt the timber fracture at the tang. He dropped the weapon beside the hand that had carried it to the inn.

'I'm goin back in and get them boots,' Jack said. 'You want that vest and breeches?'

'Bring everything we chucked in the hall. Get some sacks from Kimberley. Damned if I'm goin without a feed, either.' He looked again towards the fence. John had the revolver angled towards the setting sun for the men to view the police stamp. 'Hey!' The heads of all spun towards him. 'One of yous go fetch a blanket. You, mate, with the red hair.' The man touched himself on the chest, then nodded wildly and scampered towards the door Kimberley had left open. Ben moved his gaze to John. John stared back. Yeah, Ben thought, it's swoll you already. He nodded towards the revolver. 'Put her away, we're leavin. Go round the back and tell the cook plate up that grub and stick in a box. And some grog. And watch him round the damn bottles—make sure they're unopened.'

The youngster's face hardened. He didn't want to leave the front of the inn. The cooling corpse lying out on the road was his doing. What trap have you ever shot? his eyes said. Ben looked past him to the oldest man in his audience.

'Friend, tell all them others they can go in and take a drink.'

He saw John decide for sense. The youngster turned and stalked towards the unpeopled corner of the inn but kept the revolver in his hand. Let it go, he said to himself. And he's right, you can't know what's waitin round there.

10

His mother and Taylor had stayed up late drinking gin and were still in bed. He closed the door and crossed the verandah to the steps, unbuttoned and pissed in the left-hand tub of geraniums. He did it every chance he got. Weeds he pissed on died. Geraniums were proving to be tougher.

He buttoned himself and went down the steps and started towards the woodheap. Halfway there he remembered and glanced up to the clump of boulders at the dead wattle. He halted and stared, looked away, then looked again. The bare skull of the biggest boulder wore two bumps like the nub horns on a young ram. He studied the trees beyond the boulders, scrutinising the edges of each trunk before moving to the next with the same slow thoroughness he brought to scouting new ground for bunny sign. He saw only forms and colours that belonged. But he felt watched. He walked to the woodheap and snatched up a fistful of chips in one hand and three splits and turned and walked with long strides back to the steps, not wanting to run with those eyes on him, but thrilled to his core at the morning split open like a block by an axe.

.

In his left hand the boy carried an empty jute sack, old bloodstains along its bottom seam. His right clutched five steel stakes, their chains running over his shoulder to the traps clanking softly against his back and each other as he walked. He wore the trousers and green flannel shirt Ben had seen him first come out the door in, but on his feet he now had boots laced with twine, their leather worn through to white. Ben had unbuttoned his coat for comfort and he saw the boy's eyes go to the revolvers. Harry nodded, said hello, but kept hold of the sack and stakes. Ben forced the issue by putting out his hand. The boy hesitated, then transferred the sack and took his hand but withdrew his almost as soon as their palms met. Ben lifted a finger towards the hut.

'He not gettin up today?'

Harry shrugged.

'Been on the bottle has he?'

The boy looked past him. 'Her too.'

'Ah. I reckon we might be safe here for a bit, then.' He pulled from inside his shirt the bag from Morriss's store and held it out to Harry by the drawcord. 'These are yours. You'll have to plant em some place.'

'What's in it?'

Ben jiggled the bag, producing the soft dull clank he'd felt against his belly each step of the walk down from the ridge. 'Have to look, won't you.'

Harry dropped the sack to the ground and swung the traps from behind his back and lowered them onto it. He wiped his hands down the thighs of his trousers and took the bag. He loosed the cord and cautiously inserted a hand and, after feeling about, drew from the bag a painted guardsman standing at attention, musket on shoulder, silver helmet twinkling in the sunlight. His mouth fell open. He quickly masked his joy and lowered the guardsman back through the mouth of the bag and pulled the cord tight. 'How many's in here?'

'That's for you to find out. Later.'

'Where'd you get em?'

'A store. Don't matter where. Tuck em away.' He'd had a sudden picture of the several dozen he'd left, now cold blobs of lead. He nodded down at the traps. 'So, you been doin all right?'

'Some days.'

'Let's go see.'

Harry slid the bag inside his shirt at the waist and picked up the traps in one hand and the sack in the other and lifted the index finger of the hand on the sack to point diagonally up the ridge. Ben jutted his chin, you lead. He waited for the boy to pass, then gave the hut below a searching glance, saw the door and curtains still closed, no smoke from the chimney, and fell in behind him. Biddy would take a drink before but always stopped at tipsy. He wondered had he done this, or being with Taylor. He couldn't ask the boy when had his mother started drinking to get drunk.

'So what are you gettin a skin?'

'Threepence big ones, tuppence the others,' Harry said over his shoulder.

'Not real bad. Who buys em?'

'Mr Cellini.'

'And he's who?'

'In Burrowa. The hatter.'

Ben gave the boy a smile he didn't see. 'Hatter, eh. Long time since I forked out for a hat.' He waited but the boy didn't pick up his meaning, or chose not to. 'And . . . he straight with you?'

The boy climbed for a few paces before he answered. 'He takes em in—Taylor.'

'Ah. Well I'd reckon he'd be the one you'd have to watch.'

He waited. The boy veered to go round a fallen wattle.

Ten minutes brought them into a shaded gully, its grass cropped, dry and fresh pellets lying thickly over the circles of bare earth the animals used for their communal dung heaps. Harry didn't slow, he headed towards a dense patch of bracken in which Ben could see the crease of a path. Near the other side Harry broke and twisted off a strong green frond. They emerged into a clearing shorn of herbage and riddled with holes. The rabbit had already seen them. It began squealing and scrabbling on three legs to the limit of the chain. Harry walked to it, lay the frond and traps down and took a short club from the sack. He hauled the rabbit in, put a boot on it and killed it with a single sharp blow to the skull. The cool efficiency impressed the man. The boy released the limp animal and held it by the hind legs and beat the dirt from its pelt with the frond, then opened the mouth of the sack and dropped the body in. He kneeled and pulled up the stake by the chain and shook the dirt from the old square of newspaper that had served to cover the plate and jaws, then stood and carried trap and paper to a new hole, checked its ramp for use, kneeled again and with both hands began scooping out a well.

.

They were sitting on a log, a folded muslin between them on which lay ship's biscuits, half an onion and a serrated block of pale yellow cheese. The sack hung from a branch, its belly now full, fresh blood oozed out through the old stains.

Ben cut a vee from the block and offered it to Harry on the point. The boy shook his head. Ben lifted the cheese to his own mouth. Harry's eyes slid again past Ben to the revolvers lying along the log. His gaze had flicked to them all through the meal. Ben picked up the one beside his thigh, the Navy with the chipped grip he'd used as the model for his whittling. He removed the caps and placed the revolver in the boy's hand. Harry shifted its weight to both hands and sat staring at it.

'You lettin Charlie use yours?'

'Not use—he's mindin it.' He hefted the revolver and pointed it at the sack.

'Don't dry-fire her, mate—she's touchy that one.'

Harry moved the barrel and sighted on a trunk and clicked his tongue.

'I ain't come here just to visit. Got somethin to ask you. I'm thinkin of goin away.'

The boy swung the barrel to a crow that had settled in a tree to watch for scraps, but the changed angle of his head said he was listening.

'Pretty far.'

Harry spoke without shifting his gaze from the line of the barrel and the bird.

'Where?'

'Dunno for sure. But I been thinkin New Zealand. California, even. You heard of there?'

The boy nodded. 'They're havin a war.'

'That's the east side, the Yankees—that ain't California.' He studied the squinting profile. 'That from a newspaper too, is it?'

He waited. The boy was now cocking the hammer to watch the cylinder turn and easing it back down. War and newspapers had knocked the conversation sideways. He couldn't judge whether or not the boy knew about the second trap. He'd asked last time what happened at Jugiong. He'd have asked by now about Collector if he'd heard. He needed to get the other talked of first.

'So—she'd be a pretty big trip. First part'd be ride down to Melbourne all back ways, then get on a ship over to New Zealand. Not sure how I'll go with that. Jack's seen the ocean, reckoned it give him a fair shock first time he seen her. We think this country round here's big, ridin for days, but she's nothin to the ocean he reckons. We was just talkin one time, not about this. You're the first I told about goin away, right.' He waited for the boy to nod. 'Why I reckoned New Zealand is they got gold happenin same as here, Lambin Flat, and them places down Victoria. I'd try my luck over there first—change me name, grow a big crop of whiskers. If she's a shicer, up pegs and head to California. Won't have to hide there, I'll be a cleanskin, eh.'

The boy had lowered the revolver to his lap but was still cocking and uncocking it. Ben lifted the weapon from his hands and placed it on the log at the side away from the boy.

'Thing is, son, I could do with a mate.'

'You got some,' the boy said at his lap.

'They're still happy what they're doin.'

The boy didn't speak. Ben told himself, you said your piece, now shut up. The boy uncrossed his ankles, crossed them the other way, then back again.

'Without tellin her.'

Ben breathed in, slowly blew it out. 'Not much other choice, is there. Once we was well on our way we'd get word to her then. But first up we'd have to do like this mornin. You walk up here with a sack with whatever you want to bring, I'll be waitin with a nag for you—a decent nag, not a brum thing like that mare of Charlie's. Gives us a few hours till they'd come up lookin for you, we'd be miles gone by then.' He ran his tongue along his lips. 'It wouldn't be for good, mate, you'd see her again. Just me who'd be goin for good.'

Harry finally turned his head and looked at him. Ben thought himself good at reading eyes, he'd read many. But he couldn't read these.

'You worried about the traps?'

'What? How do you mean?'

'Why you're goin.'

'No. They don't worry me. Not in that way.' He could try to steer the talk back to Biddy. The boy was smart enough to sense he was being steered. 'You'll hear from her or him next time they're into Burrowa, so I'll tell you. Another one's copped it.' As soon as he spoke he saw the man staring at the sky, his chest like a rose had bloomed there. He shook his head before the boy could ask. 'John Dunn shot him. He told the fellow to stand and he kept comin.' The boy holding the reins and shaking was at the edge of his vision. He stared at the deep fissures in an ironbark and tried to keep him at the edge. The face of Kimberley, too, floated in, mouth twisted in the disgust he'd made no effort to hide as they gave their instructions before riding off. Can't undo none of it, he told himself, so get rid of em. You're here, bloody brighten up!

'So, what do you say? To seein all them places?'

Harry reached out with the toe of his right boot and delicately crushed a bull ant exploring their crumbs. His eyes stayed on the ground scouting for another.

'Why'd he keep comin, the trap? If John told him?'

'I think he counted on scarin John into missin.'

'So it was the trap's fault.'

'If you're told to bail and you don't, you get what comes.'

'Was other people there?'

Taylor would take pleasure in reading out that they'd half orphaned a boy.

'Yeah. An inn full. Listen, that business ain't what I come for. What do you say to what I been puttin?'

Harry sniffed, then cleared his throat, the mannerisms of an old man.

'How would we tell her?'

'Eh? Ah . . . whole lot of ways. We'd have to see what offers.'

'What if they say yes but they don't do it?'

'Who?'

Harry turned his head and looked at him. 'The person. You know, who you ask to tell her.'

'Wouldn't just ask em, mate, I'd pay em. Give em a letter.'

The boy looked down again at the ground. Ben watched as the toe of the boot again went out and crushed a bull ant just turning away from the log with a cheese crumb in its jaws. The boy waited for another to discover the crushed one and crushed it too. He understood that he'd been given his answer. He stared again at the ironbark and willed himself not to betray either disappointment or anger. The boy was choosing the safety of what he knew. But he might change his mind. He now had a prospect to picture lying in bed at night. A month or so and the hut and the life offering there might start looking damned small. That was what he had to hope.

'You better get back home.'

He'd chosen the word deliberately, let it hang in the air as he swivelled and picked up the revolver and began fitting onto its nipple each of the caps lined up on the grey timber of the log.

·

Biddy was at the splitting block. She was broader across the arse than he remembered. He watched the blade blur down and the round of wood fall in two. A second later the ring and thud rose to the boulders where they stood. She might have a sore head but she hadn't lost her knack with an axe. His wife. Still his wife,

now and forever, the two of them spliced by Father Jerome in
St Michael's Bathurst. Harry broke his thoughts.

'You want one?'

He lifted the sack, its belly bumpy with bodies. Ben thought
to refuse out of pride. Then he nodded. 'Yeah. Dinner, eh.'

Harry tipped the five rabbits onto the ground, lifted the
largest aside.

'That's your biggest, ain't it?'

'You can have it.'

Ben took the knife from his trouser pocket and opened the blade.
The boy shook his head. 'She'll ask what I done with the bunny.'

Ben looked at him, then folded the blade and dropped the
knife back in his pocket.

'Your threepence.'

Harry crouched and placed the other rabbits back in the sack.
He twisted the neck and stood clutching the twist in his hand.
Ben saw he wanted to leave but didn't know how.

'Come here.'

Harry came, still holding the sack, and halted in front of him.
Ben reached into the opening of his son's shirt and drew out the
scapular by its cord and lifted the loop over the boy's head. 'She
must've broke, eh.'

He gathered scapular and cord into his hand and put into his inside coat pocket.

•

By early afternoon he was three ridges away, in a clump of yellow box, squatted at a smokeless fire raking its coals together with a stick. Gutted and split, the rabbit leaned in a stilled leap over the coals on a fork of green wattle. Beads of juice glistened on its skin. He rotated the fork to give the pinker of the hind legs to the heat, then stood and walked to the edge of the trees, drawing the scapular from the inside pocket of his coat in a motion already on the way to becoming habit. He halted at the fringe of the shade and stood drawing the cord through his fingers and studying the sweep of country to the south. There was no wind. Nothing moved but the distant white specks of wheeling cockatoos. The thought was coming more often. That wherever he was, he was at the centre of a cage. He couldn't have said when the notion first entered his head. Some time in the last months. It was more now than a notion, he could see the damn bars. They were grey steel, the height of a man on horseback. In a dream he'd ridden out of a clump of boulders and caught them just before they retreated, how he knew what they looked like. On the ride just done they had silently followed him, settled a ridge away. In the country before him he could see where they ran, just beyond the rim of the fold marking the river then up behind the low range where he'd be by evening. But by then they'd have shifted. He knew another man could ride to the ridge he nominated and not see them. At the same time he knew he was not mad. The cage was in his mind but it was there too in the country. Jack would understand. He'd scoff, but he'd understand. So too would've the fellow on the scapular. He lifted his hand and looked at the thin flaps.

'Gone past talkin to you, but.'

He was going to scorch his bunny black. He thrust the scapular back into its pocket.

11

They were to have met at noon on the wooded hill just south of Breadalbane, but the pack mare was favouring her left hind leg and wouldn't push and it was after five by the time he rode up into the clearing on the crown. An empty Old Tom bottle standing on a stump told him they'd been there and waited. He didn't dismount. He walked the horses round the perimeter of the clearing until he found the dollops of shit where their horses had been tied and rocks dislodged where they'd started down.

It was dark when he reached the Byrne farm. They were going to lay up for a few days, then circle east around Goulburn and hit the Great South Road again at Towrang. The traps wouldn't be expecting them to repeat themselves. He halted the horses by the yards and checked the horses standing there, recognising the black racing stallion they'd relieved a groom of a fortnight back on the road near Grabben Gullen and which Jack was now riding. He clicked the horses into a walk and rode past the original slab hut and on to the brick and weatherboard house Byrne and his sons had built. Tom Byrne told the world the house grew from his being a dab sower of oats and corn. Those like Ben knew its true foundation to be lifted horseflesh. The light of several lanterns fell across the verandah from behind the curtains and he heard raised voices, Jack's the loudest. They'd kept up the gin-guzzling. He halted the horses on the dirt square before the house and gave the low flat whistle. The voices fell instantly silent. The light in one window dimmed and the door opened halfway and a bearded man in shirtsleeves and braces and carrying a lantern held above his head stepped out onto the verandah.

'Goodnight, Tom.'

'Jasus! They reckoned ye weren't comin!'

The door was snatched open and Jack stepped out holding a lowered revolver. Ben saw from the wild eyes and wet mouth he was three-quarters shickered.

'Just in time for a bloody dance, Benjamin m'boy!'

Ben dismounted and led the horses to the verandah rail. He spoke at the reins as he tied them.

'Forgot my whistle, have you? And yous don't need a lookout.'

'Don't get all shirty. Christ! Come and get a grog down you.'

Jack pushed the revolver into his belt and stood at the top of the steps, legs akimbo, refusing to let Ben pass until he allowed himself to be embraced. When he did Jack pinned his arms and gave him a smacking kiss on the earhole, laughing as Ben shoved him away.

'There, you prickly bastard, now you won't hear no bloody whistles neither!'

He herded Ben before him into the house and Byrne closed the door. The living room had a mill-plank floor and was furnished with store-bought table and chairs, a lounge, an oak sideboard with glass-panelled doors. A fire of grubbed roots was burning in the brick fireplace and the air held the smell of boiled spuds and stewed mutton. John, eyes shining, was seated at the table beside Mrs Byrne, a big woman, Kerry-born like her husband, and with a permanently red face. The two Byrne sons, both now as broad as their father, were at the table's lowly end furthest from the fire. The surprise was Jos Strickland. Ben stopped, not knowing what to make of his presence. Strickland stood, as did Mrs Byrne, she having to place both hands on the table and push. She spoke the formal welcome to house and hearth, the old words and the lilt of them stirring a memory of his own mother. He thanked her. She broke the spell by barking, 'Now plonk yer arse and I'll fetch ye some grub.' She waddled to the serving bench and took a plate from the pile of used ones and dunked it in the bucket standing by the fire. Ben walked to Strickland who was waiting to shake hands.

'Jos. I didn't know you'd gone into the liftin business, thought you stuck to duffin.'

Strickland shook his head. 'I didn't lift em, I just brung em down.'

'Bloody long way. They must be well-known nags to bring em this far.'

'He come this far for a good price!' Byrne roared from behind Ben's ear. He stepped beside him and snapped finger and thumb at the younger of his sons. 'Don't sit gawkin, go fetch a clean pannikin! Sit yerself down, Ben, sit.'

Strickland sat again too. The pannikin arrived and Byrne filled it from one of the three uncorked bottles standing on the table. Ben sniffed it to confirm that it was indeed gin and took a sip, his mind still uncomfortable at meeting Jos Strickland here.

'What way did you come?'

'Eugowra, then to the Fish and followed her.'

'On your own?'

'I had em strung.'

'Lucky you didn't meet no traps. How many?'

'Five.'

John had picked up a newspaper from the table and folded it to the front page. Jack grabbed it and tucked it under his arm. He snatched up the pannikin standing in front of the chair opposite Ben and splashed it full from the nearest of the bottles and sat. He raised it in a toast.

'Here—forget bloody nags! To bein among friends!'

There was a chorus of 'hear, hear!'. Ben drank but hadn't finished with Strickland.

'So, as well as bein well known, are they any good?'

'Jesus, Ben,' Jack shouted, 'give over!'

'Yeah, in a minute. Are they?'

'They did some travellin gettin here.'

'I might take a look in the mornin. Pack mare's goin lame on me.'

Strickland lifted his chin towards the heavy man who'd sat touching Ben's elbow. 'There's your fella now. Not mine no more.'

Byrne turned and gave him a broad wink. 'Ye're welcome to look. Whether ye get more's down to what's in yer shammy.'

'Hey! Shut your gobs.'

Jack had the folded newspaper propped against his pannikin. The others had heard the item and quietened expectantly.

'As we're talkin of prices, I can announce young John here's had his raised. For that bloody fool at Collector. Have a listen at this.'

'I seen it,' Ben said, 'I don't need to hear it too.'

'What?'

'You're drunk, not deaf. Put the damn thing away.'

'You're in it too!'

'Put it away I said.'

Even Jack saw and heard he meant it. He made a face at Byrne, rolled the newspaper and slapped it into his hand before making a performance of tipping it over his right shoulder.

Mrs Byrne waddled back to the table with a steaming plate of buttered spuds and stew in one hand and a board with cut bread and cheese in the other. She set both before Ben and said to the room, 'An empty belly makes us all touchy. There ye go, Ben, and good appetite to ye.'

.

The table and chairs had been carried to the corners of the room and the rug rolled.

Byrne was playing The Rakes of Mallow on the mouth organ and banging time with his boot, his older son was playing a jew's harp. Jack was dancing with Mrs Byrne. She was twice as big as he, but moved as lightly as a woman half her size. His face was now as red as hers. They'd been going for close on ten minutes and the fire could have roasted a bullock. He signalled to Byrne with an imaginary pannikin and the man brought the reel to a tremolo finish, took the mouth organ from his lips and flourished it as if to a floor of dancers. Jack managed a whoop and a last spin, then made Mrs Byrne an elaborate mocking bow. She laughed and slapped his shoulder. He grabbed her rolly hand and pulled her over to the chair where Ben was nursing his pannikin.

'Here, have a dance with this bugger, get his blood movin!'

'I ain't dancin.'

Jack set his hands on his hips. 'Jesus, Ben—get up, man.'

Ben spoke to the woman. 'It's not you, Liz. I'm not in a mood for it.'

She nodded and lay a forgiving hand lightly on his cheek. Then she did a half-pirouette, her eyes narrowing. John tried to make himself small but she was already sailing across the room, hauled him to his feet.

'Come on, John Dunn! Yer pa could hoof it so ye must of learned somethin!'

Later again the table was back in the centre of the floor and the chairs around it. Byrne alone was playing for Mrs Byrne, who was singing the slow and lovely ballad The Exile of Erin. A mourning for all Ireland was in her voice.

.

They were bedded down in the barn, on thin horsehair mattresses laid over straw. A low mountain of bagged oats filled the centre of the earth floor. Two plough mares, the sulky mare and Byrne's and his sons' mounts were in stalls along one wall. The sulky itself was backed into a corner. The sky when they'd stumbled down the house steps was clouding over and a cool damp wind had sprung up, but they'd left the barn doors open, preferring to hear.

The sound that woke Jack and Ben was a groan. It was not a sound a horse made. They snatched up revolvers and rose onto their elbows. The wind had died and faint moonlight was now falling through the doorway. The sound, if from outside, had not silenced a calling morepork. It came again—from three yards away. 'Christ,' Jack muttered. They uncocked the revolvers and lay them again beside their pillows. Ben drew the blanket over his head. The groaning moved from single sounds to a procession, rising and falling but growing louder. 'John!' Jack called. When there was no respite he groped with his hand for a boot.

John sprang to sitting, not yet in his body but scrabbling for a revolver. He screwed round and saw Jack.

'Me—yeah! You was moanin like Old Nick himself was after you.'

John uncocked the weapon, put it down.

'You reckon we don't bloody hear yours.'

Jack lay down without answering, slid his arms under the blanket and drew it to his chin. Ben was already snoring softly. John reached to the bottle wedged between his boots. He pulled the cork with his teeth and took a swig and, not offering the bottle, thumped the cork back in. He couldn't yet lie back down. In his nightmare he'd woken to pitch darkness and his own clammy breath, not knowing where he was until he lifted his arms and his knuckles touched wood and stones and dirt clattered suddenly on the lid. He couldn't speak of that. But he needed to talk.

'Bloody good barn, this. Good crop of oats too. Always got a warm smell, don't they, fresh oats. Minds me of the stables at the tracks. Night before race day I always come and bedded down with the nags.'

As if it had heard, one of their mounts out in the yards whinnied. Jack slowly sat up, letting the blanket fall from his shoulders, his right hand finding again the revolver and his left coming over the hammer to muffle its cocking. John had found his, coffins fled. The morepork had stopped calling. They listened until the shirts were cool on their backs. Jack had his thumb on the hammer to lower it when both heard the scuff of a boot heel. The walker stopped as if afraid he might have been heard. John looked to Jack. He wanted to whisper, that be Byrne, you reckon? but Jack's whole being was directed towards the pale oblong of doorway. The walker came on again, more cautiously. They heard then a second pair of boots, further off. Jack rose silently to his socked feet. John did the same. Ben was still softly snoring. John looked at where his head would be beneath the blanket. Even a whisper might carry outside. But to step over hats and bottles to touch him awake was even riskier. Both pairs of boots continued as if whoever the walkers were they had their sights on the house, not the barn. Then they stopped. A man leaner and taller than Byrne or either of his sons stepped half into view at the right side of the doorway but some ten paces out and peered, his head swaying as he tried to make out the barn's interior. Jack and John fired together.

The horses erupted in their stalls. Ben dropped each hand onto a revolver and scrabbled to his knees, his legs tangled in the blanket. He kicked free and rose to a crouch, not knowing where the other two were till they appeared at either side of him in the muzzle flash when Jack fired. Ben waited for a flash in the yard and snatched a shot. The flash had revealed a man half kneeling, another lying on his belly. The animals were screaming and kicking at the stalls. If the planks gave, he, Jack and John wouldn't be men, they'd just be in the road of a bolt for the doorway. He slapped Jack on the shoulder. 'I'll do the walls!' He made a swift circuit, testing slabs with his shoulder. All were solid. There were no windows. The chorus of voices shouting in the yard told him they were well outnumbered. Cutting through them came a toff English voice.

'Men, find yourselves cover in sight of that doorway! Spread yourselves, don't bunch! Greer!'

'Sir!'

'Take someone and the two of you get round the back and fire between the slabs!'

'Yes, sir!'

'Sir, it's Spall, I've lit the haystack, give us light!'

'Good man!'

Ben scuttled back, took each by his shirt and pulled them down in a huddle.

'She's solid, only way out's the front. Forget the nags, they'll have em. We're out, turn right, into the corn. Yous ready? Bloody go!'

They rose as if from blocks and, silent in their socks, burst through the doorway into pale moonlight and a low dance of flames and snapping shots right and left at the greatcoated shapes still moving to take up positions behind the horse trough and a stack of unused bricks. Expecting them to run for their mounts, the police were caught wrongfooted when they veered right and sprinted for the corn growing head-high in the field twenty yards from the barn. Ben was almost at the fence, already hunching to duck through the rails, when his right arm was punched just above the elbow. He pitched forward, landing on his knees, the finger of his left hand jammed to the knuckle in the trigger guard, his right arm suddenly useless. He abandoned its revolver and scrambled to his feet and dived between the rails and rolled, felling stalks, then rose clutching his elbow between fingers and revolver butt and dashed into a row. John and Jack were ahead of him, blundering through leaves and litter. One of them fired blind and the wind of the bullet fanned his left ear. He veered in panic to his right into the next row. His arm was dead, but from the slipperiness of his fingers on the revolver butt he knew he was bleeding, and freely. Jack or John fired again and he got a bead on where they were, twenty or thirty yards ahead and to his left. Then he heard stalks splash and topple and they were, he thought, in the parallel row. It was hard to judge above the sound of his own breathing and the rasp of the corn leaves whether the shouts behind him were truly fading, but it sounded so. They'd be through the fence but they'd be trying to run in greatcoats and riding boots, coat flaps catching, soles and heels stumbling on the clods his socked feet moulded to. The shooting wasn't fading, though. As he had the thought a cob exploded in front of him and he ran into a shower of silks, the soft damp hairs clinging to his face like spiderweb. He called 'Jack!' in a hoarse whisper.

The crashing to his left stopped.

'Over ere!'

He pushed between stalks and saw them some twenty yards further up the row, their faces dimly illuminated by the orange glow now lying along the top leaves and tassels. When they saw he'd seen them they broke again into a run, then jinked sideways, John leading, and pushed through the line of stalks at their right and were gone. He slowed and did the same and spotted them again. Their hands were empty, they'd belted their revolvers to work across the rows. That would be John's devise, he knowing best the layout of Byrne's farm. The traps would be following the rows. Unable to match the speed of the two he moved on a heading he hoped would intersect with theirs when they all three reached the fringe of the field. He passed through thirty or forty more rows and finally the stalks thinned and he saw trees. He stumbled out onto a strip of unploughed ground with a post and rail fence. The two were twenty yards away, hands on knees and blowing like bellows. His arm was beginning its first throbs. He kept hold of the elbow, fingers and revolver now glued to the sleeve, and walked to them, his pulse hammering in his ears. Their faces, shirts, the fence rails, the trunks and scrub on the far side of a gully that formed a second boundary to the farm, all were bathed orange. He turned his head and saw that the sky above the corn was a glowing ball, sparks gushing hundreds of feet into the air. A stringybark peeled to the ground grew just outside the fence, its trunk a white-orange column. He pulled the revolver free of the sleeve and let the arm hang a second and pushed the sticky weapon into his belt and gripped his elbow again and veered towards the illumined trunk for a proper look. The stickiness was a false hope, the wound was bleeding steadily, oozing through the weave of the heavy linen and dripping from the soggy elbow. Jack stumbled over to him, his breath still coming in gasps.

'Christ . . . you hit? I thought you . . . bloody tripped!'

'Just above the elbow. Don't think she's busted but feels like the bastard's still in.' He started to bring the arm round and the nerves suddenly woke, stabbing both ways, forearm and shoulder. He retched and went onto his haunches, cold sweat breaking out on his brow. John must have joined them because he heard him say, but from what seemed a great distance away, 'Purcell's?'

'Yeah.' Jack leaned over him. 'Ben. Can you stand?'

'In a tick.' His hearing had returned but he thought he might still heave his guts. He could do that as well on the run as here. 'Yeah. Give us a lift.'

They each slid a hand under an armpit.

'You right to get through the fence?'

'Find out, won't I.'

'Where's your guns?'

'Lost one. Other one's here.' He tapped the butt with his good elbow.

Jack spoke away from him. 'You hear the bastards?'

John had mounted a rail to peer over the corn. 'Still goin the wrong way. Better but if we're below ground.'

Jack spoke again in his ear. 'Ben, the dodge is we're goin along the gully. Be rougher but she brings us out by Purcell's. Gimme your arm.'

Ben let go the dead elbow and instead took the wrist and pinned it hard to his chest. Jack gripped his left elbow and together they ducked through the fence. He half slid them down a bank of crumbly yellow clay to the gully bed, then released his arm and told him they'd do a slow jog if he could. Anything he might trip on Jack would call back over his shoulder. He tried and found he could manage a jog if he dug his nails as hard as he could take into his wrist and thought of nothing but each breath, sucking it in, blowing it out. He heard the soft thud of John's feet behind him, the crackle of leaves, then suddenly he wouldn't, then a bit further along the thudding would return, and he thought his hearing was drifting in and out. Then he realised the youngster was halting to listen and catching them up.

.

Purcell's was half a mile. John knew him best, the man had been transported on the same ship as his father. When the three came stumbling in their socks up from his ploughed bottom paddock Purcell and his stockman were on the steps of the main hut staring at the glow in the sky. They were in trousers and shirts, the flaps out, Purcell with his braces hanging. They needed no lantern to see who their visitors were.

'Goodnight there, John lad, lads. Ain't seen yous in a while. Spot of bother.'

'Ben's copped one,' John called.

'How bad?'

Ben answered for himself. 'Walkin, ain't I. My bloody arm.'

When they reached the steps Purcell pointed towards the glow. 'Fred and me were hopin that weren't Tom's pride and joy.'

'We was in the barn,' John said. 'Traps fired a haystack so's they could see.'

'That what she is. Tom won't much like that, either. But I'd reckon right now he's got bigger worries. And I suppose I will too, but in yous come.'

They walked Ben inside and while Purcell lit lanterns they cleared the plank table and got him up and lying on his back. Jack asked for hot water, and carbolic if they had any. The stockman had tucked in his shirt and rolled his sleeves. He said quietly at Jack's shoulder, 'I'll have a look if you want, Mr Gilbert. I done me share of em at Lambin Flat.'

Jack turned and studied him. He'd seen him only the once before, knew nothing about him. But the man was calmly returning his gaze, and Purcell, an ex-lag, was still employing him. He turned again to Ben, who had his eyes closed.

'Ben?'

'Go to, matey,' Ben said without opening his eyes.

Purcell had hung one lantern and stood the other on the table, then gone to the fireplace and stirred the embers and added sticks and was now sliding the kettle on its hook into the centre of the rail.

'You got gin?' Jack said.

Purcell pointed towards the square bottle standing on the dresser and the pannikins hanging from nails. Jack took down three. Seeing the third, Purcell straightened. 'Not for him yet. When it's out.'

He was over fifty, but he was still a big hard man and Jack was suddenly too tired to argue. He filled one for himself and handed the second to John.

'You better take that and keep nit. Be light soon.'

Purcell was hanging corn sacks over the curtains. The stockman had cut away the bloodied sleeve and was pressing around the entry hole with his fingertips. He gave a soft click of the tongue. 'You was damn lucky, Mr Hall—the bugger who shot you didn't prime his cartridge properly. The ball's hit the bone and stopped.'

'I ain't feelin lucky.' He pushed the man's fingers away and rolled on his good arm and vomited onto the floor. 'Christ. Sorry, George.'

'You ain't the first done that here.'

As the man spoke Ben vomited again. He wiped his mouth on his sleeve and waited, chin over the edge, but his guts seemed to have emptied themselves. He lay down again.

'Give us some water, will you.'

'Just to rinse your mouth,' the stockman said. 'If you don't want to keep doin that.'

Purcell took down a pannikin and went to the water butt. Jack came and stood watching the stockman's fingers. The man was now palpating the swollen tissue above the wound.

'Can you get it?'

'I know what to do. But all we got's the instruments for treatin beasts.'

'I don't give a fig,' Ben said. 'Just fetch em.'

'Here, take this,' Purcell said, holding out the filled pannikin to Jack.

Ten minutes later the stockman had washed the arm and was holding the wound open with forceps and feeling with a probe for the ball. One lantern stood at the elbow, the other Purcell was holding and moving as instructed. Jack was seated on a bench reloading and capping his revolvers and Ben's, still coated with his dried blood. The stockman left the probe in the hole and wiped the perspiration from his face with the back of his hand, then gripped the steel again and made small scooping movements, but after a moment gave a grunt of irritation and again lifted his fingers.

'I can feel it, Mr Hall, it's movin. I just need to stop and clean the blood from the instruments—my fingers are slippin.'

'What you're feelin, I'm feelin more, friend,' Ben said. He'd opened his eyes to see something that wasn't spinning and was breathing as he had on the jog there, sucking in, blowing out, fighting down the urge to heave again, and to muffle the roaring in his head like wind that presaged passing out. He wanted to yield, knew he couldn't. As soon as the ball was extracted and the wound bandaged he needed to be on his feet. He spoke on out-breaths, his voice sounding to him as if it were coming from elsewhere in the room, not his own mouth. 'Forget what I said, matey, hurt all you have to—just get the bastard thing.'

The stockman took both instruments from the wound and held them over the basin and Purcell poured hot water onto them from the kettle. The man dried them on a strip ripped from the bedsheet Purcell had earlier taken from a trunk bearing the maiden name of his dead wife. Jack stood up from the bench and pushed his revolvers and Ben's into his belt.

'I'm goin outside.'

None of them turned or acknowledged he'd spoken.

He stepped quickly out, closing the door on his heels so as not to bare even a blade of light. It was still night but a stripe of grey low behind the trees said they had about an hour till first light. John was a shape leaning against a post halfway along the verandah. Jack walked to him, conscious of sounding in socked feet that he was creeping. He spoke before he reached him.

'Anythin?'

John didn't turn from watching the paddock they'd stumbled up. The glow from Byrne's had died. 'No. He got it yet?'

'Still workin.'

'Jesus.'

'That bloody stack's gone, eh.'

'Yeah, went pretty quick.'

Purcell's blue cattledog bitch was lying just beyond John's feet, her chin on her paws, eyes reflecting the starlight. Jack nodded down at her. 'I'd reckon keep an eye on this lady, she'll hear em first.'

'You reckon I weren't?'

'All right, I'm just sayin—don't you start gettin shirty too.'

He walked to the end of the verandah and pissed, realising as he buttoned up it was the first he'd done since lying down in the barn to sleep. A bit had happened since then.

When he went back inside the ball was lying on a tin dish with the bloody instruments. The stockman had placed a pad doused with gin over the wound and was beginning to bind Ben's arm with strips Purcell was tearing from the bedsheet and rolling into bandages.

'Do it tight,' Ben murmured.

'I am,' the man said without stopping in his winding of the strip in his hands, 'but I can't do her so tight you lose your arm.'

Purcell finished rolling a bandage and placed the roll upright on the table and said to Jack as he tore a new strip, 'I can give yous a bit but I ain't got boots, least none yous could walk in.' Ben opened his eyes and rolled his head to find the man. Purcell saw, and spoke to him. 'I'll have to make it look like you bailed us, Ben. If they got a tracker they'll know you been here.' He held out the bedsheet to Jack. 'Here—finish doin these.'

He hung the second lantern and got busy, spreading a calico on the floor and laying on it his watch, a revolver with the powder flask and caps Jack had used, two flannel shirts, a half-bottle of port, some cold johnnycakes in newspaper, tea and sugar in twists of the same newspaper. He came back from behind his sleeping curtain with a rolled blanket. 'I can only spare you the one so yous'll have to snug up.' He didn't smile. He kneeled and lay the blanket on top of the other goods and began to make a swag of the calico.

The man tied off the bandage. Ben sat up and swung his legs off the table. The room kept moving in the direction he'd swung his legs. 'Jesus.'

'Put your head between your knees,' the stockman said.

'No time, matey.' He plucked at the bloodied shirt. 'Get this off.'

The man helped him off with the shirt and got him into a shirt of Purcell's that even before he stood looked more like

a nightshirt. Jack carried the bloodied shirt and sleeve to the
fire and threw them on, the stockman followed with the swabs.

'You'll find your ticker and some quids, George, in one of
them big oaks by your creek. Can't say about your nags.'

'They got my brands,' Purcell replied from the floor. 'Hobble
em by the road when yous find better.'

·

The dawn sun when it rose above the trees gilded a grim-faced
party of troopers in bush dress sitting their mounts before Purcell's
hut. With them, wrists manacled, were Byrne and his older son,
and Jos Strickland. The two Byrnes sat calmly, hands resting in
their laps. Strickland's frightened eyes darted everywhere but
kept returning to the plaid back of the officer sitting the horse
in front of him and facing the hut. The door was open. The
cattledog bitch was standing against the wall and taking worried
peeks inside. All could hear Purcell's protests.

'What do you want? I ain't done nothin, I was here all night!'

'Sleep with gin corks in your ears, do you,' a voice replied.

He was hauled by the arms onto the verandah by two troopers.
The bitch began growling deep in her throat. 'Down, girl, sit,'
Purcell said. 'Our friends here'll bloody shoot you.' He was in
long johns as if freshly woken. He and Byrne exchanged a quick

deciding look. The troopers jostled him down the steps and stood him pinioned before the officer, who ignored him. The man had swivelled in the saddle to watch their tracker returning across the ploughed paddock. Purcell's shoulders slumped. Bluff was useless with a black on the job.

'They come here middle of the night and bailed me. What am I supposed to do against revolvers?'

The officer didn't turn his head. The tracker rode up to the side of the party and brought his mount to a halt and addressed the officer as if the rest weren't there. 'Three orses—' he lifted an arm towards a grey line of she-oaks—'ridin that way. No more blood.'

The officer turned and looked at Purcell, staring into his eyes. When he spoke it was as if a hollow bronze had opened its mouth. 'Which of them's wounded?'

Purcell lowered his gaze to a tear in the man's moleskins a couple of inches above the right knee. A triangle of white skin showed, with a small mole.

'It's Hall, isn't it. There's no point lying, he was seen to fall. Where is he hit?'

'The arm,' Purcell said at the mole.

'How badly?'

'Bad enough. He took a ball.'

'And who extracted it?'

Purcell hesitated. He had no idea where his stockman had got to. They'd have searched the outbuildings. 'I did. With no damn choice in that either.'

The officer turned his head and nodded to the man beside him. The man lobbed a pair of manacles to the man holding Purcell's left elbow. The man slid his grip to the wrist. Purcell twisted his arm free.

'You ain't takin me in these.' He flicked his fingers down the long johns. 'You're lettin a man dress!'

He and the officer exchanged glares. The officer spoke without taking his eyes from Purcell's. 'Hughes, go in and fetch for this harbouring dog the first apparel you lay hands on.'

The trooper gripping Purcell's right arm let go reluctantly and went back up onto the verandah and through the doorway. In the waiting silence Strickland grabbed the chance to speak.

'Mr Huthwaite?'

All heard clasps sprung then the sounds of a trunk being upended. Strickland gave up waiting to be invited.

'Mr Huthwaite sir I told your sergeant that I ain't from round here and Tom Byrne told him but I think he never passed it on. Please sir Purcell here can tell you too. You said yourself you never seen me before, sir ask him he'll tell you the same as Tom Byrne.

I was visitin I couldn't leave once they showed up they wouldn't let me. I've got my own place my wife's there. She's . . . expectin.'

The officer gave no sign that he'd heard. Then he drawled into the air, 'And where is your "place", Mr Strickland?'

As he spoke the trooper came from the hut carrying a striped shirt and braces, corduroys balded white at the knees, bluchers. He skipped down the steps and dropped the lot in the dewed dust at Purcell's feet. Purcell shot him a filthy look, then bent for the corduroys.

'Billabong creek, Upper Lachlan.'

The officer swivelled in the saddle and gave Strickland a searching look.

'You come a long way visiting, mister.'

'Yes sir, my wife's people are from down this way.'

The officer turned to face forward again and took a notebook and pencil from his vest pocket. 'Is that so. Well that can be checked too.' He made an entry in the notebook, closed it and nodded to the trooper who'd thrown the other the manacles. The trooper beckoned, put em out. Strickland extended his wrists. The man leaned and unlocked the manacles, caught them as they came loose. Over the trooper's back Byrne gave Strickland the faintest of winks.

'Thank you, Mr Huthwaite, sir, deep indebted to you, her and me.'

The officer swivelled again in the saddle. 'You can be very sure of a note to Sub-inspector Davidson at Forbes, urging him to keep a sharp eye on you.' He pointed along the farm track. 'I don't care it's the wrong way, ride back the way we came, I don't want you ahead of us. You circle and we see you, you're back in the bracelets.'

12

Ben had remained on the horse, arm in a sling tied from an old towel. John sat on the roadside grass pulling on good calf boots over his ravaged socks. Jack, with a pair of dusty half boots hanging by the laces from his left hand, was walking along a line of eleven men each with his right foot out, the pose that of a chorus line in a diggings music hall but all other similarity ending there. Standing ten yards to one side were a dapper young gent in a hound's-tooth suit, and a heavily bearded shearer, the two matched by reason only of their socked feet. With them stood a red-haired woman holding the hand of a girl about six. Thirty yards up the road was a dray loaded with wheat sacks, the bullocks straining against the traces to reach water lying in a shallow claypan. A fat saddle horse and a small neat grey between the poles of a sulky were hitched head to head to a wheel of the dray.

John finally got the second calf boot on. He stood and stamped both heels in. Then he strode to a man in the line and plucked the cabbage tree from his head. The man pressed his lips shut. Jack was doing a slow walk, staring down at the shoed and booted feet. John caught him up and lifted the half boots from his hand by the laces and turned and walked back along the road to the horses. Ben slipped his right foot from the stirrup. John gave him the left boot to hold and began working the right over the shredded sock.

Jack halted in front of the shearer's travelling mate and twisted himself to align his socked foot with the man's boot. He gave the man a wink, you're in luck, matey, and moved to the man next in line. He was dressed in the uniform of the itinerant farmhand, grey serge shirt, heavy belt, moleskins tied above the knees with leather thonging. Jack set his foot beside the man's boot, bent to look more closely, then straightened and grinned. 'You ain't so lucky, my friend. But you can tell folks you're the same boot as Jack Gilbert. Get em off.' The man didn't move. Then he lifted his right foot and reefed off the boot and flung it to the road, followed by the left. Even Jack was startled. Then his eyes went cold. 'Now you can bloody pick em up.'

'You're stealin em—you pick em up!'

An unpleasant smile playing around his lips, Jack stepped directly in front of the man. The man returned his stare. The man next in line stooped and gathered up the boots. Jack put out his index finger for the man to thread the heel loops onto but didn't take his eyes from the eyes of their owner. Then he gave a half-laugh and turned away. 'Mongrels,' the man muttered.

Jack spun and was back in his face. 'Say again.'

'You heard!' The man glared past him to take in Ben and John. 'There was a time you didn't bloody steal from working men!' He looked quickly towards the woman and girl. 'Beg pardon, madam, but I'm a bit upset.' He didn't wait for dispensation. 'My father was a lag, Mr Hall, same as yours. And yours,' he threw at John. 'And you're robbing the boots from off me feet! There's squatter bastards got a pair for every day of the week. I got one bloody pair and you're robbing em off me! How's that bloody fair? Eh?'

Jack pointed back along the line at the owner of the sulky. 'There's a "squatter bastard", friend.' He looked at the man. 'That's you, ain't it?' The man looked away at the hillside. Jack turned back to the angry man. 'Don't matter how many pair he's got if he don't fit me.'

'You know what I'm talking about.'

Just sitting the horse was costing Ben effort. His arm throbbed like a second pulse. He spoke through clenched teeth. 'What's your name, matey?'

'Eh? Stead. Martin Stead.'

'Well, Mr Stead, you can see how it is with us today. But I'll answer you. Time was there weren't eight traps with every coach. Time was buggers like him—' he lifted his chin towards the driver of the sulky—'were game to take us on, not have the uniforms camped permanent on their verandahs. Now it's needs must. Right now the need's boots. That's all we'll trouble you for.'

The man nodded. 'I hear you, Mr Hall. But I'm still agin you.'

Ben managed a weak smile. 'Well that's no damn good.' He looked at Jack. 'Eh, Mr Gilbert?'

'Christ.' Jack knotted the laces and slung the boots over his shoulder. He pulled the shammy from his trousers pocket, extracted a pound and handed it to the man. He fished out two more and beckoned to the men standing in socks to come and collect. The man whose cabbage tree John had plucked caught his eye and tapped his head. Jack dug in his pocket and flipped a florin towards the man who snapped it from the air as deftly as a wagtail a fly.

'There, you see, Mr Stead,' Ben said mildly, 'we done right by you.'

The man gave a grudging nod.

'So I ever hear of you not doin right by us I'll find you and shoot your heart out.'

He watched the satisfaction drain from the man's face. Then he looked along the line of shocked faces. He badly needed a swig. He couldn't here, they'd tell the traps the wound had soured his temper, he was guzzling gin for the pain.

'I reckon we'll leave yous all to get on your way.'

He clenched his jaw against making an audible cry and feigning to use both hands pulled the hard-mouthed horse of Purcell's round and kicked him into a canter.

13

Next day, ten miles north of Bowning, they relieved a squatter and his sons of the thoroughbreds they were riding and left them Purcell's nags and instructions on where they belonged. Knowing the man would make a beeline back to Bowning, Ben argued they head bush. Jack's suggestion, adopted in laughter, was to do the lunatic and continue along the road, which had the sane advantages of being faster and easier on Ben's arm. Let the traps chase east and west.

In the early evening they reached the inn at Marengo, Jack's old stamping ground when he'd been a stockman. News of the close escape at Byrne's had already travelled. The publican told them Tom and his eldest and Purcell had been charged with harbouring, but Strickland freed. Ben was put to bed in a room at the back with a door to the yard and their saddled mounts tied and standing outside. The publican's wife was doctor to the village. She inspected and sniffed the dressing and said that Purcell's man had done a good job and to leave the binding in place, but to watch for any streaking, which would signal infection. He could lose his arm. A scratch from a plough blade could lose you an arm, he told her, and if he was going to lose his he'd at least rather it was from a bullet. She'd seen both, she said, and neither was anything she'd choose. She asked how much pain he had.

'More than the other time I copped one. I'd rate this with bustin my leg.'

She glanced to see that the hallway door was still closed.

'How do you take to laudanum?'

'Had her before, she's a sweet drop. But I can't risk her. I don't want to wake up in bracelets, some trap starin down at me.'

'Then you'll have to settle for grog.'

•

Two days later they rode single file down the stony pass onto Rankins plains. Their new mounts weren't bred to rough travel. His horse kept stumbling on the loose plates of stone, every stumble driving a spike into his arm. When they reached the flat he loose-tied the reins and nursed the arm to his belly, letting the animal pick its way. Just after noon they were at the foot of the hump of hill overlooking the lower run of Billabong creek. They halted and Jack did the climb to the top. The country was so dry any patrol would need to be camped near water. He scanned the line of the creek for twenty minutes. There was no smoke, nothing rose but screeching cockatoos. He descended and told them.

'But I reckon we watch his face.'

An hour brought them to the yards and hut. Riley began barking. Strickland walked out of a new lean-to shed tacked to the barn. He hushed the dog but didn't smile, his eyes constantly flicking past them as they rode up. They halted the horses but didn't dismount.

'Jos,' Jack said pleasantly. He nodded towards the addition. 'Already spendin Tom's money I see.'

'Yeah. What of it?'

Jack shook his head. 'Nothin. Just a bit of banter between friends.' He looked past the man to the watching dog and gave it hello with a lift of the chin. The dog began wagging its tail. 'So, you had any other visitors lately?'

Strickland cleared his throat. 'Who'd be visitin out here?'

'What, we the only ones ever come callin?' The man didn't answer. Jack looked towards the closed door of the hut. Their voices would have carried. 'Susan not here?'

'In Forbes, at her mother's.' He finally looked at them without evasion. 'Yous know they took him and Purcell.'

Jack swivelled to look at John. Your mates, you answer.

'Yeah, we heard,' John said.

'I suppose then yous heard about this new harbourin law too. Purcell they're askin seven year for, Tom they're askin damn fifteen!'

'And we're damn sorry, I've known em all me life. But you ain't with em, are you.'

'Don't mean the traps have forgot me!'

Ben cut coldly through the chat. 'We need the usual. And I need sulphur and dressins for this arm. Proper dressins, not whatever rag they got torn up.'

'Jesus, Ben! I said, they're watchin me!'

He stared wildly around. Jack caught Ben's eye. Strickland's gaze returned to the ground at the feet of their mounts.

'All right. But . . . she'll cost more.'

'What will, Jos?' Ben said evenly.

'To go in for yous.'

Ben fumbled inside his coat and extracted his shammy. 'You'll get your twenty, plus the quids for the stuff. We need the grub tonight. And them dressins.'

'The grog'd be nice too, Jos,' Jack said.

Ben had managed to untie the shammy's mouth. He pulled out a rough fistful of notes, lay them in his lap and separated out five tens. The man didn't move. Ben let the hand fall with the notes to his thigh.

'You ever tallied up the quids you've had from me? Eugowra on? Not even countin, what is she, three saddles, that pretty double-barrel—'

The man flung his arm towards the hut. 'How they supposed to live with me doin fifteen year! They ain't even givin remissions!'

'That's two "theys",' Jack said. 'Who's your "they" in the house?'

'She's carryin—Susan is.' The man looked back at Ben. 'How do I even know the bastards ain't followed yous?'

''Cause we wouldn't be here. And now we are I ain't goin nowhere.' He folded the notes and tossed them to the ground. 'We get any visitors other than you, you damn well look out.'

He pulled the horse's head round. Jack hooked his head at John, go with him. He watched their backs until they were out of earshot, then turned again to Strickland and raised a disapproving eyebrow in the direction of the pair. 'That arm's makin him cranky, Jos, eh.' He nudged his mount forward, reaching into his inside coat pocket and bringing out a wad from which he peeled two tens. He displayed them to the man, then folded them lengthways and offered them tucked between two fingers. 'This'll buy yous a bonnet or two. So, the stuff and whatever papers you can get.'

He gave Strickland a conspiring wink. The wink and the tone drew the man forward, hand out. Just before they touched the fingers Jack gave the notes a flick which sent them flying past the man's shoulder to flutter down beside the fifty pounds lying on the ground. Strickland's face said he'd been drawn closer than he'd ever meant to come. Jack held him there with his eyes. Then he touched heels to his horse and turned her head.

Ben heard him join their tail.

'He pick em up?'

'No, thinks they'll bite him. But I'd reckon they're in the pocket now.'

•

They made proper camp at the pool. They would be there till the arm was useable. Ben gathered his own bed brooms, the distraction of movement being better than sitting. When his palliasse was made and blanket spread he lay down and seconds later was asleep, no gin for a pillow and none needed.

At evening there came the sound of a horse entering the belt of cypress to the south of the creek. Ben was awake and seated cross-legged on the gravel. Jack pulled him to his feet and both headed into the she-oaks, revolvers drawn and cocked. John kept going, melting into the gloom.

Strickland emerged from the oaks leading a packhorse. He splashed through the ford and brought the animal up onto the gravel, halted it and looked about. Ben stepped from behind his oak, giving the man a good sight of the cocked revolver before he lowered the hammer and slid the weapon into his belt.

'So, Jos, not as watched as you thought.' He picked up in passing a pannikin left by John on a log, tipped its cooling tea on the gravel and walked towards the man and horse. 'Pull us out a bottle,' he said pleasantly.

The tone brought confusion to Strickland's face, but he turned to the pack animal and began undoing the left buckle on a saddlebag. He spoke at the buckle. 'I paid a bloke to buy your dressins, and the powder and caps.'

Ben halted. 'Who?'

Strickland drew a port bottle from the half-opened bag and turned with it in both hands. 'You wouldn't know him. His name's Hebst. He's a German fella, down on his luck. All I told him is buy the stuff.'

'What, a halfwit too, is he?' Jack said.

'He don't know nothin about yous! I give him ten bob and he was happy.'

Ben stared into his face. Strickland met his eyes. Ben nodded. 'All right.' He walked to him and touched a finger to the bottle. 'Open her up.'

The man started the cork with his pocketknife, drew it with his teeth. Ben handed him the pannikin and motioned to be given the bottle. The man hesitated, not sure what was going on, then put the bottle in his hand. Ben tapped the neck on the pannikin's rim that the man hold it level and poured a generous tot. He lifted the bottle in salute.

'To your continuin good health, Jos, and to Susan's and the new'n's. Hope you turn out better at the fatherin game than I was.'

He put the bottle to his lips but waited for Strickland to drink before taking a pull.

14

The heat they'd ridden in across the plain continued. Lazy as cats, they did little other than eat and sleep and reread the newspapers. At the end of five days the wound had stopped weeping, the flesh around its rim pink and healed. By evening of the seventh day he could straighten the elbow and grip the butt of a Navy. In the night the weather changed, cool mist filling the creekbed and blotting out the stars and moon and the oaks along the far side of the pool. By morning the mist had turned to light rain but they'd had enough of doing nothing. They broke out their ponchos and rode to the hut and roused Strickland from bed to tell him they were leaving. Susan was still at her mother's.

They rode back south, the rain growing steadily heavier. Ben's mount had slipped and slithered on the stones coming down the pass and that had been in the dry. He announced he wasn't up for a worse jolting, they were taking the long way. Jack and John moaned about the extra miles but when pushed couldn't give a reason. South was as much as they'd agreed.

In the late afternoon they invited themselves into the hut of a shepherd. The structure looked grown from the hillside, wired-together cypress poles, bark roof and walls, earth floor. The table and the single bench were slabs on stumps. The fireplace was a circle of stones set in the floor. There was no chimney. The man, a ticket-lag of about fifty, had a beard to his navel and stank of wet wool and wood smoke. In his native Suffolk he'd been a bootmaker. He lifted a cracked black foot. 'These int seen leather in a good while.' A ewe's carcass with the forequarters hacked off hung from a scaffold across one corner. They ate a stew of mutton and thistles with damper, finished the damper with treacle. It was a long time since the man had tasted gin and they had to watch him anywhere near the bottle. But the earth floor was dry, and each had a fleece to lay his blankets on.

In the morning the rain was still falling as if night had not intervened. Ben stood at the doorway eating a cold johnnycake and drinking treacled tea and looking out at their unhappy mounts standing in the pole and bark shelter forty yards away. So much water was dripping through the sheets the animals might as well have been standing in the rain. The stallion was a toff raised to a dry stall in a snug stable. Sensing he was watched the animal turned his head and looked at him, then shivered violently and stamped his feet, sending mud flying. Yeah, matey, Ben thought, I'm with you for once. He washed down the last mouthful of johnnycake and hurled the dregs, then spun and walked to the table where the shepherd sat chewing at damper crust slathered with mutton dripping, his feet to the fire. Jack and John were still swaddled in their blankets. Ben banged the empty pannikin on the slab. It rang like a gong.

'No trap'll be out in this,' John muttered from beneath the blanket hooding his head.

Ben crossed to where his poncho hung from a nail, shook it out, wary of scorpions, and dropped it over his head. He picked up his tied bedroll and his valise.

'Where we bloody goin anyway?'

'Off this bloody hill.'

The shepherd swivelled on the bench. 'Like I already told ye, Mr Hall, I int seen a trap in weeks.' He pointed with the heel of damper towards the roof and the blue smoke hanging along the ridgepole. 'She int swell but she's dry. I int going out there today even to shit!'

Ben ignored him. He walked to where their still-damp saddles were lined along one wall, winced in anticipation and hoisted his and walked to the doorway and out. Those inside heard the instant ferocious clatter of rain on cold oilskin. John looked from under his hood to find the shepherd, then threw the blankets off and shook Jack by the shoulder, earning a muttered, 'I'm bloody awake.' John pulled on his boots and stood then picked up the revolvers one by one from the fleece, checking their caps before pushing each into his belt. He folded and rolled and tied the blankets, then crouched and opened his saddlebag and took out the last of their Old Tom. The shepherd rose on the bench like a snake. John placed the bottle on the table but didn't remove his hand from the neck. 'Uncork the bastard but I dole her out.' He waited for the man to nod before he took his hand away. Jack was out of his blankets and pulling on his boots. John looked through the doorway and saw Ben had saddled the stallion and was strapping the valise across his flanks. When he looked back at the table the bottle was uncorked and the man had three pannikins lined up, the billy waiting in his hand. John poured a good shot into each and the shepherd topped them up with tea and snatched up his pannikin. He took a gulp while reaching to hang the billy back over the fire, then lifted the pannikin in both hands and drained it in a steady throat-clicking pour and plonked it down on the table and rubbed his palms together, the sound like sandpaper on a plank.

'Wet arses and no fire today, lads.'

When neither answered he nodded towards the doorway. 'Yer mate a bit windy, is he?'

'Shut your bloody face,' Jack snarled.

.

They rode in an arc to the east around Forbes, cutting across paddocks and avoiding farm tracks and outbuildings. The first two creeks they met were running bankers. Ben knew the fords and they got across seated. The ford at the next was well under. Rather than ride miles upstream they stripped to drawers and swam the horses across, giving the frightened animals a slap on the rump and gripping hard to the root of their tails. When they remounted each was as sodden under his clothes as his horse and as cold. They came down onto the Eugowra road and crossed in running water to leave no tracks and turned south again, riding without talking, three moving islands, the smack of raindrops on hat brims and oilskins and the squelch and suck of hooves the only sounds in the sea of mud and

tussocks and sheeted water they rode through. The cattle they
met stared silently. Fences were a welcome distraction, the
chance to move cold legs. They dropped the rails, led their
mounts through, worked the tenons back into the mortices.
The few times they met wire they pulled the staples, hammered
them back in with the tommy axe. The earth retained no sign
of their passing. Mud flowed into a hoofprint even as the hoof
lifted, droppings melted.

At noon by Jack's watch they stood beneath a dripping
stringybark and ate tinned sardines and four-day-old bread,
dipping the iron crust in the brine then flattening the sardines
onto the bread with their thumbs. A bottle of port would have
warmed their bellies but they had to settle for the cold burn of
gin. The wound had begun a low ache deep in against the bone.
He wouldn't attempt any of the flooded Lachlan's anabranches
with a gammy arm. They discussed what to do, look for a cave
or overhang, or risk a hut. He needed a roof and a fire, he told
them. They were some five miles from the farm of a small cocky
named Wearne. He'd had quids before, there were no other farms
in his narrow valley. They buried the tins at the foot of the tree
and climbed back into the wet saddles.

They rode the scrub in sight of the road till they saw ahead
the track to the right leading into the valley and then rode in

sight of it. A half-hour brought them to the boundary fence. They could see the gate but they dropped and replaced a panel of rails. John rode over to the track and returned to say there'd been nags both in and out but the prints were so slushy there was no telling how recent. The two looked at Ben. The memory of Byrne's was sharp in the minds of all three. They'd risk it, he said. They entered a stand of ringbarks and passed between the shining columns till they emerged into a paddock and saw the yards and barn, their wet timbers black against the grey veils filling the head of the valley. The yards were empty, but if there was a party of troopers laying up they'd be dossing in the barn and their animals with them. They brought their mounts to a halt and studied the eaves for smoke. All they saw was a pair of swallows darting out and back in search of they didn't know what, the rain too heavy for any insect to be flying. They kicked the sullen horses forward and rode up to the hut. Ben called the cocky's name, Matthew. The door opened to the width of half a face and a woman peered through the parting. When she saw them she spoke reassuringly to someone behind her and pulled the door open and stepped out onto the verandah followed by a boy about twelve and a girl nine holding the hand of a toddler in a flannel shirt, its tail dragging on the boards.

'Ben, Jack. Rotten day for ridin.'

She wore a thin cotton dress and a man's coat. All were barefoot.

'Don't we know it, Peg,' Ben said. 'This's John Dunn.' John touched his hat brim, the woman nodded. Ben saw she'd heard the name. After Collector there were few who hadn't. He lifted his chin towards the head of the valley where the man had his muster yards. 'Matt out in her too?'

'I wish he were. He's in gaol.' She choked on the last word. She swallowed and blew out breath. 'Two weeks yesterday. "Suspicion of harbourin". They just rode up and took him! No warrant, nothin! We ain't the only ones neither.'

'What—traps from Forbes? Or where?'

'Forbes. Five of em. Wouldn't even let him pack nothin, just cuffed him in his workin clothes and took him.'

'That won't stand up. Someone has to inform on you and swear it. There weren't no one else here last time we come. So who done it?'

'What we asked em too, Ben! They reckoned under this new law they don't need no one, them sayin so's enough. And the court'll take their word.'

She hadn't asked them to step down and it was becoming clear she wasn't going to. He and Jack had played hide-and-go-seek with the little boy last time they were here, given the other two ten bob each. The older boy and his sister wouldn't meet their eyes, embarrassed by their mother's fear. His own eyes moved to the smoke trickling from the chimney. His arm was stiffening with the cold. Even the barn would do. He looked again at the woman, undecided whether to play on past quids or plain bully her.

'How long they holdin him?'

'They won't say, Jack. I went in and seen the sergeant. He said they'd have me too if it wasn't for these.' She flicked her hand towards the children. She was close to tears. She pinched her nose with finger and thumb, wiped them down the coat. 'I can't feed three of yous, I got barely enough for these. Or sleep yous.' Her voice broke and she began to cry. She smeared her hands angrily up her cheeks, angry at her helplessness, not at them. 'I'm sorry Ben, Jack. You've always treated us good. But if they find out yous were even here . . . ohh. Mother of Jesus, Ben, they said they'll stick him in for seven year! What would I do? We'd lose the place.' Her mouth twisted and she began to sob. She grabbed up the flaps of the coat and smothered her face, but they could see the heave of her shoulders and hear the wrenching sounds her mouth was making. The boy and girl were staring at their feet.

'You, boy, what's your name again?'

'Fred, Mr Hall.'

'Come here.'

The boy pulled the tail of his shirt over his head and stepped down the one plank onto the mud. In the six paces it took to reach where they sat their horses his shirt and he were soaked. Ben had his good arm up under the poncho and was fishing with cold fingers for the mouth of his shammy in his inner coat pocket. He managed to extract a note and held it at his waist under the umbrella of his hat brim to see what it was. A fiver. It would have to do. He crumpled it in his fist and handed it to the boy as a ball he could enfold in his own fist and keep dry.

'Watch where you change it, eh.'

The boy nodded.

'We're goin over the barn and give our nags a feed of oats, then we'll leave you be.'

.

The rain had stopped and a breeze was breaking up the cloud and sending it scudding east.

They dismounted on a ridge with a wide view of the lower Belubula valley, cleared fields and farms along the river and trees and scrub up into the foothills, all rippling with cloud shadow. There was plenty of wood but all wet. They'd got many a fire going with wet wood, but the smoke would be visible for miles.

They'd have to wait for dark. At least with the rain gone, and patches of blue, it wasn't too cold, despite the breeze. They left shirts and coats on but pulled off their squelching boots and propped them upside down and peeled the socks from their frogskin feet followed by their strides and draped them over bushes. With their white legs and brown coats they looked a giant perambulating species of mushroom. Jack opened his poncho over a rock catching sunshine in the breaks. They stood around the rock and removed caps from nipples, then broke the cylinders from the revolvers, reassembled the barrels and stood the revolvers on their butts and barrel tips with the air moving through the mechanisms. Jack asked did anyone have gun oil in his kick and was told no. 'Got half a Old Tom, though,' John said. He walked to his mount and brought the bottle back to the rock. 'Couple of swigs each.' They passed the bottle. Jack drank the last, then flipped and caught the bottle by the neck and lobbed it high out over the ledge projecting from the side of the ridge.

'What else we got?' Ben said. 'I got sardines and a heel of that bread.'

'Trumps me, just sardines.'

'John?'

'Sardines. And I think I got an onion.'

'Christ.'

A pair of crows had settled in separate trees twenty yards apart and were watching them and conversing in undertones. Jack lifted his finger, grinned. 'Can do you crow and onion boil-up.'

Ben scowled and left the rock and went to his mount. He untied the valise and opened it standing and took out a tightly rolled bundle, his second pair of trousers, and sat the valise mouth open on a drying log. He flicked the trousers out, having to do so three times before the legs stopped looking like curled tongues and hung nearly straight. The clammy corduroy refused to slide on the skin. He struggled into the legs, hopping on one foot then the other. It was a funny sight but the glimpses the other two got of his face told them laughter would lead to words. He got the waist up and buttoned and belted, then walked to the edge of the ridge and along to the jutting ledge and squatted facing out to the valley. Jack caught John's eye and hooked his head towards the trees that he go fetch some wood. He watched the youngster mooch away but switch after a few yards to using the patches of stone erupting through the thin grass as stepping stones. At another time he would have challenged him to a contest, who could find the route that took him the furthest clean-footed. He turned and started towards the ledge, the breeze tickling the hairs on his legs.

Ben wasn't surprised to hear the muted crack of a wet stick.
Jack had been reading people to stay alive for even longer than
he had. The whisper of feet stopped when Jack reached rock but
Ben sensed also that he'd halted and was studying him. It was a
minute before he spoke.

'Still a bloody lot of country, Ben.'

Ben spoke at the valley. 'You reckon? I can see a bloody big
fence around her. Been seein it for months.'

'This just your arm talkin? Or somethin else?'

Jack appeared at his right hip but remained standing.

'Both, but more the somethin else.'

'What—this harbourin act?'

'That, yeah. And the plainclothes. And bigger escorts. And
damn cheques instead of notes. Bastards are startin to think with
their brains instead of their arses.'

Jack was silent, both of them looking over the valley.

'I been toyin with chuckin her, Jack. Now I'm more than toyin.'

'You reckon I haven't been watchin? Been on since Collector,
ain't it.'

'Parry was fair game. That other bastard should have stayed
home.'

As soon as he spoke he saw not the body in the road but the
shaking boy, piss running a black stain down his trousers.

'So when are we talkin?'

'I ain't decided that. Won't be for a bit yet.'

'But it's why we're headed south.'

'No. I got other business too.'

'You gonna ask him? About goin with you?'

The question startled Ben into turning. Jack had read deeper than he'd suspected.

'Who?'

Jack glanced down at his face then returned to looking out over the valley.

'I'm not talkin about a dead trap, am I.'

'I already asked him. Last time. He . . . ain't sure.'

'What ain't he sure of? You?'

'More leavin her, I think. But me too, yeah. He don't know me. What he does is what she tells him and out of the bloody papers.'

'Take me. I'll set him straight.' He looked down and winked, then away.

'He'd be up for meetin you. Don't mean he'd believe anything you told him.'

'I can tell him more about you now than either her or Taylor. He wants proof I'll tell him how bad your farts are.' Before Ben could react he spoke again, all play gone from his tone. 'How long you givin him?'

'Like I said, I ain't clearin off tomorrow. We work our way down and yous go to Fogg's and I'll go see him.'

'But you're still chuckin her, whether he's yes or no.'

'We could all chuck her.'

'The lad and me ain't got your reason.'

'Harry aside we all got the same reason, Jack—a rope.'

Jack shook his head. 'Can't rope me with a gun in my hand.' He looked down. 'I'm not sayin anythin more by that neither, all right?'

He waited for Ben to nod.

'So where you thinkin?'

'A damn sight further than Frank went. Queensland didn't do him and Katie much good, always some bastard wanderin through knows you. So I'm thinkin right out, New Zealand. Down to Melbourne back ways, then across. The traps know I've took breaks before. Or you spread that my arm's gone bad, gonna be weeks before I'm back on a nag. Time they figure I've left New South I won't be on a nag I'll be on a bloody ship.'

'When I took breaks them times, I was livin with family. Waitin to sail, and when you get over there, you'll be stayin hotels, buyin your grub. You're talkin serious funds.' He looked down and gave a sly grin. 'Unless you go back to this game.'

Ben grunted a laugh. But Jack had put his finger on the subject that most worried him. The papers told that even traps from New South had quit and gone over to the New Zealand fields, some even working there again as traps. He'd need to be wary of staying in any one place for too long and that meant trouble earning. And if he had Harry with him it would be hard to earn at all.

'Serious meanin what?'

'What have you got planted?'

'Dunno. Never tallied her. Might be a couple of thousand.'

'You'll need more than that. I spent half that in five months.' He sank to a squat, his bare knee touching Ben's corduroyed one. 'Bigger escorts is only a problem *now* with doin coaches. The other one's always been there, you gotta wait for the bastards. Banks stand still. And they hold a damn sight more than a coach. Whole string of towns where they never seen our faces. I reckon we can all use more than just road pickins.' He fired into space a pebble he'd been rolling in his fingers, then stood and padded from the ledge.

15

For two days they watched the straight stretch of road a few miles north of Canowindra, letting wallets and watches pass. Late on the second day the object of their wait finally hove into sight, the high-sided wagon of one of the Syrian hawkers who plied the roads and tracks, calling at hut and station alike. Each of the panels bore a painted miscellany of what was to be found inside, pails, pots and kettles, cotton reels and scissors, pipes and tobacco, and, of most interest to the three, suits, waistcoats, dress boots and hats.

A cocked revolver persuaded the Syrian to drive his wagon a quarter-mile into the bush. They then calmed the frantic man by pushing the revolvers back into their belts and producing their shammies.

A half-hour saw Jack and John fitted out like squatters' sons, in knee boots, pinstriped breeches, frock coats. Jack selected a small leather valise. They admired themselves in the folding mirror. Then they took off the finery and told the man to fold and wrap each outfit separately in brown paper and tie it with plenty of twine, supervising the care with which he did so. He was asked then what they owed him. The man, by now more calculating than afraid, totted up on the inside of his wrist with a pencil wetted on his tongue. Ben subtracted ten pounds from the figure he named and paid him.

They escorted him back to a stand of wattles overlooking the road. Had they done fairly by him, Jack asked. They had, the man replied, even the 'discount' fair. So how would he return the favour? No fool, he put a finger to his lips. Each shook his hand as bond. And, Ben added, if his finger happened to slip and they met a party of traps coming along the road—well, they knew his face, they knew his wagon, they'd wait for him again, maybe not on the Canowindra road but on another. They held him in the wattles until the coast in both directions was clear. Then he and the wagon were sent bumping and lurching down to the road.

They rode to a hill a half-mile off and sat their horses and watched the wagon shrink. When it sank from sight they dismounted and ate hard bread and cheese but drank only water, not wholly sure of the man. They waited for the hour they reckoned it would take for him to make Canowindra and the traps to ride back at a gallop. The empty road was their answer.

•

Unshaven, clothes sprinkled with dust, he rode in from the north, down the steep hill he remembered and past the Anglican church and the Joint Stock bank he also remembered, both of the same distinctive orange brick, and into a street he didn't remember, shopfronts now completely lining its western side where once there'd been a blacksmith's with yards and stables, and the old weatherboard inn on the eastern side joined now to more shopfronts stretching all the way to the intersection with the road that ran along the riverbank to the trestle bridge across the Belubula. In the five years since he'd last seen Carcoar the village had grown to a town. A prospering town meant a fat bank. He could be on his way south in a week. He felt a tight cold excitement start in his balls and spread like a queasiness to his bowels. He dismounted at the inn, aware that he'd attracted looks, but less for himself he thought and more for the quality of his mount, its racer's breeding impossible to disguise, and just possibly for the fact of his coat being tightly buttoned on a warm morning. In the looks he'd returned, though, he'd read curiosity more than suspicion.

He set the stallion to drinking at the inn trough and fiddled for a few minutes with girth strap and stirrups as if they'd given trouble. Then he took out pipe and pouch and filled the bowl while giving the shopfronts opposite a frank appraisal, occasionally breaking off to lift his gaze to the ring of hills, the very picture of a man stretching his legs after a long ride. The doorways of the shops were busy, people in and out. A tubby fellow, ginger hair and muttonchops and wearing a black suit and bowler, caught his eye, but more for his obvious air of authority than for anything catching in his appearance. He was addressing a gaunt man in a full-length leather apron, all the while stabbing the air with a finger. Ben tried to catch words but the street was too noisy. Two shops along from the steps at which they stood was a bootmaker's, almost certainly where the gaunt fellow had been returning to when waylaid. The boots displayed in the window looked to be very fine and if he'd not had larger things on his mind he'd have crossed for a closer inspection.

He smoked one pipe, knocked it out, and took the pouch again from his pocket, glancing up the hill as he did. Where in hell were they? As his mind spoke the two rode into sight round the bend at the church.

They sat their mounts as if honouring the street and indeed the town with their presence. Earlier at the creek where they'd camped the three of them had washed and groomed the two horses till they shone. He'd left while the two were still dressing. In their full finery they too shone. The frock coats, Jack's emerald green, John's royal blue, caught the sunlight and threw it into the morning's eye, the ball of the sun itself was emblazoned on the calves of their knee boots. Strapped prominently to the saddle between his thighs, as if requiring ceaseless watching, Jack had the leather valise. Ben saw the eyes of those who paused to gape at the mounts and the men go next to the valise. Alerted by the bootmaker, the tubby man too had stopped talking and swivelled to see. When the two turned in at the row of fluted iron hitching posts at the foot of the bank steps he thrust his hand at the bootmaker and scurried to the plank that stepped down to the roadway from the boardwalk, his shoulder colliding with that of an elderly woman in widow's weeds who stood furling an umbrella. Ben's intuition about the man had been correct. He glanced again towards the bank. They'd tied their mounts and were climbing the steps, nearly to the porch. The altercation with the woman had delayed him, but the manager was now in the roadway, and in a hurry. Ben headed him off, not obtrusively, as if only now spotting him as a likely person to ask.

'My friend—a minute of your time?' He put out a hand, not touching the man but a barrier, and hooked his head towards the inn. 'What's she like, your hostelry? Clean beds, the grub all right?'

A pained look crossed the man's red fleshy face at a second delay when a valise of money had just entered his door. His feet continued to take nibbling steps.

'The beds I can't vouch for, sir, but the food is fine, excellent in fact, I dine there myself when the need arises. Now if you'll excuse me.'

'And my host? If I could have a moment more.'

'Mr McIntosh, a thorough gentleman.' He pressed a hand apologetically to his heart. 'I really must depart you, sir, I've urgent business.'

To attempt to keep him longer would risk creating a small theatre in the roadway. Ben touched his hat brim. 'My thanks to you. Sorry to have been a bother.'

The man was backing away. 'Not at all, not at all.' He turned and broke into a half-run. John was leaning now against the porch wall as if taking the sun while his elder brother executed their transaction. Ben saw him realise who the approaching man was and stand away from the orange bricks. He pocketed the pipe and walked to the stallion and untied the reins and, holding them in his left hand, turned to watch John deal with the man while with his right he gently unbuttoned his coat from the bottom, all the buttons but one. The man had climbed to the porch. John gave him a grin and moved to open the door, his voice unnaturally loud, a warning to Jack of the impending visitor. 'Lovely morning, sir! You're heading in, I take it? I might join you.' Ben clicked his tongue at the stallion and began leading him up the roadway.

Jack was at the counter, a revolver aimed at the teller's face. The valise stood open on the waxed cypress countertop. The manager came through the doorway and stopped dead, unwilling to believe his eyes. A squatter's son was robbing his bank! Jack glanced over his shoulder and the teller dived to the floor. There was the click of a hammer and a second later a shot exploded into the ceiling, deafening in the confined space. Plaster cascaded over him and the counter. He swiped his eyes and spat. He couldn't see over the counter but heard the scrabble of heels as the man began wriggling on his back towards the door of the inner office. Hands clapped to his ears the manager spun and barrelled into John a yard behind him. The man was in such a panic he didn't register that the polite young fellow who'd conducted him to the door now held a revolver. His belly bounced John hard into the timber. In the seconds it took to recover the man was past and out on the porch. He stopped to bawl, 'Help! Robbery!' then ran down the steps yelling the same two words and waving his arms.

Ben played as dumbfounded as all the other faces that had turned towards the man, but undid the last button and swept the flaps of his coat open. The manager had halted in the centre of the roadway and was bawling at the shopfronts and pointing to the bank.

Jack was in a rage, torn between backing to the door and jumping the counter. 'Jack—I reckon hook it!' John called. The teller fired a second shot into the ceiling. Jack vaulted the counter. Seeing him come flying over, the teller flung the revolver skidding away over the floor. Jack seized the terrified man by the shirtfront and slammed his head on the boards.

'You bastard! Get up! Give me the keys!'

He hauled the man to his feet. The man was protesting, 'I don't have the safe's, I don't have the safe's!'

'Jack, leave him, she's bust!'

A revolver in each hand, John was standing with his back against the door, his gaze whipping between Jack and the street where the manager was keeping up his bawling. People were pouring from shops and crowding verandah rails to gawk. He couldn't find Ben. Then he heard him.

'John! Your nags!'

He strode to the balustrade. A young woman, quicker-witted than the rest, had sprinted across the roadway and was at the reins of Jack's horse. Without mounts they were dead men. He uncocked the revolver in his left hand and pushed it into his belt and stepped over the wrought iron and dropped the eight feet to the ground, falling to one knee, then rising. The woman saw him and bit her lower lip but continued working at the hitch, somehow not knowing that it pulled. She was about his age, with large frightened blue eyes and blonde hair. None of that could matter. He slapped the Colt's barrel across her cheek and she reeled from the post and sank to the roadway on her knees and one hand, the other clutched to her mouth. Ben was beside him, revolver in one hand, reins in the other.

'Where in hell is he? Bastards are fetchin guns!'

More than one shopkeep had gone back inside and emerged with a revolver or shotgun. The gawkers began to scatter, men shepherding their women, women grabbing children. There was a distant confused shouting, then a hard voice bawled, 'Stay uncocked, just get up there, move yourselves!' Six or seven uniformed troopers had turned the corner at the river end of the street and were now footing it. The closer danger though was the armed shopkeeps. Even a nervous miss could cripple one of the horses. He cuffed John on the arm and the two advanced into the roadway, revolvers levelled. Ben watched one man's courage falter and break under the gaze of the barrels. The man lowered his gun and scuttled back inside the haberdashery, slamming the door. The shotlike sound galvanised them all into a dash for their doorways.

The teller was sitting against the wall with hands on head. Two drawers lay upside down at his knees. The floor was awash with coins, they sprinkled the man's lap and thighs. Jack unlocked a third drawer and pulled it off its runners, coins splashing and rolling everywhere, coins, coins and more coins. The few notes that fluttered down he snatched and stuffed in a frock coat pocket. He looked towards the doorway, then began testing keys in the next drawer. John, on horseback, appeared framed from the waist up. The first shot, a long-range chancer, whanged up the street.

'Jack! Traps!'

But he knew the sound of a police carbine. He vaulted the counter and sprinted to the doorway.

He flew the steps in two leaps. John held the reins of his horse. He half-propped when he saw a woman in the roadway on her knees and drooling blood but it wasn't the time to be puzzling her out. He ran past her, snatched the reins and launched his foot at the stirrup. No words needed, the three flattened themselves along the horses' necks and kicked them into a gallop, not up the steep hill but along the street, firing as they came, expecting the troopers to scatter. They didn't, they stood their ground. A trooper went down clutching his thigh. Ben saw Jack's arm whip and the revolver fly. Then they were in clear street.

At the corner they met the object of the charge, a trooper running with saddled mounts. The man had reins in both hands. His mouth opened in soundless shock. John fired, the bullet taking the man's cap. The man dropped the reins and fell to one knee, fumbling at his revolver case. Ben laid two shots inches over the horses' ears, sending the animals wheeling away in panic. The three rode for the trestle bridge, the first carbine balls whining over them, and clattered across its planks. Twenty yards put them in the lee of a house, letting them straighten in the saddles. A blacksmith was out of his forge. Further along a butcher in bloodied apron had come from his premises and onto the road to find where the shooting was. John pointed a revolver and each man turned and leaped back across the roadside drain, the blacksmith flinging away the hammer he held and jamming a finger in each ear. The sight set Jack giggling. Ben glanced back at him. He held the reins in his left hand and was swayed far back in the saddle, his right arm high in the air and the hand streaming a banner of blood.

He wasn't laughing when they drew rein on a crest a mile to the south of the town. The deflecting bullet had cut a jagged path through the palm, skin and flesh hanging. His blood was all down the emerald green frock coat and over his horse's flanks. John was delicately fingering his bleeding left ear where a piece was missing. He took off his hat and in some awe examined the hole in its brim. His mare was distressed, snorting and shuddering, blood sheening from an ugly gouge across her rump.

Jack straightened his arm so the drips fell to the road rather than down his trouser leg.

'Well that was a rum result. Bastards are gettin gamer, mateys.'

16

Before they saw cleared land they heard the sound of a maul. They walked the horses to the fringe of the scrub. The run was leased by a man named Partlett, married to a Dunn cousin. A man too far away to identify—but him, John reckoned, from his hair—was working alone at the far side of the paddock where a line of trees marked a creek. A felled ironbark lay in its bark, the trunk sawn into post lengths.

His hobbled mare looked up from her grazing and watched them all the way across but didn't snicker or whinny. The man was going hard with the maul, moving from wedge to wedge, and didn't hear the walking horses until they were ten yards from him. He looked round in surprise, which turned to a wince of not wanting to own his eyes when he registered the faces under the hat brims and Jack's blood-spattered coat and his bound hand jammed hard into his stomach.

'Oh Jesus.'

He lowered the maul head to the ground.

'Hello to you, Ned,' John said.

The man let go the handle and turned up his palms in supplication. 'I can't, John! Please! They was here last week—bloody camped here!—they damn near tore down the hut lookin for listed notes!'

'Good job you spent em. We need to patch up Jack's hand and have some grub.'

'For the love of God! You've heard about Tom Byrne and them, you must've!'

John lifted a hand towards the hobbled mare. 'Go fetch your nag. Leave your tools.'

The hut was a single room, the walls undressed slabs, stringybark roof, earth floor with sacking rugs. There was a woman's hand in the curtains and the ordering of the kitchen bench. Three small cowhide satchels and a girl's grubby bonnet hung from a row of whittled pegs beside the door. John asked after his cousin. She was close to her time and crook with it,

Partlett told him, they were all gone to her parents' to be near the midwife.

They seated Jack at the table and while the man found sulphur powder and castor oil Ben unbound the hand on a square of clean sacking. The palm and fingers were purple and swollen. But he'd been lucky, he could move all five digits, the deflecting bullet must have dished and somehow slid between the bones. The man didn't drink but had a dusty bottle of brandy. John sniffed it, then poured Jack a short measure, his good hand shaking too much to be trusted with more. Partlett was put to ripping a flannel nightgown into strips while John mixed powder and oil into a paste for a poultice. Ben poured brandy into a saucer and wetted a fold of flannel and cleaned the ragged hole. The man tore and rolled six strips of nightgown, then gathered the bloody bindings and took them over to the smouldering fire and pushed them into the embers with the poker, agitating them until they burst into flame. He leaned the poker against the fireplace stones and sidled to the half-open door for the third time. Even through pain Jack was alert to the whisperings of the devil. He said into the air, 'I could go a tea too, I reckon. With a spoon of honey.'

'I reckon we all could,' Ben said. He'd done the back of the hand and was laving the poultice over the hole in the palm. 'And we need grub. Flour and soda, sugar, tea.' He paused the spoon and nodded towards a hung flitch of bacon. 'A couple of pound of that. And eggs. And whatever tins you got, sardines, lobster, limas.'

'I can do the other,' the man said, 'but I ain't got no tins except treacle.' He pushed himself reluctantly away from the doorframe. 'I'll do yous the tea first.'

He walked to the fire and made to lift the lid from the kettle. The knob slipped from his fingers, the lid clanging on the rim and making them all start. John looked at him.

'You a bit windy, Ned?'

The man gripped the knob again and looked into the kettle and replaced the lid.

'Yeah. Why wouldn't I be?'

'I dunno. You tell us.'

'I told you out in the paddock, John.'

'Tom and them.'

'He's copped fifteen, and there's talk of chargin her now, his missus.'

'Who told you this, your traps? The ones lookin for notes?'

Partlett nodded.

'And what else they say?'

The man looked down at the sewn sacking rug he stood on. When the silence grew Ben stopped winding the flannel strip round Jack's hand and both looked at the man. All heard the click in his throat as he swallowed.

'They're offerin a amnesty. Don't matter who you are—even you've harboured in the past—anyone willin to shop yous can do it on the sly and they'll pay em sly.'

The room fell quiet, the only sounds Jack's breathing and the cheerful crackle of the rekindling fire.

'Tempted are you?' Ben said.

The man flared. 'Course I bloody ain't! Wouldn't be tellin you, would I. Just lettin yous know what they're offerin.' He turned and went towards a bought cypress dresser where a teapot stood and china mugs hung from hooks.

John looked at the other two. If anything was to be done it fell to him. Jack whistled softly through his teeth, a shivery whistle, the last two lines of Pop Goes the Weasel. He winked, then tapped Ben on the arm that he resume bandaging and looked at Partlett, who had his back to them and was taking down mugs.

'Ned, I'm changin me order, do me a brandy and hot. And double up on the honey.'

17

At first light he walked down and placed the stones, then moved back to the treeline.

It was forty-two minutes by his watch before he heard the clank of trap chains. He didn't want to distrust his own blood, but Carcoar had made him edgy. He stayed hidden until certain the boy was alone. He had then to hide that he'd been in hiding. He called that he'd caught him having a shit and to find a patch of sun.

He came from the scrub relooping the tongue of his belt. The boy shook his hand. Ben removed the caps from a Navy and pocketed them, then lifted the traps and sack from the boy's other hand and gave him the revolver to carry. They walked up through the ironbarks and granite to the clearing on the ridge. The boy halted when he saw the stallion head down and pulling at the mean grass about the wattle to which the reins were tied.

'You got a new horse.'

'Yeah. Had to leave the lady.' He thought to show the boy the puckered purple hollow in his arm, decided against. 'He goes better, but he's a bit of a toff, he don't like the rough feed.' He looked down at the boy. 'What about you, you eat anythin?'

Harry shook his head. Ben touched him on the shoulder to steer him towards the log where they'd sat last time and went to the horse and opened the near saddlebag and took out cheese wrapped in muslin and a tin box of ship's biscuits, then pannikins and the water flask.

Harry kept hold of the revolver and ate with his left hand. Ben noted that his wrist and arm were stronger, he could raise and level the Colt one-handed. He watched him sight on a trunk then bite off a second corner of the biscuit as he swung the barrel.

'You're liftin that easy now. You won't even want your wood one soon, I don't reckon.'

The boy lowered the revolver instantly to his lap. Ben wished he'd held his tongue.

'You seen any more of your cousin?'

Harry had turned the revolver on its side and was thumbing

the cylinder through the chambers. 'Once. In town. I was with her, but. He give me a nod and I give him one back.'

'Well you're up on me—I ain't seen him since we seen him together.'

'You can tell him use mine too. If he wants.'

'All right. Don't know when it'll be, but.'

Will had sent word not to come near them, the traps were a constant presence. He saw no need to tell the boy. A female magpie alighted on the ground ten yards away and gave them the haughty stare of her tribe, then hopped to a patch of dead gum leaves and began flinging them aside looking for skink eggs. The boy couldn't resist lifting and cocking the revolver and sighting on the bird. He made a soft 'pchrr' with his lips, the sound Ben had heard him make at the woodpile. But he remembered not to pull the trigger, and Ben remembered to hold his tongue. Harry kept the bead on the magpie until she stood erect and stared at him, when he quickly uncocked the revolver and lowered it to his lap.

'Yous were in the *Illustrated*. For at Carcoar. They done a drawin. They reckon you didn't get nothin.'

'Got out. That weren't nothin.'

Harry pulled a wry face and thumbed the cylinder through another chamber. Ben began to reach for the weapon, then drew back his hand. He'd been given his opening.

'Good paper, ain't she, the *Illustrated*? All them places.' He swallowed, his stomach fluttering more than on the ride down the hill into Carcoar. 'I seen a picture in her once of Port Melbourne. There were so many masts it was like a paddock of ringbarks. Be good to see the real place, I reckon.' He waited, looking down his shoulder. If Harry had made the connection he gave no sign.

'Never mind we got nothin. I ain't short, mate. Got more than enough for what me and you talked about.'

Harry glanced at him, the glance not reaching his face, then looked away as the stallion squealed and lifted his tail and shat a stream of dry pellets.

'I'm stayin.'

Ben went to speak and couldn't. His lungs had climbed in his chest. He swallowed but it made the constriction worse. He sat straighter and watched the magpie. She'd moved from the leaves to the base of a rotted stump and was hacking with her beak at the powdery timber. Another creature's busy indifference restored him to himself.

'That's you decidin—you ain't talked about none of this.'

The boy nodded.

'Well . . . I reckon you're old enough to know your mind.'

18

Jack had told him they'd be on Mount Wheogo.

The mount was a miles-long hump but Ben knew where he meant, Frank's old camp just below the summit. They'd assembled there, the eight of them, to ride to the rocks outside Eugowra and await the gold escort. Each had ridden from the plundered coach a rich man that winter's afternoon. But two and a half years had passed. That money was long gone, most of it on buying safety. Their shares hadn't done the others much good either. Frank was in Darlinghurst, along with Fordyce and Bow. Harry Manns was made gory example of, strangled more like than hanged. John O'Meally was dead from a shotgun. Only he and Jack and Dan Charters were free to sit a horse, and only Charters, turned Queen's Evidence, was free to ride it anywhere. He'd always promised himself a visit to his former mate if ever he learned where he'd cleared out to. 'Fat chance now,' he muttered as he started into the dense cypress at the foot of the mount.

He got slightly bushed, so long since he'd been here. Frank had drummed into them that every time down or up they ride apart, create no track. Then he spotted the two giant boulders against the skyline.

The campsite as he rose up to the level ground looked much as he remembered, thin scrub, nests of smaller boulders. Then a scatter of rusted sardine cans and dusty gin bottles brought a hard lump to his throat. His emotion must have transmitted itself to the stallion as danger, for he propped, danced sideways. Both were relieved when John called, 'About bloody time, we was startin to think you was lagged,' and he stood up from behind a boulder. He held a double-barrel gun he'd not owned when Ben parted from them.

Ben kicked the stallion forward. 'Weren't no hurry. Where'd you get that?'

John grinned. 'We met a fella tryin to pot chickenhawks. Told him I had a better use for it.'

He opened his mouth to ask where Jack was, but passing round the boulder he saw a low tarpaulin stretched between a ledge and three gum saplings, at its mouth a stone circle enclosing a dead fire and at the back against the boulder wall two palliasses of cypress brooms. Jack stepped into sight from its far side, revolver already back in his belt and his bad hand buttoned into the opening of his shirt.

'Benjamin, my boy! You've grown in name they tell me since last you were here. You'll join me in a tipple?'

Jack often for a lark fell into Frank's light Caledonian burr, but to hear it in this place was eerie. To let him see, though, he'd touched a nerve would be to have him prattle on as Frank for another hour.

'How's the hand?'

'Pus and hurts and don't let me sleep,' Jack said, returned to his own voice. 'Apart from that, hardly notice the bastard.'

Ben dismounted and tied the reins to a stunted tea-tree. The stallion, he'd learned, was not a horse you could trust to stand. 'How much grog yous bring? Not enough by the sound.'

'Don't bloody help.'

Ben began untying his bedroll. 'I'll peg this bugger out, then I better have a look.'

•

They stayed nine days, eating cheese and oysters and herrings in sauce with bread then spuds then biscuits, and lighting a fire only after dark. Jack and John had loaded the packhorse with three corn sacks of tucker and grog, not wanting to announce their presence on the mount by running short and having to ride down to the Pinnacle store or McGuire's for more. By the time the sacks were empty Jack's hand was crusted but clean and he was sleeping. They filled the sacks again with bottles and tins, new and the old, and dropped them down a crevice. Their last afternoon they amused themselves by carving their names with the tommy axe into the boulder where Frank had scratched his the night before Eugowra. Jack, first meeting him at sixteen, had been both wild younger brother and son. When they'd finished their own names Jack traced the letters of Frank's with the tip of his index finger, the grooves now grey and starred with lichen.

'Don't reckon he'll ever see this again.'

'Who's sayin we'll see ours.'

'Me and John yeah, damn you! Don't fancy the odds from bloody New Zealand, but.'

They came down the mount through the heavy scrub on its south flank. Ben wanted a jeweller, so they camped in sight of the road from Forbes waiting for Cope, who still, as far as he knew, did the circuit between there and the Flat, and from whom he'd bought the tie pin and links he'd been married in.

The man turned up late on the second day, dressed, it looked to Ben, in the same brown suit, but on a better nag. It didn't need three to bail him, Ben rode alone down onto the road. Cope remembered him. He got windy only when Ben led him up into the trees and into the presence of the other two. They gave him a shot of his own brandy to settle his nerves. Then Ben had him lay out on the square of purple velvet the man carried for the purpose the watches from his valise. Most were silver or chromed, reflecting what the main of his customers could afford. The few gold ones were plate. Ben lowered the one he'd just examined back onto the velvet by its chain.

'This trash doesn't interest me, Mr Cope. I'll take a look at yours.'

'Mine? They're all mine.'

Ben pointed to the man's vest pocket and chain. 'The one you're wearin. Haul her out.'

So slowly as almost to risk insolence, the man did as ordered. The watch was large and carat gold. Ben motioned to be given it. The man lay it reluctantly on his palm, still attached to his buttonhole by the chain. Ben tipped the watch onto his fingers and hefted it for weight, then sprang the lid. The casing was thick, the movement good. He grunted.

'This's more the ticket. What'd it set you back?'

'I beg pardon?'

'I ain't brought you here to rob you, Mr Cope—what'd you pay for it?'

The man's lips refused to work. Then he said breathlessly, 'Fourteen guineas.'

'Christ. You're not tellin me that's wholesale?'

Insulted, the man recovered his dignity. 'I am! It's a very fine piece! As I'm sure you're more than capable of judging.'

'He bloody should be,' Jack laughed, standing at one side with the man's open brandy bottle.

Ben handed the watch back. 'Okay, unclip her, I don't want the chain.'

While the man worked at freeing the watch Ben brought out his shammy and extracted the notes. The wad had shrunk in the last month. He separated out a ten and a five, grimacing at how few tens remained. He refolded the wad and pushed it back through the shammy's mouth. The man had the watch free.

'No, hang on to her.' Ben lay the notes on top of the watch. 'There's fifteen quid, so you made a profit. I need a receipt. You got writin things?'

The man, now utterly confused, nodded.

'And you'll need your tools.'

Ten minutes later the jeweller was seated at a log with loupe in eye and his suede tool sleeve open under his right hand. He was graving on the inside of the lid to Ben's dictation, pausing after every letter to wet the tip of his little finger on his tongue and dab up the tiny curls of gold and deposit them on the suede. The three stood at his back, leaning to see over one or other shoulder. They had lifted dozens of inscribed watches but had never seen the work done. Their combined breath on his neck was causing the man's own breathing to be faster and shallower. It was a strain to concentrate on the graver's point. He couldn't, though, summon the courage to ask that they stand off a little.

19

Autumn found them trying their luck between Orange and Molong. The weather was cold winds and whole days of drizzle. They no longer trusted barns. They camped under thin overhangs or in the lee of boulders, enduring wet wood, the monotony of sardines, damp blankets. Just when it looked to be healed, the hole in Jack's palm again began weeping pus. Ben, getting up at first light for a piss, was bitten through his sock on the right big toe by a bull ant. The toe turned blue and swelled so much a boot was agony. He hacked the leather away and wrapped the gape with a piece of oilcloth. They needed to do their quota of bailing up simply to eat, and did, hiding their handicaps from those they stopped. But in camp Jack was one-armed and Ben one-legged. Having to do all the scouting for wood and humping of water, John got cranky and bucked up. Ben offered to thump him. Jack stepped between them with revolver drawn and offered to shoot them both. They saw he meant it.

The game itself had a hard new truth, the ready money of even just six months ago was drying up. Working men still carried cash, but the squatters and storekeepers and cattle buyers had their wallets filled now with bank drafts and cheques. Notes and gold were still being moved by coach. But since Jugiong the escorts had doubled to eight and sometimes ten troopers, most still armed with single-shot carbines, but one or two in every escort now carrying the new five-shot Colt revolving rifles. It became the reluctant custom that after a count of the approaching uniforms they retreated to cover and watched a coach and its padlocked bags go by.

·

They rode down the familiar stony pass and out onto Rankins plains, the now equally familar drizzle accompanying them.

It was late in the afternoon when they saw Strickland's hut and barn through the screen of stringybarks they used always for their approach. The crowded yards made them draw on the reins. There were at least six mounts, maybe more. It was possible they were lifted nags yarded overnight for moving out in the morning. But the man had pole yards in the scrub for that. The door of the hut was shut and smoke from a good fire was pouring from the chimney. Unless one of the visitors stepped outside there was nothing more to be learned from where the three sat their horses. John was waiting. Ben gave the nod. The youngster slipped from the saddle and drew a revolver and wove away at a low crouch through the trees.

They lost him behind grass when he dropped into the shallow gully that ran to the back of the yards. He was gone from sight only minutes before his head rose again from the grass. As he wove back through the dully glistening trunks he caught their eyes and drew his left thumb across his throat. There was no humour in the gesture.

He waited till he was almost at the horses before he spoke.

'Seven clean Crown brands. Bastards'll be tucked up round the fire gutsin stew. Couldn't see no black but he's probably in the barn. We could take em, I reckon—shoot the bloody hut to cheese and to hell with Strickland, he can cop it too if he's feedin traps!'

'That's a serious plan, John,' Ben said quietly.

'Too right! Damn the bastard.'

'The act don't give him no choice. And who do you reckon dished up that stew you're talkin about?'

He pulled the stallion's head round and kneed him into a walk.

They rode a mile and made camp in a stand of tea-tree. John found dry bark and sticks at the base of a leaning gum. Jack nodded, good man, then shook his head. They kicked leaves and strips of paperbark together and unstrapped their bedrolls. Then they squatted in their ponchos and ate biscuits and cheese and sardines, sharing a bottle of port. The drizzle had turned to rain. Its steady hiss made other sounds distinct, the snap of a biscuit and the grind of teeth, the rattle of a knife blade in the corners of a tin, the tick of each drop falling from leaves onto stiff hat brims.

·

In the morning a watery sun was showing through the ground mist. The three kneeled in the belt of stringybarks and watched six plainclothed troopers and a tracker saddle up and ride away east along the creek. Strickland stood on the verandah and watched them go. When they were gone a safe distance he spat after them and went inside and shut the door.

The three watched for an hour in case the troopers played cute and doubled back or circled. Then they walked to the patch of scrub where they'd left their mounts and removed and rolled their ponchos and unbuttoned their coats so the revolvers were in plain sight.

Strickland came onto the verandah when he heard the horses. They saw from the angry flush to his face that he'd thought they were the troopers returning. He whitened when he saw them. His eyes flicked along the creek, then he attempted a smile. Susan had come to the doorway. She was showing now, her belly pushing out the apron. Her gaze too went first to the creek before she managed a smile more convincing than her husband's. The three halted their mounts at the steps.

'Mornin, Jos,' Ben said. He touched his hat brim. 'Susan. Back a bit sooner than we planned on.'

She looked at her husband. When he didn't speak she said, 'Always a welcome, Ben.' She nodded. 'Jack. John.' They returned the nods, but the refusal to speak and the grimness of their stares unnerved her. She flicked another glance along the line of box mallees bordering the creek.

'Wet night we had, weren't it.' He waited till he saw she'd caught his meaning. 'We could go a brew if there's one offerin.'

'I . . . think we can find you more substantial than just a brew, Ben.'

'That'd be much appreciated, Susan. Thank you.'

He made no move, though, to step down. Strickland still wouldn't meet their eyes. He began to ball and open his hands. Ben relented, lifting a finger towards the orchard. Leaves were turning but branches were still hung with fruit, empty tins strung in pairs to bell the cockatoos and rosellas.

'Rain's good for somethin but, eh. We was talkin about pies on the way. We all remember that peach you done us once, best we ever ate.'

'Oh . . . no peaches . . . I—I've got apples—and quinces—good quinces this year—we've not got the moth out here.'

Jack cleared his throat. 'Speakin of out here, you haven't had the traps about? Keepin their eye on you, Jos?'

Ben kept his gaze on Susan, saw her wish words, the truth, Jos, please, into her husband's mouth.

'No,' Strickland said. 'Nor heard of any.'

She closed her eyes. Ben looked from her to the man. 'So,' he said softly, 'you didn't see the six that rode away from here about an hour ago?'

Strickland's face flushed with the shame of being caught, then darker red with anger.

'Yeah, we bloody seen em! And fed em—and slept em—same as we'll have to for yous!'

'The difference is,' Jack said, 'we ain't traps.'

'You'll scoff our grub just the same!'

'And thank you for it.'

'And pay for it,' Ben added. 'Notes, not bloody chits.'

'They don't bother with chits for the likes of us,' Susan said with quiet vehemence. She placed a hand on her husband's arm. 'Jos, go in and put on what chops are left—and some eggs. I'll be in directly.' When he didn't move she shifted her hand to his back and said softly in his ear, 'Go—please.' She lifted her other hand towards the line strung between two trees. 'You can hang your blankets if they're damp.' Strickland spun and strode to the doorway. She waited till there came the clang of a skillet on the rails.

'There's no harm in him, Ben. He's angry at them usin us how they do, expectin to be fed then speakin to us like we're dirt.' She pointed along the verandah. 'There's pegs there, the biscuit tin. They finished my bread but I can do you johnnycakes.'

Ben nodded. 'Johnnies is fine, Susan.'

She smiled and wiped her hands down the apron covering the slope of her belly, then turned and went in. Ben twisted in the saddle to find Jack, who for answer arched an eyebrow.

They hung and pegged their bedrolls and rinsed the sour smell from their hands in the trough.

When they walked into the hut Strickland was at the fire with the wire fork in his hand. He didn't look round. Chops were sizzling in the big skillet and the smaller was on the rails, a gob of dripping at its centre and melting. Susan stood at the bench with her hands in a mixing bowl. The teapot and sugar bowl and three pannikins stood on the table. She looked at them over her shoulder.

'Sit yourselves down. Jos's done your tea.' She turned to her husband. 'Leave that. Why don't you see to the horses?' She half turned to address them again. 'I'm sure after bush pick they could go some oats.'

'Might go em myself,' Jack said.

No one laughed, even smiled. Strickland lay the fork across the skillet and, looking at the floor, moved towards the doorway. Ben slopped tea quickly into a pannikin and lifted it between finger and thumb, offering the handle.

'Take a brew with you, Jos.'

Strickland stopped and raised his eyes. Jack and John too looked at him, as alert as Strickland to the oddness of this affability. Ben nodded reassuringly at the man. Strickland hooked his finger in the proffered handle and walked to the doorway and out onto the verandah. Ben glanced at Susan. She'd turned back to her dough. He looked at John, inclined his head towards the window.

John glided to it and put one eye to the gap between frame and curtain, in time to see the man take a sip, then set the pannikin on the top step to free his hands for the reins. He nodded and stepped away. Ben lifted the teapot and filled the two pannikins, then stood it again on the table and walked to the dresser for another pannikin.

Jack carried his tea to the fire. Susan, with floury hands, was breaking eggs into both skillets. The chops, fat browned to a crisp, were already lying on china plates, three to each. He stood his pannikin on a stone in the hob and picked up the shaped and hammered lid that did as a slice.

'I'll look out for the googs, Susan.'

'Oh? Would you, Jack?'

She handed him the egg in her hand, gave him a smile grateful for more than the simple offer, and returned to the bowl and pulled a lump of dough and began slapping it into a johnnycake.

•

They stayed only as long as it took to eat.

Their bedrolls were back on the horses' flanks and tied. John sat his horse. Ben stood with Strickland. All were watching Jack

and Susan walking back from the kitchen garden, near invisible
behind its palisade of woven wattle wands, she carrying carrots,
turnips and onions by their tops, he his inverted hat filled nearly
to the brim with peas. He was cracking pods one-handed as he
walked and thumbing the fat peas into his mouth. Susan said
when they reached the horses, 'I'll get a sack for these,' and went
on to the steps. When she disappeared inside Ben took a counted
fold of notes from his vest pocket and passed it into Strickland's
hand, who palmed them into his trouser pocket.

'Sorry for earlier, Ben. Them bloody traps, and then yous
arrivin on their heels. And her bein . . .' He made a belly with
his hands. He turned away to catch Jack, who'd taken the reins
of his horse from John and was juggling the inverted hat in his
right hand. 'You'd know that lady's goin lame on you.'

'Who do you reckon's ridin her? She was brought up to lanes
and meadows this one.'

'You want, I could try re-shoein her.'

'Ain't her shoes.' He stepped up into the saddle balancing
the hat. 'She'll last till I find better. You ain't got better by any
chance? Tucked away?'

Susan came onto the verandah with a tied sack. Strickland
gave a small shake of the head. She came down the steps and
walked to Jack's stirrup.

'Here you go.'

'Green in my hand but none in my eye I hope, eh Susan.'

'I think we all keep a bit in our eye, Jack.'

He laughed, then looked from her down at the sack and busied himself with forming a loop in its twine.

Minutes later they were riding across the creek paddock to cut the meander the stream made, the horses at a slow walk, each man now bareheaded, pea pods in his hat and its crown wedged between his thighs. They were thumbing peas into their mouths and dropping the shells to the ground. The peas were cold, exploding in the mouth. Chilled teeth and tongues were a delicious contrast to the sun on their faces. The thoughts of the younger two were far from bushranging.

'My ma grew these bastards,' John said, firing a shell away with his thumb. 'Damn good to eat but Christ the buckets we donkeyed up from the river!'

'These don't drink it! Beet—that's the bastard drinks it! All them big-leaf bastards.'

'Least he's made her that little sled now with the butt. Wouldn't have no garden otherwise. How long's she got to go you reckon?'

Jack swivelled in the saddle to look at him. 'What—you the youngest are you? You never seen your ma carryin?'

'Not the youngest, no, got a sister after me, but only two year. Ain't gonna remember me ma carryin at two year, am I!'

'She'd be seven months,' Ben said flatly. 'So what sense you get of him, Jack? I don't want to be haulin my whole damn bank around.'

Jack had been enjoying the banter as much as he had the peas. For a half-minute the only sound was the swish of the horses' legs through the tussocks.

'He's windy, yeah.'

'More of us, or the traps?'

'Both. But I'd reckon more us.'

'Bastards can soon change that, threaten to do him like they done Wearne and them, on suspicion.'

'I'd go by her, Ben, not him.'

'That's not a hatful of peas talkin, is it?' John said.

Jack laughed and threw a full pod at his head, which the youngster easily evaded. He was right, though, too fine a morning to let one of Ben's moods cruel it.

'Bein jealous ain't stopped you bloody eatin em.'

'Too right! Best ones to eat—that I didn't have to slave waterin!'

'I'd reckon Nelson's made you safe from waterin peas, John,' Ben said.

Jack glanced at the youngster. His cheeks were burning. Jack whispered 'Jesus' and raised his eyes to the sky. He felt for a pod and split it, thumbed the peas into his mouth, dropped the shell. Then, chewing, he twisted in the saddle and looked back across the paddock, barked a laugh, turned forward. When he saw the other two emerge from their thoughts he hooked a thumb over his shoulder.

'Them traps come again, they won't need their bloody abo.'

Ben and John swivelled. Stretching away into specks was a trail of bright green shells.

·

Ben parted from them at the edge of the belt of cypresses, rode on for a further five minutes.

He tied the stallion twenty yards from the blazed box, removed his boots and wove through the cypresses to the giant box and the clump of boulders at its base. An animal had been scratching there, a goanna from the deep claw marks, but the bank was undisturbed. He rolled and lifted away the stones, then made a mat of shed bark. Unbelting his revolvers, he sat cross-legged and lifted the topmost tin from the cavity, thumbed off its lid and extracted the tight roll of notes. They wouldn't stay flat. He reached around him for stones, then sorted the notes into twenties, tens, fives and ones, placing a stone on each pile, then relidded the tin and stood it against the base of the cavity boulder and reached in for the next.

When every tin stood empty he did the count, starting with the twenties and scratching tally marks with a twig in the hard earth at his hip. Divvying hauls for more than two years had made him as fast as any teller and he soon had the total, twelve hundred and thirty-eight pounds. He stared at the four piles, his mind sliding between what he needed now and what to keep for the year ahead. He made himself face the truth that he was making provision for just one. The stallion whinnied, snapping him from calculation. He snatched up and cocked a revolver and rose to a crouch, looking towards the blazed box. He could just see the animal through the cypress trunks. The stallion was looking back at him. He did a slow scan of the trunks to either side, then past the animal, as far as he could. Nothing moved. The damn toff was just venting his impatience. He uncocked the weapon and sank again to sitting cross-legged and took up the thick pile of tens. He peeled through, selecting the cleanest, until he had twenty and set the thin pile at his hip. He placed the tens down again under their stone, then hesitated, picked up the fives and peeled off another fifty pounds and lay it on the two hundred. Then he reached for a tin and, starting with the twenties, stuffed it full and lidded it and placed it back in the cavity and picked up another.

The door stones again in place, he took from his coat pocket the scrap of twine he'd lifted from a shelf at Strickland's and bound the two hundred and fifty in a tight cigar and slid it down into his shammy beside the spending wad. He picked up the three revolvers and stood and pushed them one by one into his belt, then stepped away and inspected the door. A clean edge showed. He crouched and turned the stone through a few degrees. When he stood again the stallion gave another short indignant whinny.

'Yeah,' he muttered, 'and I'll be damn glad to see the arse of you too, matey.'

·

After weeks of rain they no longer trusted their caps and cartridges. Strickland was buying fresh, and waterproofs to keep them in.

He arrived in the late afternoon with three oilcloth drawstring bags drooping with the weight of lead each held. He brought too a placatory quince tart. He refused a slice, insisting there was another at home, but accepted a pannikin of the port he'd brought. He asked how long they were staying. A few days, Ben told him.

They left next morning at first light, headed south-east towards the Lachlan. The day's rest hadn't cured Jack's mare of her lameness. She could get him taken or killed if they needed to leave from anywhere in a hurry.

At noon they stopped in a wooded creekbed for a brew and to give her a spell. While John scouted rocks and sticks, Jack unwound the strapping he'd put on the right foreleg and began running his fingers up and down the skin, she snorting and trying to pull away each time his light touch became more searching. Ben stood and watched, his opinion already formed, that she was good only for a bullet. He took the shotgun and climbed the bank to keep nit.

He found a shaded possie among spindly tea-tree and watched a family of roos grazing sixty yards away. The male had seen him and was sitting on his tail watching back while the females and joeys returned to feeding. He'd probably seen men before. When this one made no attempt to approach he too lowered his head and resumed nibbling.

When a second man appeared the male made a cautionary hop towards the females, then stood alert again. John slid in beside Ben and set the pannikin on a pad of dry litter. Ben said without turning his head, 'What's he doin?'

'Still workin on her.'

'You give her a look?'

'His nag.'

Ben took up the pannikin by its belly, extended one finger. 'You reckon I could drop that bastard?'

Beyond the roos the grassland swam in the haze of an unseasonally warm autumn day. Stared at, each animal floated, shimmered.

'He'd have to be damn unlucky.'

Ben twisted. John ducked his face and said into his pannikin, 'Don't suppose they got roos over New Zealand.'

From behind them came a scrabble of stones. Jack joined them in the thin shade.

'That lady's busted.'

Ben lowered his pannikin.

'Took you a while.'

'Well even busted I'd have her over that brat bastard you're ridin.'

'I'm ditchin him too soon's I find somethin with as good go.'

A third human had panicked the male, he was rounding up the females. They were pocketing joeys. Ben watched the family move off, a lone joey that had outgrown the pouch still with its face turned towards them and unaware it was being left.

'Where you thinkin?'

'I reckon we hit Cropper. Bastard blows in the papers about all the times he's been out with the traps huntin us, startin way back after Eugowra. I reckon we save him the sore arse. Teach him too to stick home.'

'Might be a big job for just three of us. He'd have a fair mob of men workin there.'

'Not if we time it right. Come on em about dinner, not from the road, from the river.'

Ben turned the pannikin in his fingers and stared after the roos.

'What's up with you? You've said before we should do the bastard.'

'Ain't sure this's the day, Jack.'

'I bloody am, I need a new nag! You don't want to come, stay by the river and John and me'll do the place.'

'You're gettin holes in your memory. Burke and O'Meally. Them names mean anythin?'

'We ain't mountin sieges no more, it's in and out.' He flung the dregs of his pannikin. 'There's careful and there's windy, Ben. Windy gets you killed.'

'And you be damn careful who you're callin windy. I'm sayin there's easier places to hit for a horse.'

'Christ, man, it ain't just his bloody stables, we need a decent hit of funds! You the most!'

20

The station, Yamma, ran for three miles along the north bank of the Lachlan. They had used Cropper's riverbank many times travelling to and from the Fish, always at night, no benefit to be had from needlessly provoking the man, and always well clear of the station buildings. Now they rode up from the river directly towards the homestead.

The sun was an hour from setting when the cluster of buildings came in sight, their shingle roofs and limed walls washed pink. Oateries and poultry sheds afforded a blind approach. They halted the horses at a hayrick and studied the maze of outbuildings. Jack muttered how well the bastard must be doing, the place was the size of a small town. No one was moving about. It seemed work had finished for the day. They kneed their horses into a walk, John holding by the foot and ready to lob the stinking shank from a dead ewe. But no barking dogs appeared. They rode single file to the large fieldstone building they took to be the stable and brought the horses to a halt again in the shadow of its eastern wall.

Jack dismounted, drawing and cocking a revolver, and walked to the corner and peered round. The heavy adzed-timber doors were still open, a chain running from the brace of the nearer door to a hook in the mortar of the wall. Someone was about then, if the nags hadn't been shut in for the night. He ghosted along the wall to the doorway and saw to his annoyance that the floor was cobbled. A broom lay on a swept pile of straw and manure. He stepped inside on the balls of his feet keeping heels well clear of the cobblestones, picked up the broom and knocked on a beam with the handle's bald end, the revolver pointed at the doorway of the tackle room. No head appeared in answer. He lowered the revolver and looked inside the room at the walls thickly hung with rope and leather, then crossed the floor less wary of heel taps to the row of stalls. A prowling glance into each stall was all his practised eye needed to assess the merits of the animal it held. He returned to the doorway and looked towards the homestead, all but its roof hidden behind a rose hedge. A woman's voice came, too distant to make out words. He waited but the voice remained at a distance. He flitted along the wall and round the corner and told them there was a racing mare named Danserey he'd take for himself, and three other mounts nearly as good, two stallions and a mare.

Ben and John got down and drew revolvers and they led the horses to the rose hedge and along it to a gate whose hinges they checked were oiled before opening it and leading the animals through into the house garden and quickly from the gravelled path onto the dense grass of the lawn, Ben having to snatch the stallion's head from the prospect of decent pick at last. Even from close the house was half hidden by grape trellises and fruit trees, most nearly bare of leaves but the wands unpruned. It was a long low red-brick and stone structure with a shingled roof and a wide verandah. At the foot of each verandah post was an earthenware planter sprouting a blackboy. A pad worn in the lawn led between the ends of two trellises towards steps. As they came nearer the verandah they heard the rhythmic shick-shick of a wood plane. Ben nodded towards a wisteria vine growing on a frame. They hitched the reins loosely to the timber uprights and walked towards the steps. A second path of river gravel barred their way. The planing was coming from the front of the house.

Ben waved them towards the sound and tapped himself on the chest and pointed back along the building.

The two walked in the newly turned and manured soil of a flowerbed, their heels sinking silently into its wormy richness. On the path, his back to them, a man in shirtsleeves and waistcoat was planing a new plank for the verandah. The warped and removed plank, its dimensions chalked on it, lay on the gravel beside the sawhorses. They walked the bed to three yards from the man and halted. The plane faltered as the sense grew in him that he was no longer alone. He straightened and looked round into the mouths of four barrels. His own mouth fell open. Jack raised the revolver in his right and took his finger from the trigger and touched it to his own lips. 'Bail up, friend,' he then said pleasantly, 'give your arms a rest.' He stepped onto the path and lifted the plane from the man's unresisting hands and lay it correctly on its side on the plank and with a flick of the revolver barrel motioned that he walk ahead of them to the front steps.

Through an open window Ben heard the strident voice of a woman he guessed to be the cook giving instruction about a soup she wanted creamy this time, no damn lumps. He retreated from the window to the doorway he'd passed, a laundry, and on tiptoe climbed the three steps of soft brick hollowed by feet and walked in onto a floor of the same bricks. He lay both revolvers on the steam-furred boards lidding the copper, then leaned his buttocks against the firebox and pulled off his boots. He pushed one revolver into his belt and threaded a finger through the loops of his boots, picked up the other revolver and moved to the door, its hinges leather to escape rusting. The door pulled silently. He put an eye to its edge and was looking into a hallway with yellow plastered walls and an oiled plank floor. Through a closed door to his right at the end of the hallway he heard the cook's voice still issuing orders over the thud of a heavy blade on a board. She sounded angry enough without having her evening's preparations further interrupted. He started along the hallway in the other direction, soundless in his socks. He'd gone only six paces when a door ahead of him opened. He froze. A woman in her mid-forties wearing a green crinoline dress and maroon shawl, her hair up, stepped into the hallway carrying a grey woollen comforter. She didn't see him, intent on picking fluff from the wool, then did, and gave a start. But after her initial shock she didn't appear overly worried at finding in her hallway a man dressed for the bush with boots in one hand and a revolver in the other. She had high cheeks in a broad face, a large brown mole beside the mouth. The eyes were blue and shrewd. They raked him down and up.

'You must be Mr Hall.'

She offered a cold smile with the pun.

'And you'd be Mrs Cropper. You don't keep dogs, ma'am.'

'About the stables, yes, about the house, no. I don't share my husband's fondness for them.'

'We come by your stables. Your dogs there seem to have took their leave.'

'We?'

'I ain't visitin you on my pat.'

'Ah. No, of course.' She lifted the comforter. 'My youngest son is indisposed with a boil, Mr Hall—and I have a visitor of my own. I suggest we join them.'

'I'd rather I knew the whereabouts of Cropper.'

'Bathurst. With our overseer Mr Arndell.'

'That's a pity. What other men are about the house?'

'Besides my son, none. Why a pity, may I ask?'

'He's been blowin in the papers about what he'd do if he met up with us. As I'm sure you know. We're savin him the saddle sores.'

She spun on her heel and moved off down the hallway, forcing him to follow in his holed socks. She opened the door of a room and walked in, leaving the door open and not glancing behind her. He halted and peered in, then entered, revolver levelled. The room was crowded with furniture, a large parlour or sitting room. A fire was burning in the grate but the lamps had not yet been lit. A boy about nine was sitting in an armchair before the fire and a young woman in a sky blue dress sat on a straight-backed chair between two windows, a leatherbound book lying open on her hands but her eyes now on him. Ben nodded to her, then lay the revolver on the sideboard beside a china bowl painted with red and gold dragons and leaned against the wall and pulled on his boots. The young woman had lowered the book to her lap and was looking now towards Mrs Cropper for a sign as to what she should do. The boy was staring open-mouthed. Mrs Cropper lifted a hand to each in turn.

'My son Samuel, and Miss Farrand, a guest from Forbes. This is Mr Hall the bushranger.'

The name Farrand he knew, but it was the boy who commanded his attention.

'Pleased to meet you, Samuel. Your ma says you've a boil. Beasts of things, ain't they. Where is it? If it's—' he glanced towards the young woman—'a place we can mention.'

The boy closed his mouth and swallowed but couldn't speak.

'Answer Mr Hall, Samuel,' his mother said. She turned and looked Ben in the eyes. 'He's not intending to harm us.'

He returned her stare. 'Without we're harmed first.'

She opened her hands to say, how, pray, two women and a child?

'On my neck,' the boy stammered.

There came a timid knock on the room's second door. Ben snatched up the revolver from the sideboard. The door opened and the carpenter, red-faced at the trespass, was prodded into the room. Jack followed, then John. They saw Ben and lowered the revolvers.

'Our bravo's in Bathurst.'

'So I been told.' He lifted his hand towards them. 'Jack Gilbert, John Dunn—Mrs Cropper, Miss Farrand and Samuel.'

Jack swung towards the windows and gave the young woman a piercing look. 'Farrand? The magistrate?'

'My father,' she said coldly.

'Makes you a valuable woman, Miss Farrand.'

Ben saw her stiffen. 'Don't scare the young lady, Jack.' He turned to the older woman. 'I expect you have a plant for your cash, Mrs Cropper. Tellin us would save sackin the place.'

'Our only "plant", as you term it, Mr Hall, is my husband's wallet, and that has gone with him to Bathurst.'

'And you reckon we're such donkeys as'll believe that?'

She pressed her lips together and stared at a point on the wall above the picture rail.

'Jack'll keep you good people company. We'll have both doors open if you don't mind, Mrs Cropper.'

John joined him in the hallway and they went in search of the master bedroom.

They turned the room over, finding coins and costume jewellery which they left, and a man's ruby dress ring which Ben pocketed. John stood at the foot of the bed. He'd checked along its edges and under. Now he suggested they tip the mattress onto the floor.

'No. He won't be divin into his beddin every time he wants notes. I reckon that study we come past.'

The drawers of the work desk were not locked and contained only ledgers and correspondence. A closed rolltop desk in the corner when levered open yielded an envelope inscribed *Martin* containing eight pounds, and a gold watch with a broken winder. They heaved the rolltop away from the wall but it had no hidden panels. Ben told John to lift down each painting and print while he pulled out likely books from the shelves and shook the pages before dropping the books on the floor and tapping the panelling behind. Neither the clean bare patches on the walls nor the bookshelves revealed any secrets. They turned the prints and paintings and went over the backpapers looking for slits and any suspicious bulges. Lastly they kicked their way around the skirting boards. No spot rang hollow. They stood surveying the mess.

'You want to try the other rooms?'

'We done the two likely ones. I reckon put a small fright on those who do the cleanin and dustin. You up for that?'

An already frightened maid about eighteen was lighting the lamps. Miss Farrand had moved to the couch beside Mrs Cropper. The woollen comforter was now tucked around Samuel's neck. Jack was seated at the round table opening a bottle of Jerez. Sherry glasses and two more bottles stood on the table beside his revolvers. He welcomed the two back as if the sitting room were his, then hooked his chin towards the maid.

'I've told Edith here it's three more for dinner. Crab soup and roast beef.'

The girl had lit the last lamp and come to stand obediently at the table.

'John,' Ben said, 'escort Edith to the kitchen, will you.'

The appalled girl looked at Mrs Cropper, who nodded it's all right. She curtsied and waited. John opened his hand towards the doorway and in her confusion the girl curtsied to him also then scurried to do as bidden.

Ben walked to the centre of the rug and turned to face the couch. He drew the eight pound notes from his coat pocket and held them dismissively by one corner.

'From the rolltop in the study. As you didn't offer any keys we had to bust her, I'm afraid.' He flicked the notes so they rustled.

'If you swear honour bright this's all you have in the house we'll leave the other rooms be.'

Her face had flushed with outrage. She swallowed whatever words she had thought first to say and said as coldly as anger permitted, 'You have my word.'

'Keeps you on short rations, does he.'

'By no means.'

Ben folded the notes in two fingers and slid them back into his pocket. When his hand re-emerged the ruby dress ring was on his middle finger. He displayed it to her eyes.

'You can tell Cropper he's keepin me close company.'

She looked past him at the fire, placed a hand on her throat and breathed until she was calm.

'I will tell him nothing of the sort.'

John came back in and stopped beside the dragon bowl on the sideboard. Ben looked at him above the women and he gave a small shake of the head. Ben returned his gaze to Mrs Cropper.

'As you like. Be a juicy secret for you.'

She didn't deign to answer.

Jack had filled five glasses. He walked to the couch with a glass in each hand and offered them with a bow to the women. Mrs Cropper refused and Miss Farrand followed her lead. He shrugged and gave a glass to Ben, carried the other to John. John carried his untasted across the room to the open piano. In lamplight its polished walnut panels and brass candleholders gleamed, the ivory of the keys was a rich waxen yellow. He'd seen pianos in shanties, even had a tinkle. His fingers hovered. But he couldn't bring them to touch this beautiful thing. A double sheet of music was open on the stand. He turned towards the couch.

'Do you play, miss?'

She didn't turn her head. 'Yes.'

'Do you know The Exile of Erin?'

'I don't play for the outlawed.'

Ben was raising his glass a second time. He lowered it. 'You've misread the notice, Miss Farrand,' he said mildly. '"Liable to be declared" ain't declared. Am I right, Mr Gilbert?'

Jack balanced his glass on the arm of a chair, drew out his watch and sprang it open. He tut-tutted theatrically, then looked round their faces, grinned.

'We're gonna be late, though, I fear—stiff ride from here to Goulburn by noon Wednesday.' He dropped the watch back into his fob and turned to the women. 'Your father could answer this I'm sure, Miss Farrand, but you're both ladies who might know your law. If we turn ourselves in, can we claim the rewards?

Thousand each on Ben and me, seven-fifty on young John there. We could buy our own clink.'

John and Ben laughed and Samuel giggled, but quietened instantly when his mother gave him a ferocious stare. There came a knock on the jamb of the open door. Jack called come and the maid, Edith, stepped into the doorway. She stood gulping before words emerged.

'Cook is ready to serve, ma'am.'

'Thank you, Edith.'

Mrs Cropper gathered her skirts and stood. The carpenter was still perched where he'd been pointed to put himself, on a chair by the second door. Seeing Mrs Cropper rise he shot to his feet, then as quickly sat again when he saw their heads turn.

'Yeah, you too, matey,' Jack said.

The man glanced towards the women.

'My . . . jacket, Mr Gilbert. It's outside.'

'Well go fetch it. You're not back in two minutes I shoot Edith.'

He kept his face so straight the poor man gaped in terror, then made a dash for the hallway.

·

The dessert bowls had been cleared away. The three were drinking brandy from elegant balloons and smoking Cropper's cigars. The women had glasses of port in front of them, untouched. Samuel had eaten with the comforter wrapped about his neck. With the distractions of food and cutlery gone he was putting fingers gingerly to the wool covering the boil. Ben had kept him in the corner of his eye throughout the courses. He put down the balloon and lay the cigar on the plate he was using for ash.

'That thing botherin you, son?'

The boy spoke at the tablecloth. 'Yes, Mr Hall.'

'Come here.'

Samuel looked at his mother. She nodded. He got down from his chair and went to Ben, who pushed back his own chair.

'You got a decent nag?' The boy nodded. 'Show me your seat.' He thrust out his knee, patted his thigh.

The boy looked at him, back at his mother, then made up his own mind and straddled Ben's thigh, facing out. Ben corrected his posture, then began to jig him. The boy held his seat well. Ben bucked his leg more vigorously and the boy broke into a chuckle. Ben began making every third or fourth buck bigger, laughing 'whoa there!'. Mrs Cropper caught his eye and touched her own neck. Ben ended the game and lifted the boy off, but kept a hand on his waist.

'You're a plum. How would you like to spend some time out with me?'

'I'd rather you didn't put thoughts in his head, Mr Hall.'

'A week or two, Mrs Cropper, I guarantee he'd see us in a different light to what Cropper paints us.'

'I very much doubt that.'

'Bein married to the painter.'

'The opinion is my own, Mr Hall.'

Always restless, Jack had stood, brandy in hand, and walked to the fire. He kicked a smouldering log further in then bent and snatched another from the box and threw it on. Ben turned the boy the more clearly to see his face in the kindled light.

'Do I look like vermin to you, Samuel? Would you have burned my house?'

The boy studied his face seriously, shook his head.

'Mr Cropper roundly condemned the burning of your house,' Mrs Cropper said. 'In the press, and in public in Forbes.'

Ben let his eyes roam meaningfully around the room. The look was not lost on the woman but her alarm showed only in her eyes.

'Did he. No matter, I'll have another one day.'

He gave the boy a gentle but firm push to return him to his chair, then reached to the brandy bottle. Mrs Cropper cleared her throat.

'Mr Hall, if you gents intend to stay the night I would like Mrs Arndell to keep Miss Farrand and me company. Edith can fetch her.'

'A maid done for Daniel Morgan, Mrs Cropper—down Vic. Did you know? Only two, three weeks back.'

'I recall reading that, yes.'

Ben placed the balloon on the tablecloth.

'Company or not I don't reckon we'd any of us sleep too well. We'll take a visit to your stables again shortly.'

She bristled. 'I'm sorry, but is that absolutely necessary? You've dined well, you've drunk our brandy, we've been, under the circumstances, civil to you in every possible way. I take it you came on horseback.'

'Jack's is lame.'

Jack was still standing at the fire toasting his loins. At his name he looked round, his expression worried, even solicitous.

'But *is* it necessary, Ben? Really? I mean, I could walk.'

Samuel laughed outright. Even Miss Farrand couldn't suppress a smile. The older woman's cheeks burned.

•

They rode for two miles along the river flats, getting the feel of their new mounts. Jack, in the lead on the racing mare, was the first to slow. He reined in at a stand of scribbly gums.

'This'll do for me and the lad.'

John walked his horse in a tight circle round him. 'The lad? So you're squire now are you?'

Jack laughed. 'Easy—I got the bottles.'

They got down and led the horses into a natural bay in the trees. While Jack and John untied their bedrolls then kicked together leaves, Ben scouted sticks. Soon the bedrolls were open by a small fire and a bottle of Cropper's brandy was warming at the flames. The white trunks reflected the firelight eerily like the dining room walls an hour ago.

Ben drank two rounds with them then set the pannikin on the ground and stood. He adjusted the thick comforter he'd found hanging in the stables and buttoned his coat to the top, glancing higher, while his chin was raised, to a gap in the leaves. The sky was a clear deep blue, ablaze with stars, the moon risen. It was a good night for a ride. He settled his shoulders and looked down at the two lying on their sides on the bedrolls, noticing in the firelight gilding his face that in the last week John had grown a downy stubble.

'Don't let this rash bastard talk you into takin on a bloody coach, eh.'

Jack's teeth glinted orange. 'Nailed or hanged, what difference.'

'What difference? This—you might change your damn minds! You can't, but, with a bullet through here.' He tapped a finger on his forehead. Not waiting for retort he spun and walked towards the chestnut mare he was now riding and the pack mare standing quietly behind.

21

He reached Will and Ann's a little after three by his Jugiong
watch, the moon again low but on the opposite rim of the sky.
The yards were empty, the barn door was shut and barred. If
there were traps Will had them locked up. He allowed himself
a silent chuckle. It was a further fifty yards to the three stunted
gums left growing between track and yards. He brought the
horses to a halt in their shadow.

It took three of his low-pitched whistles before a lucifer
flared behind the curtains. Will appeared in the doorway in his
nightshirt and holding a lantern. He raised and lowered it then
held it out to throw light into the yard. Ben walked the horses
into the open and dismounted at the trough and tied the reins

to the pump handle, its iron sparkling with frost. He punched open the skin of ice in the trough. As he turned a puff of smoke blossomed from the chimney. Will met him at the bottom of the steps and they gripped hands.

'We got your message. Quittin's the wise thing, Ben. Even Frank knew when the game was up.'

'Jack ain't convinced.'

'Jack's never known nothin else.'

Their breath bloomed and collided. Ben nodded out at the blue paddocks. 'I circled the place before I come in. How close they watchin yous?'

'Close enough. But you picked your night, they buggered off yesterday. We been encouragin the bastards to believe you've give up comin here. They ain't far, but.'

'I'll head off before she's light.'

Will clapped him on the shoulder. 'That's hours. Get in here and get somethin hot in you.'

Ann was at the fire in her nightdress and a coat over it. Flames were already dancing along the bark and twigs she'd lain on the embers and blown up. She added sticks and a split and moved the kettle over the flames then came to him, surprising him with an embrace. 'Ben. It's very good to see you, it's been a while.'

'Not by choice, Ann. I heard they was stickin close to the place. Didn't want to give em even half the excuse for hittin yous with this new act.'

'It's been more than hinted at, I can tell you.'

'You'd know they can have us on just "suspicion" now,' Will said as he hung the lantern. Its light fell on the sleeping face of Lizzie in her crib. Ben had a sudden picture of the three at Wearne's, and his sobbing wife. He pushed the memory away.

'Yeah.'

He caught the look Ann gave her husband, enough, not tonight. He walked to the crib, breathed on the backs of his fingers and stroked his niece's cheek. She was a little furnace. He turned and said so.

'Will's and your blood,' Ann said, 'not mine. Soon as autumn comes in I'm wishing for spring.'

Will had stood two pannikins and an opened bottle of Old Tom on the table. From his coat pocket Ben pulled a bottle of Cropper's brandy and placed it on the table beside the gin.

'How about a nobbler of this instead.'

Will leaned to peer at the label.

'My word yes!'

Ann was moving to the fire. She halted and looked back at the bottle.

'I'll have a drop of that too, Will, thank you.'

She fried him four eggs and two thick rashers of bacon. She carried the plate to the table with butter and bread and sat opposite, beside Will. He'd sent word only that he was getting out, not where. Between mouthfuls he told them. Melbourne, then to New Zealand, and if that was a shicer a second and much longer ship ride, to San Francisco. No shortage of colonials there, either, according to the newspapers. And no one would care who he'd been here. Will asked his proposed route and Ann how he might get word to them that he'd reached Melbourne. He told them he needed to clean out his bank on the Fish and see Harry, then they'd let themselves be seen tracking towards the Great South as if planning to hit her again near Towrang. But at night they'd swing north, back to Strickland's. Clean out his bank there, put new shoes on his nags, then down between the lake and the Weddins and hit the Melbourne road below Junee. To Ann's question he had no answer. A letter was dangerous. Just, if they didn't read about him being taken then he'd got clear.

He wiped up the yolk and fat from the plate with buttered bread then lifted the plate aside and brought out his shammy. He extracted the cigar of notes and untied the twine and flattened the notes on the table and weighted them with the handle of the butter knife. Neither Will nor Ann spoke. From his road wad

he peeled off five twenties and placed these in a separate pile
before them.

'That'll get yous that paddock off Mahon. They're all clean.
His will be I'm figurin by the time he needs em.'

Will tapped the table beside the thicker pile.

'How much is this—his?'

'Two hundred and fifty. I don't want him rich, just ahead.
Plant it till he hits sixteen. If he clears off from her and Taylor
before then and needs funds let him have half. If he don't, like I
said start him at sixteen. Dole her out, I'm thinkin, fifty a year.
The first dose'll get him a lease if that's what he wants, and some
stock on her. With the rest, and what he starts makin, he can
turn his leases into titles. Really be able to forget I was his old
man then, eh, when he's turned squatter.'

'That's in your head, Ben, not his,' Ann said. She stood and
went behind the blanket hung as curtain over the corner holding
the second bed.

Ben looked at Will, who shrugged, I never heard him disown
you neither. Her voice reached the two men as a murmur,
answered a moment later by a boy's slurred voice. The bedframe
creaked. Then the blanket moved and Charlie, more asleep than
awake, in a flannel shirt of his father's, stumbled into the light.
He blinked, then shuffled round the table and put out his hand.

'Uncle Ben.'

Ben stood. 'Charlie. You'll be a man, matey, I reckon, next time I see you.' He slid his hand from the boy's and lightly clasped his neck. 'Jesus, you're a furnace like your sister.'

Charlie came awake, realising that what his mother had whispered to him was true, it was happening now.

'How long you goin?'

'I'm hopin not for good, but that's how she might turn out.'

'Is . . . Harry?'

Ben looked away at the fire. So it had been talked about. He looked back at his nephew.

'No. Stayin.'

'I still got his gun.'

'I seen him, he said hang on to her.'

He saw a look of alarm cross Charlie's face, the strict honour among boys.

'I reckon you'll run into him someplace, town, or over McGuire's. Yous can work it out.'

Charlie nodded, unconvinced. Ben turned from him and nodded to Will, then to Ann standing behind her husband. She placed a hand on Will's shoulder and gripped. He rose unwillingly to his feet.

'So, no letter—we don't hear nothin, you've made her to Melbourne.'

'He's said, Will.'

'Worst way of drawin attention's tryin to stick too much to the scrub. Most people other side of Cootamundry won't know you, so I'd reckon—'

'Will,' Ann said gently.

She came round the table to Ben and embraced him, short yet fierce. Ben put out his hand to his brother, not trusting his eyes if they embraced. Will ignored the hand and threw his arms round him and clutched the back of his head in strong fingers.

22

Two mornings later, first light, even the stones white, he was at the dead wattle looking down on Taylor's farm. His wife had never risen with the chickens and the man was mud lazy, but he kept his eyes on the curtained windows and on the door as he carried up one at a time and placed the round stones on the boulder, cupping his palms when he'd placed the second and breathing hard into them.

Back again above the treeline he walked in circles to stay warm, stopping only to stamp his feet. When the sun at last rose he chose a patch that would be in its redness for a while and squatted to wait.

Harry came barefoot, old dirt between his toes and the feet and toes raw-looking from the frost. He wore the same man's tweed coat that came to his knees, its cuffs rolled and grubby. He transferred the sack to his left hand with the chains and put out his right. Ben gripped for too long, the boy worming his fingers to tell him. Ben looked at his raw feet.

'Where's them boots you had?'

'She got em back. Hers the heel come off.'

'Christ.' He began to reach into his coat for his shammy before it dawned that he couldn't give the boy a note that might be listed. He let his hand drop, nodded down at the traps. 'They're mongrels to set with cold fingers. You bein careful?'

The boy held up fingers as answer. An awkward silence grew, the boy avoiding his eyes. Ben knew what was worrying him.

'I ain't come here to try and change your mind. I got somethin for you.'

Harry looked at his pockets. Ben hooked his head towards the ridge. 'Not here—she's a walk. Leave your traps.'

Thirty yards below the ridgeline was an outcropping of granite. Ben led the boy between boulders and onto a slanting ledge which widened as they climbed. At the point where it began to narrow again he squatted. Harry had halted.

'Nothin to see from there.'

He patted the rock beside him. Harry came and squatted, leaving a careful gap between their knees. Ben reached both hands into the shallow overhang and lifted aside a small slab. Cupped in the hollow the slab had covered was a package wrapped in oilcloth and cross-tied with a leather bootlace. 'Take her out, open her.' The boy broke the bow in the lace and peeled open the oilcloth to reveal another wrapping, of jeweller's velvet. He unfolded its petals and was staring down at a gold watch. Ben lifted the watch, whipped the velvet from under it, and placed the watch on his palm.

'She's bought, mate, she ain't lifted. Open her.'

Harry had never held a watch before, gold or otherwise. He fumbled with the hinge, then the winder, then gave up.

'Give here.'

Ben thumbed the winder and sprang the lid, revealing a tightly folded square of paper. He tucked it back in place, then pressed the lid closed and handed the watch back. The boy did as he'd seen and the lid once again sprang open with its soft meaty click. He took out the folded paper.

'That's your receipt, eh. Case anyone ever questions she's yours.'

Harry nodded. He placed the folded paper on his knee and turned the watch and began moving his lips. It was a moment before Ben could credit what he was doing. The jeweller, Cope, had graved the letters with loops and curls.

'You readin that?'

'Yeah,' the boy murmured, not looking from the watch.

'Go on.'

Haltingly, but without error, he read, *'To Henry Hall. From his father Benjamin Hall. 1865.'*

Biddy could scrawl her name but didn't read.

'Who taught you? Him?'

Harry nodded.

Angry, and shamed, Ben stared at the flecked granite of the rockface.

'You keep her here, mind, nowhere else. Or find another place, but up here. You got your excuse for comin.' He let the boy hold the watch for a moment longer, then he stood. 'All right, wrap her how she was and plant her.'

They walked along the ridge to the clearing where the horses were hobbled. The shaded half of their sitting log was still frosted. Ben spread his poncho on a patch of leaves from which the ice had melted and laid out Ann's bread and apples and the cold leg of mutton and opened two tins of sardines. He trickled port into a pannikin and topped it with water and gave to the boy. Harry ate his aunt's bread and mutton but wouldn't touch the sardines, saying he didn't like their taste.

'Cripes, mate, you can't live in the bush and not eat sardines.'

Harry shrugged but maintained his refusal. He drank all of the watered port.

They walked back down through the ironbarks and cypress to where they'd left the traps.

'What're you gonna say?'

'Didn't get none. Native cats got em.'

Ben studied him, both pleased and made uneasy by how glibly he lied. He delved into his coat pocket and drew out a small shammy. The coins inside clinked. He lifted the flap on the right-side pocket of Harry's coat and dropped the shammy in.

'That's ten quid. Find your own plant. Or put with your skins money. I'm guessin you got that planted.'

'I was gonna.'

Ben nodded. 'Yeah, I'd reckon you'd know as much as me about gullin your mother.'

It was more than he'd meant to say. Harry stared at him. Ben looked away over the valley that contained the farm.

'I seen Charlie couple of nights back. He was askin about you.' He looked down at the boy. 'I don't mean now, cause you ain't got the say. But when you're older you need to visit em, your uncle and aunt and your cousins. They're blood to you too.'

Harry now looked out over the valley. After a moment he nodded.

'No, mate, noddin ain't enough for this neither, I need your word again. It's to your own good too.'

'I give my word,' the boy intoned.

'And your uncle'll hold you to it. Anyway, you'd like to see your Aunt Ann, eh? And Charlie?'

The boy nodded.

'All right then. Plenty more I could say but that's the important part. How about you?'

'Nothin.'

Knowing it would be folly to try to elicit anything warmer, Ben put out his hand.

'Goodbye, son.'

'Goodbye.'

He'd hoped, though, for more than the unadorned word.

Harry slid his hand free and bent and picked up the sack and trap chains.

Ben watched him down to the gully which always took him from sight. He held a hand ready should the small figure turn. His son sank into the ground without a backward glance. Ben slapped his hand softly against the cold smoothness of the scribbly he stood at and let his arm fall to his side.

23

He got no answer to his whistles. He led the two horses from the she-oaks and down to the ford, the creek so low and narrow as to be crossed dry-foot, and left them drinking.

Fresh sardine and oyster tins and three Old Tom bottles, corked but empty, said they'd been there. He looked in the cave for a tin with a note but all there were rusting and powdered with dust. He didn't want to empty his bank before he knew where they were. He arranged the bottles in a blunt arrow pointed towards Strickland's and walked back across the gravel to the horses.

He sat the mare in cypress saplings with the lowering sun behind him and studied the hut and yards. The only animal visible was the plough mare hobbled on pick fifty yards from the barn. Susan came from the hut with a basin and emptied it onto the herbs growing at the steps. She was big, her movements stately. She stooped, back straight, and picked up firewood one-handed from a barrow beside the doorway, trapping the splits against her hip, then rose slowly upright and went back inside, heeling the door closed. A minute later the trickle of smoke from the chimney turned to a billow, then subsided to a steady stream that rose a few feet in the cold air before flattening and flowing lazily towards the orchard. He tugged on the pack mare's lead and nudged the mare into a walk. When he came abreast of the corner of the barn he saw its doors were open. He felt foolish but drew and cocked a revolver and rested it on his thigh to pass by the dark opening. The plough mare raised her head and looked at him. In the straightness of her stare was reassurance. He gave the interior of the barn a last glance, then studied the hut as he approached. The depth of dust in the yard rendered the hooves of the animals soundless. He brought them to a halt twenty yards from the steps.

'You there, Jos?'

A curtain flicked. Then the door was snatched open and Susan came onto the verandah wiping her hands in her apron. He silently lowered its hammer and pushed the revolver from sight between his thighs.

'Ben, hello—they said to expect you. I told Jack he should be measurin out a patch of ground here for a hut.' She smiled to take any sting from the remark. 'Jos's gone to his brother's, day before yesterday. They're musterin.'

'Ah.' He lifted a hand towards the dense belt of scrub a half-mile away, out on the plain. 'Well, I'll take—'

'Come in and warm yourself. Please.'

'If that's all right. Mug of tea'd be good.'

He clicked the mares forward and got down, then walked to the pack mare and began to untie the sack with his food and grog.

'Leave that,' she said quickly. 'Long way to fetch more.'

'You got enough?'

She nodded. 'It won't be flash, but more than I can eat right now.' She placed a hand on her belly.

He retied the sack. He turned again to the steps and lifted a hand towards the distant cypresses, now a band of dark blue, that marked the pool.

'I checked the creek, seen some fresh bottles. When were they here?'

'Day before Jos left. John's got a tooth givin him curry and wanted fever drops. Then some stockmen come through and they must have thought they was traps—I ain't seen em since. I promised Jack some marmalade.'

'Thought I could smell it.' He glanced over his shoulder at the sun. 'I wouldn't reckon they've gone far—I said I'd meet em here.'

'Jack said.'

He took up the mare's reins. 'I'll hide these two. Can I treat em some oats?'

'Of course. There's loose, or open a bag. And could you save me the job of gettin that lady in.' She pointed with her chin towards the plough mare, gone back to cropping.

·

She'd trimmed the wicks of the lanterns. Burning clean and bright, they and the fire threw a warm glow over everything in the hut. As well, to light her work, she'd stood a candle in a brass holder on the table. He was seated at the other end from her workplace. A plate streaked with mutton gravy was at his elbow and in front of him he had a second and clean plate with a thick slice of damper and a saucer of new marmalade with a spoon. A pannikin of tea was in his hand. Strickland didn't use tobacco and he'd asked her permission to light his pipe and she'd given it, saying she liked the smell, it brought back her father.

She ladled the last of the marmalade into a dark green ginger jar and placed it with the miscellany of china and glass jars lined up on a folded cloth, then stood the ladle in the boiler and stooped slowly and deposited the boiler on the floor. She swivelled, still stooped, and pushed on her thighs to straighten and went to the fireplace where she'd set beeswax to melt on raked-out coals. Ben watched in quiet fascination, memory stirring. Long white wisps were rising into the chimney, the wax was crackling in the saucepan. She wrapped the handle in her apron and gave the pan a last swirl, then lifted it from the coals and was carrying it held before her to the table when a startled look came on her face and she stopped as if a hole had opened in the floor. He knew what had happened.

'Kickin?'

She closed her mouth and gave a small shake of the head and came on to the table. 'Turnin over.' She brought her other hand to the saucepan handle and began pouring the clear liquid into the first in the row of jars.

'That's a healthy sign.'

She nodded, but couldn't meet his eye. He reminded himself that it was her first. He said, to cover her discomfiture, 'I had a couple of orange trees at my place, Sandy Creek. Good bearers, too. My wife made marmalade. I expect she still does. I venture you'd know her—Biddy Walsh? As was. The Walshs down at the Weddins?'

'I've . . . seen her. We've not ever spoken.'

'I suppose you know where she's livin now.'

She glanced at him before starting another pour. 'I've heard, yes.'

'So you'd know too she took my son Harry. But I been seein him again. He's a fair bit like his old man—' he smiled without humour—'don't give much away. At least he ain't shopped me. That's somethin.' He'd spoken down at his hands resting on the table. He raised his face. 'So, what you hopin for?'

Her smile was a far remove from his forced one, both excited and shy. She poured the seal into another jar before she spoke.

'I'd like a girl, but of course Jos wants another pair of male hands about the place.'

'No law sayin you have to stop at one. I'd have wanted a girl for my next.' He touched the butt of the revolver lying at the corner of the table. 'Would've been safe at least from takin up this game. Though with my blood in her . . .'

Susan had stopped pouring and was watching him through narrowed lids.

'What?'

'Are you . . . gettin out, Ben?'

He looked at the minutely pulsing flame of the candle, then returned his gaze to her face.

'I'm showin too, am I?'

She placed the saucepan carefully on the corner of the folded cloth and with both hands smoothed the wrinkles from the apron covering the mound of her belly.

'Just you?'

He'd said enough. But her kindness this night, and near two years of other days and nights, had been unquestioning. Even now she was risking giving birth in a cell. She deserved an answer.

'Yeah. They're stickin. John's still well up for it, and Jack's been at the game longer than me, ain't hardly known nothin else. I didn't want nothin but the road life neither after we done Eugowra. You get the taste for wakin up in the mornin not knowin where you'll be by noon, what you'll be doin. Even if you'll see the sun set. I ain't sayin the life was all honey. You know what we done lately. But she's still better than walkin the day behind a plough mare knowin you'll be doin it again tomorrow and tomorrow, or lookin at ten mile of paddocks need fencin. That's why Jos does his bit of duffin. Gets the blood movin. I reckon you'd know that.'

She nodded.

'He won't go no further, Susan. My feelin of him. And I'm thinkin you've had a word or two.'

'More than two.'

'Yeah.' He picked up the spoon and stirred the stiffening marmalade in the saucer before him. He spoke down at the spoon. 'Only thing was, I never wanted to cop one in the guts. I seen a mate go that way, Micky Burke. So bad he shot himself. But it's never worried me I might be nailed cold. And I ain't followed round by dead traps, nothin like that. Not sayin you're thinkin it, just tellin you.' He lay down the spoon and lifted his other hand towards the folds of hessian curtaining off the bed, its outer face sewn with velvet stars. 'Partly your fault, Susan. All this, eh.' The swing of his arm encompassed hearth, kitchen bench, the row of marmalade jars. He gave her a thin smile. She didn't return it.

'Where'll you make for?'

He knew she wasn't trying to worm information, it was the sensible next question. But it was time to end the line of talk.

'If I answered I'd have to be gullin you, and I don't want to.'

She blushed crimson to her hair, only now hearing that the question held wider implications than she'd intended, which was simply wanting to know more about this man she'd grown to like and who was alone for the first time and speaking of himself.

'No harm, Susan.' He stood up from the table. 'I got a bottle in my kick if you'll take a drop with me.'

'Ah . . . no.' She patted her belly.

'You don't want to give her a first taste?' He saw her brow crease and realised she didn't even now know him well enough to tell when he was chaffing. He waved the remark away. 'While I'm out there, I think your barrow's near empty. Where's your heap, round the back of the chimney?'

'Yes. Take one of the lanterns.'

'Thank you, I will. Prefer to see what's livin in her.'

He picked up the revolver from the table and pushed it into his belt and reached to the lantern above his head.

.

The sealed jars were covered with a clean muslin. Susan was seated with him at the table, she drinking tea, he gin. There was damper and cheese on a board and homegrown walnuts in a china bowl. He was cracking the nuts in pairs in his hands, prising out the crinkled flesh and laying the pieces on the board for them both. She began to yawn, stifled it, then couldn't and covered her mouth with her hand. He popped a half-kernel in his mouth, brushed his hands over the bowl and picked up the closest of the three revolvers lying on the bench at his hip.

'Better let yous both get your rest.'

He stood and pushed the revolver into his belt and picked up the next.

'You're welcome to a roof and a fire, Ben.'

'I don't think that'd look too good, Susan.'

'If that mattered I wouldn't have said it.'

'All the same I'll take myself off.'

He kept the third revolver in his hand and walked to his hat hanging with a frayed work bonnet on the row of nails beside the door.

'Come and have some tea and eggs before you go lookin for em.'

'I will.' He didn't reach for the door handle. 'She . . . movin still?'

Susan nodded. 'Slowin down, but. I think she's sleepy too.'

He pushed the revolver into his belt and put out his hand, palm up.

'You reckon could I . . . ?'

She stared at him. Then she stood and unbuttoned the coat she'd earlier put on and exposed the bulge of her belly hard against the linen of her dress. He walked to her and proffered his hand. She took his wrist and guided him to the underside of the bulge.

'You might have to wait. Oh—no . . . there!' He nodded to say he'd felt it. 'A big one! She knows the different hand.'

He kept his hand there, hoping for another. But to keep it there too long would embarrass them both. He stepped back and began to button his coat. She began to rebutton hers. Neither could quite look at the other.

.

The clear sky promised a hard frost. He could already smell it, the air stinging his nostrils. He carried the revolver at half-lift, thumb on the hammer, and walked to the barn. The mare gave a low whinny. He stopped in the doorway. No one was there. The mare was still new to his step. He pushed the revolver into his belt and walked to her and placed his hand on her neck, then stood looking across her back into the pitch dark of the underloft. His shoulders began to work and a wrenching sob erupted from his mouth. He clenched his jaw but another broke from him. He clamped his hand over his mouth and rested his forehead against the cold nap of the mare's neck, the sobs breaking painfully from him, dribble coating his hand. He allowed the sobbing to spend itself. When it did he sucked air through his fingers until the shuddering in his chest also stopped. He took his hand away and thumbed the water from his eyes, wiped his palm down his coat. The mare had swung her head to look at him. He patted her and ran a reassuring hand up her neck to her cheek and down her muzzle and out onto the cold leather of the reins to where they looped about the barked cypress trunk that rose to the invisible ridgepole.

He rode to the belt of scrub half a mile from the hut. He kept his mind deliberately blank, taking in not thinking. Beyond the creak of leather and swish of grass the night was silent, no wind, no bellow of a beast, not even plovers. His breath and that of the horses made extravagant blue plumes. He tilted back his head and had a contest with himself to blow the highest, but stopped when he neared the scrub and concentrated on spotting the big yellow box they used when they didn't use the pool. He saw it, closer to the tip of the scrub where it poked out into the plain than he'd always thought, or else there was another further in the same size. But this would do. He headed the mare with his knee and rode to the edge of the scrub. There he dismounted, unstrapped his bedroll and valise, and carried them through the tea-tree and stunted hickory wattles to the foot of the box and dropped them on its thick sheddings. He walked back out and unsaddled both mares, laying each saddle and the rugs on the dense tea-tree, then found the hobbles and led the animals out to a patch of pick and put the leg ropes on and removed the bridles.

Rugs, saddles and bags took two more trips. When all was stacked at the foot of the box with the rugs over he undid the tie on the grub sack and brought out the port bottle, uncorked it and took a long swig, and another. There was no heat in the syrupy liquid as it slid down his throat but when it hit his gut he felt the glow. Go easy, he told himself, you only got the half and you'll need her a damn sight more in the morning. He thumped the cork back in and shoved the bottle under the rugs, then picked up a fallen branch and began sweeping leaves and bark into a bed.

.

The only light in the hut came from the smouldering back log. The figure removed boots at the door and crossed the floor in socks and parted the star curtain and sat on the bed. Susan woke with a startled, 'Oh!', her hands going instantly to her belly.

'It's me.'

'Jos! God. My heart's thumpin. I didn't hear the door.' She struggled up onto one elbow. 'There's stew there. And some spuds.' Her speech was slurred, tongue only half awake. She fumbled for a lucifer and struck it and reached the flame towards the candle on the bedside shelf. He leaned and blew it out.

'I'm all right.'

He pulled his shirt over his head and draped it over the foot of the bed then stood and began unbuttoning his trousers.

'I thought I only just fell asleep. What's the time?'

'Dunno.'

She lay back down.

'Ben was here.'

He replied with a grunt. He stepped from his trousers and hung them by feel from one of the nails in the wall, then slid into bed. She snuggled into him, then recoiled.

'Goodness—you're shiverin like a pup.'

She lay a hand on his singleted chest. He kept his arms rigidly at his sides. Her breathing slowed and deepened until she was lightly snoring. The back log collapsed with a sigh and the underside of the roof lit up and flickered. He lay staring at the ridgepole, ears tuned to the night, his mind, too, out there.

24

He woke at first light. He lay with eyes closed, reading sounds. Above his head was the quiet chatter of rosellas. Further off magpies were abroad and carolling. The distant bellowing of a beast of Strickland's. No wind, the foliage about him still. He listened for sounds under those he could hear, sounds sensed rather than heard. The hush of cold, that was all. And the rustle of something small, a wood roach maybe, in the leaves below his right ear, because at some time in the early morning his head had slid off the pillow of his folded coat. He opened his eyes and began on the job of feeling out his limbs. He was lying on his side, tolerably warm to the hips, but below them nothing. He moved his left leg and cold instantly replaced numbness as if a bucket of water had been tipped on him from the thighs down. He'd be damn glad to be done with sleeping on the ground! He drew his left hand from under the blankets and pushed the hat from his face and rolled onto his back, the poncho crackling. Between the leaves was a pale blue sky. He'd be riding in sun at least. The day's work was find them. The hut first for some fried eggs. Leave her ten quid, tell her it was for the girl. Then up to the pool, see if they'd come back. If no, circle out and cut their tracks. They wouldn't be far, a mile or two. Probably doing the same, lying in their rolls wondering to one another if he'd arrived. Or they might already be saddled and on the move.

He sat up and found his boots under the blankets and pulled them on, remembering when he felt the patch of what felt like wet but was cold leather that the heel of the right sock was gone. He pushed forward onto his knees and fetched out the revolvers from under his folded coat and shoved them into his belt, then stood and hobbled two paces and unbuttoned. His member didn't like his cold fingers, he held it lightly as he could between index and thumb. Steam rose from the splash of his stream on the leaves. He shook dry and rebuttoned, then dribbled spit on his left middle finger and cleaned the crust from his eyes. The poncho and horse rugs were silvered with ice. She was going to be heavy out on the paddock. He needed a nip before facing the walk to the nags. He bent and found the bottle under the rugs and pulled it out by its neck. The glass burned on his lips but the dark sweetness tasted good, cleaned the mouth. He took a second long swig, then corked the bottle. No guarantee the other two had any. Not from the evidence of the bottles at the creek. If they wanted grog for the road they'd have to stay till Jos got back, get him to go in. He'd need to give him extra quids too for a full grub bag. And fresh caps and powder, just in case. He shook the thoughts loose, returned to the day. If they reached the pool before him they'd find the arrow of bottles and mightn't hang around. Maybe a better plan if he went there first and emptied his bank, then find them and all come back to the hut for eggs. He bent and lifted his coat by the collar, shook it out, pulled it on, leaving it unbuttoned. He picked up the bridles and pushed through the tea-tree and wattles to the fringe of the scrub.

The horses were a hundred yards away, straight out across the frosted grass. Ground mist filled the dip where he knew the hut to be. No smoke rose above it. This close, she needed her sleep. He brought his gaze back to the plain and began searching the enclosing fingers of scrub, hunching instinctively and his hand going to his belt when there came a blur of movement to his right. But it was a butcherbird spearing down to take a hopper that had stretched its frozen legs. He watched the bird fly back up to a branch and begin beating the hopper against the bark, then returned to searching. No odd colour snagged his eye, nothing glinted. He set out into the open, the grass crackling beneath his boots.

He was half the distance to the horses when something flashed red in the corner of his right eye. He turned his head and saw three men, two whites and a black, clutching shotguns and running to head him off. He gaped, more in wonder than fear. Where had they appeared from? And how were they running without sound? And the red nightcap on the one in the lead. Were they apparitions? The questions occupied a half-second. He dropped the bridles, drew a revolver and was himself running at an angle to draw away.

Within a few steps he knew he was in trouble, running in knee boots and they in socks. He glanced over his shoulder. The tracker and the red nightcap had gained on him, they were only forty yards behind. He couldn't get back into the scrub, he set himself towards a patch of cypress, lose them, or fight if he had to, shoot the tracker first. But she was two hundred yards, all open ground. He'd done it before, outrun traps, but in scrub not in the open. They must be about ready to take a pot at him. He began jinking left and right, clumsy in the boots but needing to put them off their aim. If he stopped for a shot he'd be giving them first crack, then they'd be on him. How did the bastards even come to be here! Jesus, he didn't want to face this alone. Show up, boys, damn yous, give em a fright! A voice, had to be the nightcap, yelled, 'Stand, Hall, and you'll live!' That's it, matey, his mind spat, waste your breath and I get a couple of yards! The jinking, but, was costing him ground. On the next he dug his toes and broke into a straight sprint running on the balls of his feet. A searing fist studded with nails punched him between the shoulderblades. His feet left the ground, touched again. His legs, not he, kept running.

.

Snatched from sleep, Susan Strickland started upright in the bed.

'My God—that's Ben!'

She swivelled and saw her husband lying awake beside her. He didn't look at her, he went on staring at the stalactites of ice piercing the bark roof, the muscles of his jaw standing in his face.

She moved to the edge of the bed and lay down again, face turned to the wall, hands crossed on her belly.

.

Jack was stirring the embers of their fire with a stick and placing the twigs he'd kept dry under his bedroll. Doped on fever drops, John was snoring.

At the first boom, distant enough to sound harmless, he grabbed up a revolver and sprang to his feet, eyes darting everywhere in the surrounding tea-tree.

The boom was followed by two more, overlapping.

.

The second blast of shot caught him in the ribs, the third just below the first. He slowed to a staggering rolling jog. Moaning was coming from somewhere. A bullet hummed past his face, not from behind, from his left. He turned his head and saw figures. More of the bastards. Oh Jesus. They were already between him and the cypresses. He veered from the figures towards a stand of gum saplings. A bullet slapped into his left elbow, another into his thigh. A jubilant Irish voice cut through the roar in his ears of his own breathing. 'Ye're done for, Hall, ye mongrel!'

He reached a sapling, gripped it in his armpit and sagged to his knees. A blow hard as a horse kick slammed into his hip and the weight of belt and revolvers fell away. It was better, he could stand now and face them. He couldn't lift his arm. The Colt was too heavy. He was sleepy. How was he sleepy? Because you're dying, a voice, his and not his, said. The voice that had called on him to stand was bawling, 'Hold your fire, damn you, hold your fire!'

'No—I'm dyin—shoot me dead!'

He found the trigger guard, felt the shock in his foot of the bullet bury itself beside his boot heel. The shot set them firing again. He registered three more blows, without pain. The sapling's smooth bark slid up his cheek.

A wild capering dance began around the body. The officer, a sub-inspector named Davidson, doffed the red nightcap and stood staring down at the slack face, blood trickling from the nostrils and three slug holes in the forehead. There was no use yet attempting to assert control over his prancing men. They'd been out a week, eaten possums, slept on the ground. They'd lain awake all night with the frost settling on them, the last hour with greatcoats and boots off so they could run. And they'd bagged him! Faces alight, they were laughing and shaking hands, slapping backs, hugging each other round the shoulders. A trooper named Hipkiss threw his hat to the ground and danced a jig on its crown. Dargin the tracker was grinning but standing apart, uncomfortable with this elation in the presence of death, the spirit not yet departed. Then one of the Irish, Bohan, leaned down close to the face and spat, the gob landing on the ear. That snapped the sub-inspector out of his suspension of command.

'Bohan! Move away—there'll be none of that! Move away, man. That's an order!'

•

The volley, then its echoes, ended. Jack continued to stand, arms and revolver hanging at his sides. Then he brought the revolver across his body and changed hands and lifted his right and made the cross, his hand clumsy, so long since it had performed the rite.

•

The troopers had sloped emptied carbines and repeaters against other saplings. He'd been turned onto his back. The blood that had trickled from the nostrils was beginning to darken and clot. The eyes were lazily open, the right filled with blood. Hipkiss on one knee was going through the coat and trouser pockets a last time, wiping his fingers on the coat flap each time he withdrew them smeared. The revolvers and the contents of the pockets were laid out on the grass, a gold watch and three chains, a worn keeper ring in the shape of a belt, Cropper's ruby dress ring, a powder flask and tin of caps and a leather bag of bullets, Harry's scapular. On the other side of the body a trooper named Buckley was counting and calling the tallies of the banknotes he'd sorted into piles. Davidson stood with pad and pencil.

Dargin arrived back at the saplings leading Ben's horses fitted with the flung bridles. The spitter, Bohan, had been sent to the patch of scrub and was walking back across the trampled frost carrying poncho and blankets, pack straps and a length of rope in a loose coil.

Davidson looked up from his pencil and caught the two kneeling troopers as they exchanged silly grins.

'That'll do, you've had your fill. Caban, here, help lay him out.'

Buckley lifted the half-tallied banknotes clear and the other two pulled the arms in flush against the sides and brought the legs together ready for trussing.

Bohan came up. He glanced to see where the sub-inspector was looking, then worked his mouth as if gathering another gob and gave Buckley a wink. He dumped the blankets and poncho at the head, dropped the rope and pack straps beside the hands of the other two, then stepped back and folded his arms and stood brooding down at the dead face through slitted lids.

25

Upwards of fifty people, men and women, were crowded into the foot constables' locker room. Excited male voices and laughter came through the open doorway leading into the barracks proper, but in the locker room was silence, deepened rather than broken by the whisper of pencils.

One belonged to the man in a suit who stood before the riddled and bloodstained coat and corduroys slung from wire hangers against one wall in a parody of their wearer. He was glancing up at the clothes between rapid bursts of writing on a fat notepad. The other pencil belonged to the man sketching the corpse. He was seated on a folding stool with a folio pad on his knees, a fan of pencils in his left hand and drawing with his right. Behind him stood the reporter who had commissioned the sketch. He was taking each pencil handed up to him and resharpening it with a pocketknife.

Ben lay on a low stretcher in the centre of the room. His head, shoulders and chest were exposed, the head supported by a thin gaol pillow, its ticking yellowed, the lower body covered by the poncho they'd rolled him in for strapping to the pack mare, the oilskin dark with soaked-in blood. The face was languid, but the lips had drawn up, accentuating the hook to the right corner of the mouth. The eyes were opened a fraction as if peeping to see who might have come to view him.

There was a quiet commotion at the street doorway, then the raised voice of the constable stationed there, followed by the shuffle of people moving or being moved aside. Will, wearing mass suit, white shirt and black tie, and Ann in sombre brown came through with Harry, each holding him by a hand. When clear of the gawkers Will halted them and they stared at the form on the stretcher. Will bowed his head and made the cross. Then his stare shifted to the man sketching. He pulled Harry by the hand and led him and Ann into the narrow gap between the man and the corpse. The sketcher, taken by surprise, looked up to protest, but a man was already bending to speak in his ear. The sketcher glanced around the circle of faces. Cold eyes

were on him. He stood, folded the stool, and he and the reporter
retreated to the wall.

Harry stood between his aunt and uncle. They had released
his hands. He knew he should be feeling something. But what
interested him was the evidence of how this man, his father, had
died. The heavy mottled bruising that surrounded the encrusted
hole in the shoulder, and another in the chest like a burst
carbuncle. The blood that had trickled from the nostrils and
dried. The three small but deep holes in the forehead, each as
sharp as the slug holes in the smooth white bark of the apple
gum near the woodheap. He wanted to reach out and touch a
fingertip to each hole, and might have overcome the certainty
that the man and woman standing either side of him would
disapprove except that he felt a gentle tap on the shoulder. He
turned his head and a woman he didn't know reached for and
gripped his wrist and with her other hand placed a lock of hair
on his palm and closed his fingers with her own. She blinked
to say, I took it for myself but it's yours now, and stepped back.
He half opened his hand and glanced in. She'd tied the lock
neatly at one end with strands of itself. He didn't want this
piece of his father. He turned his anxious gaze to the matted
brown hair on the head. If somehow he could lay the lock there

it would disappear. But he couldn't. Aunt Ann had looked down and seen that he had it. He felt tears begin to burn at the back of his eyes. He would have to keep it, bring it out when asked. He didn't want to.

ACKNOWLEDGEMENTS

Roger McDonald and Bette Mifsud read earlier drafts of the manuscript, and I thank them from the heart for their insights and suggestions.

Kerry Guerin and Brian Maloney of the Lithgow Small Arms Factory Museum placed in my hands firearms of the era and explained their workings. I thank both for an initiation into the thinking of men who know and respect guns.

Ali Lavau did a wonderful job as editor, picking up things I could no longer see, and I thank her.

And at Allen & Unwin, my thanks to Jane Palfreyman and Siobhán Cantrill for bringing the manuscript so professionally to publication, and for their enthusiasm for its contents.